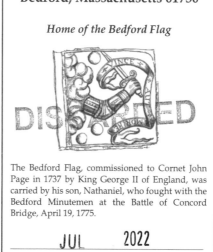

A HEAVY DOSE OF ALLISON TANDY

A HEAVY DOSE OF ALLISON TANDY

JEFF BISHOP

putnam

G. P. Putnam's Sons

For my parents—Charlotte, Finley, and Steve

G. P. Putnam's Sons
An imprint of Penguin Random House LLC, New York

First published in the United States of America by G. P. Putnam's Sons,
an imprint of Penguin Random House LLC, 2022

G. P. Putnam's Sons is a registered trademark of
Penguin Random House LLC.

Visit us online at penguinrandomhouse.com

Library of Congress Cataloging-in-Publication Data is available.

Book manufactured in Canada

ISBN 9781984812940
10 9 8 7 6 5 4 3 2 1
FRI

Design by Eileen Savage | Text set in Dante MT Pro

I thought that I was dreamin'
when you said you loved me

—Frank Ocean, "Ivy"

1

If I were to ask you "Where is the worst place to run into an ex?" you might say "the supermarket" or "on a date with somebody else" or maybe even "at a family reunion." To which I would reply, (1) "wrong," (2) "wrong," and (3) "for the love of God, man, stop hooking up with your cousin."

There is a right answer, by the way.

I can tell you—with absolute certainty—the worst place to run into an ex is inside your own home, while you are splayed across the bathroom floor, neck-deep in porcelain, your stomach hollowed out like the inside of a snare drum.

Should I elaborate?

Say you're me. (Hi, I'm Cam.) You're a senior in high school, just two weeks from graduating. Best time of your life, or so you've been told. Results may vary.

Say you're head over heels in love with a girl—let's call her, oh, I don't know, Ally. You and this Ally had been dating for over a year. Everything with you guys was good—no, better than good. Phenomenal. Stupendous. Second to none.

Say that very same girl blindsided you, ending things abruptly and without explanation. Shredding your heart in the process. Real hatchet job. *I've been thinking about this for a while . . . It's not you, it's me . . . I still want us to be friends.* She played all the hits.

That was in January. Now it's late May. The two of you haven't spoken since. Not even a text.

Say a couple months after the split, you found out she was seeing someone else. But not just any someone else. The very someone else who you'd always known had a thing for her. Who she swore to you was "just a friend."

Here's where it gets fun.

Say that ex (you know, the one with the hatchet) was driving home from school one afternoon in late March when suddenly—inexplicably—she lost track of the road. Wrapped the hood of her car around an oak tree at the bottom of the Shermer Ravines. The skid marks are still there, branded on the pavement. So is the puncture her sedan left in the guardrail.

Say she's been in a coma ever since, confined to a hospital bed just a few miles up the road. Unable to walk, talk, or breathe without the assistance of a ventilator. Unable to—hypothetically—materialize out of thin air. Inside your bathroom. At three in the morning.

So I'll ask again: Where is the worst place to run into an ex?

The answer? Anywhere.

2

The sun isn't up yet and my mom is trying to kill me.

The dash clock reads just before six, so we're the only ones on the road, thank God. The good folks of Shermer, Illinois, must be sleeping in, staving off their Monday mornings for as long as their snooze buttons allow.

I'm not so fortunate.

Attempting to doze with Dr. Cindy Garrity behind the wheel is an exercise in futility. Mom isn't a fan of posted speed limits. Or stop signs. Or the Rules of the Road generally. As we speak, she's driving with her knees, one hand on the stereo, the other fussing with the elastic holding back her sandy blond hair.

"Shit, my turn!"

Suddenly we're Tokyo Drifting through an intersection, my forehead bouncing off the passenger window. (Note to self: Ask Dr. Vernon to check for a concussion.)

"Jesus, Mom!"

"Language, Cameron!"

"Why you have to drive like someone on bath salts?"

"How would you know how someone on bath salts drives?"

Things are extra tense this morning since this little trip over-laps with her breakfast spin class. She looks the part at least, dressed head to toe in black athleisure, save for her clean white trainers. The official uniform of North Shore moms. They hand them out at PTA meetings.

"I spoke with your father last night," she says, pausing to sip from her travel mug. "He's looking forward to seeing you walk the stage at graduation. He's making a special effort to fly in, so I expect you to spend time with him. Okay, Cameron? Will you make sure to spend time with him?"

Mom has this aggravating-as-all-hell habit of telling me some-thing, then immediately following up with a question about the thing she's just said. She does this, apparently, because I don't listen (her words). Mom prefers people listen to her. Probably why she became a pediatrician; people are extra attentive when it comes to their kid's health.

"Cameron?"

"Yes, I'll spend time with him."

"Don't take that tone with me."

"What tone?"

"*That* tone."

"No tones were taken!" I turn my attention to a battle I can win. "Do you really need to have your window open *and* the AC on? It's, like, sixty degrees out."

"How can you say that?" Mom switches her mug from one hand to the other. "You know my hands get sweaty when I drive. What if I lost my grip and we ended up—" She cuts herself short, but we both know where she was headed. The eight-hundred-thousand-pound elephant hanging over all of Shermer.

"Wanna finish that thought?"

Mom wrestles a tickle from her throat. Suddenly it occurs to me. "Wait, are we going to the hospital or to Dr. Vernon's?" My pre-op visits took place at his satellite office. I'd just assumed that's where he'd perform my surgery.

"Rich"—my mom calls Dr. Vernon *Rich*—"only operates out of the hospital. It's standard procedure. Where did you think we were going?"

The truth is, I hadn't. *Thought*, that is. (I try avoiding it, as a general rule.) Not about where the surgery would be, how long it would take, what my life will look like once it's over. No, I'm allowed exactly one thought, played on a loop.

I am over Allison Tandy.

My mantra for the last five months. They say if you repeat something enough times you start to believe it. Jury's still out. Just don't ask me to say it out loud.

"Why should it matter?" Mom asks. "It's not like you haven't been to visit her in the hospital yet, right?"

I turn and face my window.

"Cameron? You have gone to visit her, haven't you?"

"It's on my to-do list."

Look, I know we just met, but if there's one thing you should know about me, it's that I have never written a to-do list. Things sort of just . . . happen with me. I'm like a substitute teacher; just trying to run out the clock until the end of the day. Compared to my mom, who writes to-do lists in her sleep. Seriously, if I croak before her, you can bet your sweet ass she's sending me up to Saint Peter's Gate with a list of shit she wants done by the time she arrives.

"You're kidding."

I can sense Mom's eyes on the back of my neck. Knowing Mom, I'm sure she'll process this new information with the patience and love any parent would grant a child struggling to cope.

"That is totally unacceptable, Cameron!"

Just kidding.

"I didn't realize I had to go, okay? I must've missed that day of ex-boyfriend school when they went over what to do if your ex winds up in a coma. How do we even know I'm wanted there? It's not like anyone invited me."

"It's a hospital room, not a Fourth of July party! You don't wait for an invitation! I realize the two of you had a falling-out, but that's no excuse."

A *falling-out*? Is that what we're calling it?

"You need to stop letting your pride and self-pity get in the way. If the roles were reversed, I'm sure Ally would've been at your bedside on day one."

I'm not so sure about that.

"Alright, sorry! The minute she wakes up, I'm there."

Mom's still fuming, but she knows better than to touch that one. It's been sixty-two days since Ally's bumper met the wrong end of a tree trunk. Sixty-two days without an update beyond the standard "she's stable" and "we don't have a timetable."

At first, Ally's accident was all anyone could talk about. But once her forecast became less-than-fatal, people felt justified shifting their attention to more *important* matters, like their summer plans, or the latest couple inflicting their continued bloodline on the rest of the world.

Ally's being in a coma became just another fact of life, like traffic on the Kennedy, or the impending climate apocalypse. People still donated to the Save Ally Fund, established to help her mom with the rising medical bills, but that was it.

For the record, I never thought for a second this would be the end for Allison Tandy. Not when she still had so much left to accomplish. Namely, ruining my life.

By some small miracle, we pull into the hospital's parking lot. Mom whips into the roundabout and brakes in front of a sign marked AMBULANCE ONLY.

"I'll pick you up in a couple of hours," she says like I'm here for a playdate.

"You're not coming in?"

"I have to run to the office; we have some of the equipment you're gonna need. You have to be careful, though, especially with our ice machine. It was very expensive and we only have one, so if you break it, the money's coming out of your college account."

Fiscal threats are Mom's go-to.

"Since you won't be able to climb stairs while the cast is locked, I'll set things up for you in the family room. You can sleep in there for a few days, but only if you agree to keep things neat. Can you keep things neat, Cameron?"

"Yes, Mom."

"You weren't supposed to eat or drink anything this morning. Did you?"

"No, Mom."

"Meds, what about meds?"

"Haven't taken any of those either."

"Are you sure? When was the last time you took your Lexapro?"

"Last week."

"Adderall?"

"Last month."

"Ativan?"

"I stopped taking Ativan in March."

"Who told you to do that?"

"My doctor."

"Which one?"

"You!"

Mom stills. Probably trying to recall why she made the switch. Hell if I know. She prescribes, I consume. Simple as that. I think for a moment she's about to release me, but then she's like, "Oh, Cameron. Before you go, there is something I need to have a talk with you about."

"Oh my God," I groan. "Can it please wait until after they rip my knee apart?"

I brace myself for a lecture, but it never comes.

"Okay" is all she says. "We'll talk about this later."

Huh. Mom never lets me get the last word in. Weird.

"Thank you." I unlock my door and spill out into the crisp

morning air. Just as I slam the door closed, Mom summons me back.

"But sass me like that again, and I will not hesitate to write you out of my will."

There she is.

"Name?"

"Cameron Garrity."

"Birthday?"

"November seventh."

"Height?"

"Six three."

"Weight?"

". . ."

"Body weight?"

"Oh, I thought you meant *wait*, like *hold on*."

"Body weight."

Instinctively, I suck in. "Two hundred." Nurse Molly could just as easily glean my info from any one of the half-dozen forms I filled out in the waiting room. I don't point this out to her; she doesn't strike me as the type that appreciates it when teenagers tell her how to do her job.

"How many drinks do you have in a week?"

"Who can count, amirite?" Her expression assures me that I am not, in fact, right. "None," I lie.

"Drugs?"

"Only ones with needles."

Again with the scowl. The faded whites of her eyes match the yellowish stains on her scrubs. "Please answer the question, Mr. Garrity. I have other patients to attend to."

"My bad, Molly. Can I call you Molly?"

"No." Nurse Molly finishes jotting something down on the side of her form, then gets to her feet. "Everything off except your underwear. Dr. Vernon will be with you in a minute."

I start to apologize, to explain that hospitals make me nervous, and when I get nervous my brain goes into overdrive, and when my brain goes into overdrive I start to ramble, and when I start to ramble I usually end up saying something I regret or pissing someone off. But Nurse Molly's already gone.

I really do hate hospitals, comatose ex-girlfriend notwithstanding. I can't help but imagine all the dead and dying people being visited by other soon-to-be dead and dying people.

Mom's had her own private practice for a few years now, but she used to be in pediatrics here at Shermer General. Sometimes, when her appointments ran late, I'd roam the endless taupe hallways. The geriatric wing freaked me out the most. Walk through it and you'll hear *Family Feud* in almost every room. Forget loved ones; Steve Harvey is the last face most people see before they meet their maker.

I wonder what's playing on the TV in Ally's hospital room. Her mom—Mrs. Tandy—is too classy for the Game Show Network. Probably something highbrow, like C-SPAN or *Real Housewives*.

Per Nurse Molly's directive, I start to strip. As I'm reaching for the hospital gown, I catch a glimpse of my reflection in the full-length mirror hanging from the back of the door.

Two hundred pounds—that's what I told Nurse Molly. My listed weight in the Shermer Wasps basketball program last season. The same weight I reported to my new coaches at the University of Chicago (Go Maroons) when I signed my National Letter of Intent to continue my basketball career a few months ago. Right before my knee turned to Jell-O. I've all but given up since then. What point is there in exercising, eating healthy, bathing, or general personal upkeep if the only person whose opinion I value isn't there to see it?

At least the surgery'll give me an excuse to avoid the beach and any other clothing-optional summer activities. I pile my stuff in the corner of the room, grabbing my phone from my shorts in the process. It's compulsive at this point, opening my Messages app, scrolling to her name. Nothing's changed, of course—we hadn't even texted since January. And still I find myself doing the same ritual a few times a day.

There's a knock at the door. In walks the executioner: Dr. Richard Vernon.

"Cameron! How are we feeling this morning?"

I force a smile. "Every day's a dream."

My mom's known Dr. Vernon forever—they went to medical school together. She handpicked him to do my operation. I might've found him forgettable—balding, vertically challenged white dudes are a dime a dozen in Shermer—if not for the bizarre handlebar mustache tacked to his upper lip. The sort of mustache you'd expect to see on a guy being handcuffed and loaded into the back of a squad car, his hard drive in tow.

"Today we're going to take care of your left knee, correct?" Vernon strolls over to the sink and runs the water. "The procedure is fairly standard. We should be in and out in about forty-five minutes. You'll be under a general anesthetic, so it will be over before you know it."

Two months is a long time to wait between injury and surgery, but for a while there my knee was the size of a grapefruit, far too swollen to operate on.

"I've never seen one this bad," Vernon told me during my intake appointment. *Stop it, Doc, I'm blushing.*

It happened during a routine warm-up, not five minutes into practice. Someone took a shot from outside, missing long. I tracked the ball off the back iron. Leapt after it. Then—*pop!*

It felt like my leg had snapped clean in half. I fully expected to look down and see my femur bursting through its fleshy cocoon, emerging into the world like a skeletal butterfly.

I did the smart thing after that and passed out. Woke up in the hospital a few hours later. My best friend Chevy Wyatt was there, which didn't strike me as odd. At first.

"Cam, there's been an accident."

I thought he was doing a bit. "Yeah, dude, I know. It was *my* goddamn leg."

I grinned. Chevy didn't. Single-car wreck, he explained. Only the driver had been hurt. Ally's ambulance arrived at the emergency room just two minutes ahead of mine. I'm not sure I buy the whole "we live in a simulation" theory, but as far as coincidences go, that one felt too cute by half.

The first few days were awful. That old cliché, the one about being in a bad dream you can't wake up from? Turns out, not bullshit. I left welts up and down my arms from pinching myself so many times. Nothing worked. It was the real deal. Eventually Ally's condition stabilized, but ever since, we've all collectively been playing the waiting game.

My injury turned out to be a blessing in disguise. Finally I had an excuse to bum around the house all day, feeling sorry for myself. Visible pain is much easier to understand than emotional, and anyone looking at me could tell you I was broken. Finally my outsides matched my insides.

Shit, I think Dr. Vernon's been talking this whole time. I start nodding like I've been paying attention.

"One last thing. In the coming days you will likely feel some . . . *discomfort* in your knee. For a tough guy like you, it shouldn't be a problem. But don't go overextending yourself. I need you taking it easy for a while. Be sure to get lots of bed rest."

You read my mind, Doc.

"To make life easier on you, I'm writing you a script for painkillers. Two-week supply. Once we've cleared that hurdle, we'll start weaning you onto a standard anti-inflammatory. Sound good?"

"You had me at 'Oxy,' Doc."

Dr. Vernon stuffs his pen in the front pocket of his lab coat. "Actually, we aren't prescribing oxycodone anymore."

"What then? Percocet? Morphine? Horse tranqs?"

Vernon kicks his stool to the cabinet and sifts through the drawers. "It's called Delatrix." He hands me the sampler pack. "Just approved by the FDA. Treats pain just as effectively as those other options without causing the same habit-forming afflictions. Incredible stuff—it's even safe to drive while taking it. So long as you haven't had anything to drink. But since you're underage that shouldn't be an issue."

Vernon shoots me a look. I pretend not to notice.

"The only downside is a higher likelihood of certain less severe side effects. So there's a greater chance you'll experience some nausea, bloating, headaches, vomiting, involuntary meta-physical phantasmal visitations, constipation—"

"Wait, what?" I really need to start paying attention. "Can you repeat that last one?"

"Constipation. Just take a laxative and you'll be squared away."

Weird. I could've sworn he said . . .

Eh, whatever. Let's just get this over with.

"Those are side effects? But they sound like so much fun," I deadpan.

Dr. Vernon chuckles to himself. "I get it, you're ready to go. But this is important. Just because we haven't seen the same level of abuse with Delatrix that we have with opiates doesn't mean it can't pose a risk if abused. Which is why we recommend you dispose of any excess capsules at the end of treatment. Did you see our drug take-back bin in the lobby?"

I shake my head.

"I'll have Nurse Molly point it out to you before you leave. Looks like a mailbox. Once you can comfortably go twenty-four hours without taking Delatrix, just swing by and drop any left-overs in there." He slaps me on the back. "Use your best judgment."

I compose a convincing smile. Lying to doctors is second nature.

"I always do."

NURSE MOLLY MOSEYS back in a few minutes later. She coaxes a vein out of hiding, snares it with an IV, and slips something in my drink. Next thing I know, Dr. Vernon's jostling me awake, his tire fire of a mustache inches from my face. Mom's there—I think? I don't know, man, everyone's just blobs to me. One way or another I make it home. That should be the end of it—the details from that hour the casualties of the powerful sedatives.

Unfortunately, no one thinks to confiscate my phone, so there exists textual evidence of what occurred from the hospital to my house.

To my best friend, Chevy.

> **CAM**
> Chevrolettttt
>
> the mustache man took my coloring book

CHEVY
> Someone's having fun. How're you feeling bud?

> I count get to waffle before Mary had a little lamb

Hahahaha sounds about right

> Chevy

> I'm fine

> Can I ask you a question?

Of course

> Can we go to the levy???

We sure can, big guy.

To my other best friend—and Chevy's girlfriend—Lisa:

> **CAM**
> hey

LISA

Well hello drugged-up Cameron. Chevy tells
me your surgery went well.

> are you with Chevy please tell him I say hi

"Hi Cam!"

-Chevy

> SORRY IF I INTERRUPTED I DON'T WANT
> TO GET IN THE WAY OF YOUR SEXY TIME

Is your keyboard stuck in caps lock?

> WHAT IF ALL THE FISH IN THE LAKE
> STARTED DROWNING

> WE WOULD NEVER KNOW

Chevy again.

CAM

CHEVY I DID SOMETING BAD

I ATE ALL THE OREOS

FOR BREAKFAST

CHEVY

Dude, you're not supposed to eat anything
before surgery! You're gonna get so sick later!

NOOOOOOOOOOREO

DON'T TELL CHEVY

And finally, to a number I haven't texted in almost five months.

CAM

ALLLLLLLLLLLYYYYYY

AYE GURL

WHATCHU ON LATER

Not Delivered

3

Imagine, if you will, a hangover. (I've never actually had one since I'm not geriatric, but I think I get the gist.) Your head's thumping, your body's desperate to vacate the previous night's mistakes, there's a malnourished honey badger on the loose inside your throat. Take all that unpleasantness and move it about four feet south. *Then* you might have some clue how my left leg feels when I come to.

The house is pitch black. Dead quiet, if not for the antique grandfather clock. I squint at the brass hands, trying to make sense of them, but the longer I stare, the more I forget how to tell time.

Fukkit, that's what phones are for.

2:14 . . . a.m. *The next day.*

Vernon said the anesthesia would wear off in a couple hours, not an entire goddamn day. My arm's still asleep. I unearth it from my ribs, muster what little strength it has, and prop myself up.

Big mistake.

Newton's first law of motion tells us an object at rest stays at rest unless acted upon by a force that sets it in motion.

The narcotics in my stomach were at rest. The second I move, they're set very much in motion.

Suddenly, the pain emanating from my knee is the least of my concerns. I snatch my crutches, falling once . . . twice . . . *three* times before successfully making it upright. There isn't time to secure them under my arms. I squeeze the handgrips in the crooks of my elbows and army-crawl into our front hall, dragging my decrepit leg behind me.

The next few minutes are . . . let's say *rough*. Chevy loves to brag about his ability to throw up on command, then proceed with his evening like nothing happened—aka "Boot and Rally." Not me. If I boot, just call it. Night over.

Once there's nothing left to purge, my stomach and throat manage to call a momentary truce. Extracting my head from its unfortunate helmet is its own challenge, so I rest my cheek on the cool bowl. Allow my eyes to creep closed. Finally, a moment of peace.

"Jesus, Cammie, what have you done to yourself?"

I don't move—couldn't if I tried. I simply open my eyes. There, leaning against the door frame, an imposing five feet two inches, weighing in at "I'm not telling you," is Allison Tandy.

My Ally. In all her ginger glory. My gaze travels naturally, starting with her feet—size seven—her bony ankles. Her warm, dimpled tummy. Her boobs—all two of them. Her lips. Soft. Pink. Full. Her eyes. Big. Blue. Aimed right at me.

"Al?"

The smirk falls from her lips.

"Cam?" she says breathlessly. "Can you see me?"

I don't respond. Or look away.

"You can, can't you?"

Ally lets out a strained laugh, then stumbles. Weak knees. I know the feeling. I watch as she weaves her fingers together and balances them behind her head.

"Holy shit . . . holy shit."

Her eyes haven't left mine. Like she's worried if we break eye contact, I'm the one who might disappear. Not the other way around.

"How is this even possible?"

She's asking me, I realize. Fuck if I know. I'm still charging.

"You know what—" Ally throws up her hands. "Doesn't matter, because *holy shit*! How are you not freaking out right now?"

Good question. Because I should be shocked, right? So why aren't I? The answer hits me, seeming painfully obvious; this isn't real. Do you know how often I see Ally like this? Every. Single. Night. She was a mainstay in the Cameron Garrity REM extended universe well before her accident.

Granted, this does feel different. My memory never quite gets all the details exactly right. Tonight is as close as it's come to reproducing the real thing.

"Can we not," I'm finally able to say, my cheek still glued to the toilet seat. "Not tonight. I can't do it."

Ally's hands find her hips. "Can't do what?"

"*This* . . ." Motor function isn't coming easy; I barely manage to flop my noodle-like arm in Ally's general direction. "Another dream. In a few seconds, I'll wake up, you'll be gone, and everything will be fine."

An unsettling grin spreads over Ally's lips. "Cameron Alan Garrity, are you saying you dream about me?"

"No—NO!—that's not what I meant!"

"Too late, you already admitted it." Ally cracks up. She's actually enjoying this. *Why's she looking at me like that?*

"I wonder . . ."

I blink, and she's on me, erasing the gap between us in a split second. Crouching down to my level. An arm's length away. Close enough for me to make out the bump on her bottom lip, a keloid scar from when she was a kid. You can't see it from a distance, only at close range. Kissing distance. My favorite place in the whole world.

"Touch me," Ally says next, and suddenly this dream just became *way* more interesting. "You want to make sure this is real, don't you? So do I. So, touch me, and let's have our answer."

"No, Al. I'm not gonna do that. And you know why?" I dig deep, summon the strength to lift my head. Face her straight on. "Because this isn't real. You're not really here. I'm not really covered in vomit. And—"

Just like that, Ally plants one on me. The soft part of my cheek, where there's untrimmed stubble. Never saw it coming. Her lips are soft and gone much too soon. She takes me by the chin and turns my head to the side, then gasps.

"What—"

Again, I don't see it coming, only this time it's her palm, open-handed, fingers spread wide.

The crack of her hand connecting with my face leaves behind an echo, pulsating off the walls in lockstep with the searing rhythm bleating in my cheek.

"Ow!"

Ally jerks away from me, looking panicked. Like she's the one who just had the shit slapped out of her.

"Ow!" I holler out again.

Is she laughing? Even with a hand—the culprit—over her mouth I can still hear her cackling. "Shit, I am so sorry. That was uncalled-for. But I had to be sure. Cam! I can touch you!"

Yeah. I'd noticed.

To herself: "That's impossible!" To me: "Do you have any idea what this means?"

Walking on her knees, Ally draws near. This time I'm not taking any chances. I feel around for a weapon, er, the closest thing in my vicinity.

"Stay back!" I thrust the plastic toilet brush at her chest. Ally looks at it, amused, and bats it out of my trembling hand.

"What exactly are you afraid of here? You just said this isn't real. And if it isn't real, that means it's all in your head. And if it's all in your head . . ." She shrugs. "Then technically, you slapped yourself."

"That's not what . . ." *Is it just me, or is the room spinning?* "You can't just . . ." *Jesus, I'm gonna yuke again.* "Goddamnit, Al . . ." *Don't throw up on her.* "Just—just gimme a second."

The floor's gone, replaced by a Gravitron. My elbow buckles from under me. Going down. The room fades gradually, color and light fading until all I can hear is my own heart drumming in my chest and the sound of Ally cackling in delight.

IT'S BRIGHT. Too bright. I'm an amoeba under a microscope. Impossible to open my eyes all the way. I'm left squinting through my lashes as I wait for them to adjust. I'm still in the bathroom, I realize, when I try moving my arms and ding my funny bone on the toilet. Status update.

Knee: inflamed, but still in one piece.

Tummy: growling, like the masochist it is.

Cheek: tender. *Tender?*

I straighten suddenly, forcing my eyes open. Just like my dream, I think. Only no sign of Ally. Because of course there isn't! Why would there be?!

I touch my cheek again. Still stings. I probably just slept on it funny. Yeah, that's it. The other stuff was just a dream. A hyper-realistic, weirdly painful dream. My subconscious can object all it wants; that's my story and I'm sticking to it.

Just to be safe, I don't get up right away. I wait. And watch. Glancing at the door every few seconds, wondering what it would mean if my dreams actually came true.

———

If you're looking for a meet-cute, you've come to the wrong place.

Nothing could be less cute, at least on my end. See, my mom has this really annoying habit of seeing patients in our kitchen, even though she has a lovely office, complete with exam tables, stethoscopes, the works. And Dr. Garrity is Shermer's preferred pediatrician, which means it isn't uncommon to run into one of my classmates while making a PB&J. (I'm still haunted by the time I overheard her ask Johnny Bowden to "cough twice.")

It was an otherwise unremarkable late August morning, the waning days of summer break. Around noon-ish I rolled out of bed and plodded to the bathroom. While I waited for the shower to warm, I noticed a small group of bubble-gum-colored bumps clustered on my left shoulder.

Atopic dermatitis, also known as eczema. I had it bad when I was little. Not so much anymore, but I still get flare-ups sometimes.

"Moooooom?"

Did I put a shirt on before bumbling downstairs? No, no I did not.

"Hey, Moooooom?"

Did I put shorts on? No, no I did not.

"Moooooom, can you look at this? I think the eczema is back—"

Was I wearing only a towel when I walked into the kitchen and saw Allison Tandy sitting on a barstool? Of fucking course I was.

"You're not my mom."

Ally snorted. "God, I sure hope not."

It took me a second to gather my wits. "Ally. Allison Tandy."

She mirrored my cadence. "Cam. Cameron Garrity. We're using full names, then? So formal, I like it." She tilted her chin at me. "Cameron Garrity, you forgot your shirt."

"Oh, right. I was about to shower, but then . . ."

"Something about eczema."

"Right. Eczema."

Ah, yes. Nothing like a recurring skin condition to set the mood. Sparks were flying.

I knew of Ally, I just didn't really know her, you know? That's the trouble with Shermer Township High School (STHS for short). With over thirty-five hundred students, you can go all four years without crossing paths with some people. Even the most important ones. I knew she was pretty good friends with Chevy—they were in a bunch of the same extracurriculars. Debate/speech, community service club, Best Buddies, stuff like that. Chevy was thrilled later when I told him we'd started talking. "Of course you should go out with Ally!" I remember him shouting. "Why didn't I think of this sooner?!"

Otherwise, Allison Tandy was a mystery.

That morning, Ally had her hair tied back in a ponytail. She's a redhead, but not a full ginger, as she's quick to point out. Her hair actually gets darker during the cold months, but summer brings strawberries. She was wearing this enormous tattered Cubs sweatshirt, baggy enough that when she went to stand, it concealed her track shorts. You just had to assume they were there.

Eventually I scooped my jaw off the floor long enough to ask, "What're you doing here?"

"Picking up a new script for my birth control. Dr. Garrity—your mom—ran upstairs to find her pad."

"Oh, awesome." I remember sweating up a storm. "Birth control is . . . awesome." And nodding profusely. "I mean, it's awesome you're on it. You know. Because . . . of . . . babies." And fitting my whole-ass foot in my mouth. "Unless you want babies. Which is . . . also awesome. You know. Your body, your choice. And all that."

"Uh-huh."

I noticed then her eyes kept flitting to my chest, and I suddenly regretted skipping voluntary lifts that morning. Really wished she was seeing me post-pump.

"Cameron Garrity, can I ask you a personal question?"

"Yeah, sure." I straightened my back. Flexed my stomach muscles.

"You don't have to answer if you don't want to."

"I don't mind."

"Since we don't really know each other . . ."

"Go for it."

Ally motioned at me, her hands still bunched in her sleeves. "Is one of your nipples an innie?"

And that, ladies and gentlemen, is where it started. Really. With eczema and concave nipples. And yes, technically Tyson (my name for my left nipple) is an innie. But he's just a shy guy. Eddy (my right nipple) and I respect his decision.

Ally wouldn't get a closer look—at least not yet. Mom returned soon after and shooed me away.

But the damage was done. I was hooked. No doubt about it.

4

"Cameron!"

Meet my little sister, Maizy.

"Caaaam-roooooon."

Maizy's ten years old.

"Camroncamroncamroncamron!"

We're still working on boundaries.

"Go away," I mumble into my pillow, pulling the blanket over my head.

"Mom says you're not allowed to sleep all day again," Maizy continues. "She says if you sleep now, you won't be able to tonight." When I don't respond, she jostles my shoulder. "Cameron! Did you hear me?"

"Tell Mom I'm dead. She'll know what that means."

It's just the three of us here—me, Mom, and Maizy. People usually assume, because of the age difference, that we must have different fathers. Not the case. My parents separated shortly after they had me, then reconnected a few years later. Popped out another kid. Dad didn't stick around too long after. He works some fancy corporate job. Travels a lot. Calls on occasion. Sends gifts when appropriate. Otherwise, he's not really involved. Word of advice: Whatever you do, don't ask Mom about him. The company line: "As long as his child support comes on time, I couldn't care less what that man does."

In the wake of Ally's accident, Mom insisted we tell Maizy about what'd happened. I lobbied against it; Maizy and Ally were close while we were together. Ally and I used to go to her soccer games and take her for ice cream after.

Ally'd tell her things like, "You're a much better athlete than your brother."

Maizy would start cheesing and say something cocky like, "I know," then proceed to order the maximum number of scoops allowed. Her brother's a real pushover.

A moment passes without further inquisition. Maizy's breathing dwindles until all I hear is a faint whir—the dehumidifier maybe? My body relaxes and sinks deeper into the cushions. I begin to drift, completely unaware of the hyperactive fourth grader hurtling my way.

Her piercing battle cry—"WAKE UP!"—is the only warning I get. My eyes split open just in time to see her five-foot frame take flight. Miraculously, she avoids the cast, but the surprise causes my body to tense. Including my knee. The pain is instant and excruciating.

"JESUS CHRIST!"

"Sorry-sorry-sorry-sorry," I can hear my sister repeating, her voice shrinking, as the virginal tendons binding my leg together continue howling in agony. "Please don't be mad at me."

Too late.

"What did I tell you about sneaking up on people like that?" I shout.

Maizy turtles into her T-shirt. "Don't do it."

"And what did you do?"

"I snuck up on you—"

"You snuck up on me!"

It takes another minute or so for my defenses to fully recoil, and even then I can still feel my heart beating at the point of incision. With all the action last night, I didn't have a chance to check out Dr. Vernon's handiwork.

The cast is unlike any I've ever seen, nothing like the one I had when I broke my arm in fourth grade. Looking at it now, I'm realizing just how much of a tank it is. The thing completely encases my leg, with thick straps woven down the front, securing the generous padding in place. On either side are these black coaster-sized dials locking the joint in place at 180 degrees. I unbuckle the straps and find a second layer, a translucent ice pack hooked into the dehumidifier-looking machine at my feet. *That explains the whirring.* Underneath, a taupe-colored bandage provides the final layer of protection.

I look part cyborg. Sure as shit don't feel like it, though.

Curiosity getting the better of her, Maizy pokes out of her shell and hurries closer. "Does it hurt?"

"Yes."

"How much?"

"A lot."

"Like, a lot, a lot?"

"Do you remember learning about the Civil War?" She nods. "Imagine my thigh is the North, and my calf is the South. And this . . ." I land on my knee. "This is Gettysburg."

Maizy scrunches her cheeks, confused. I don't know why; it's a spot-on analogy. "You're weird, Cameron."

"Thank you, Maizy."

My phone's lighting up. I have Maizy get it for me, and I start thumbing through my missed notifications. Only then do I learn the extent of drugged-out Cam's damage.

Maizy doesn't sit idly; I track her progression peripherally as she scooches closer . . . and closer . . . and closer . . . until finally—

"Maizy."

"Uh-huh?"

"Why is your finger in my face?"

Maizy counters with a question of her own. "How come you have a mark here, Cameron?"

"I don't." I swat her hand away, but it boomerangs back.

"Yes you do! See, right here."

Maizy pulls her iPad out of nowhere. Shoves it an inch from my face with the front-facing camera open. I grab the tablet from her, take a look for myself.

"I already told you, Maiz, I don't have a—"

Well, shit. Just below my left eye is small pink blemish in the shape of a kiss.

My equilibrium comes roaring back. *But . . . that's impossible.* I must've slept on it funny. That tracks, right? It certainly makes more sense than Allison Tandy rising from the (almost) dead.

"Are you okay, Cameron?"

"Huh?" Maizy's gawking at me. "Yeah . . . Yeah, Maiz, I'm fine." Just then, my phone dings again.

CHEVY

You up yet?

Idk why I asked, I'm already headed over

Maizy curves her neck so she can read the banner. "Chevy's coming over?"

"Looks that way," I say. "Don't you have a crush on—" My audience is already on the move, dismounting off the couch and vaulting over the coffee table before I can finish my thought.

I wait until her footsteps peter out before switching the camera back on. My hair is a wreck—cowlicks for days. The three-day stubble I'm working on isn't doing me any favors.

But I could give a shit about any of that. What concerns me is my cheek—or rather, the residue left on it. That, and the strangely crystalline memories I have from my dream last night. Memories I'd prefer to forget.

You don't realize what a luxury bending your knee is until, suddenly, you can't.

Case in point, there are two stairs—two literal *steps*—that lead up to our kitchen from the rest of the first floor. Two stairs

I'd never given a second thought to in the eighteen years I've lived here.

Until now.

After staring at them a solid thirty seconds, I make my move. I plant a crutch on the first step, then leverage my weight, swinging my immobilized leg over the landing. But before my foot clears the edge, momentum takes the wheel, followed swiftly by its co-conspirator, gravity. I crash instantly. The floor and I are becoming well-acquainted.

Mom doesn't flinch. "Good, you're awake." She's stationed at the counter—her de facto desk when she works from home— rapping on her keyboard like she's mad at it.

I prop my chin on the cool lacquered wood. "No, no. Don't get up. Really, Mom, I'm all good down here."

Mom ignores my crack. "You left the powder room light on last night. Do you have any idea how much electricity that wastes?"

"I wanna say . . . six? Is that right?"

Mom's nose twitches. Tough crowd. "Are you going to lie there all day or are you going to pick yourself up so we can finish our conversation from yester—"

Just then, the patio door careens open, cutting Mom short. Enter The Happy Couple.

"Cindy!" Chevy hustles over to the counter and gives Mom a wraparound hug over her shoulders.

"Hi, Chevy. How are you?"

"Better now that I'm with you. You're looking lovely today, as per usual." Mom rolls her eyes, but there's a whiff of a smile on her lips. Chevy's the only one of my friends Mom allows to use her first name. To everyone else, she's Dr. Garrity. But Chevy gets away with all kinds of shit like that. I know it, and Lisa does too. She sticks to formalities.

"Hi, Dr. Garrity." Lisa steps out from behind Chevy and—Jesus Christ, they're wearing matching outfits. Identical STHS girls' lacrosse pennies and Creamsicle Hawaiian-print shorts. You see the kind of shit I have to deal with? It's like, *We get it! You're dating! Good for you!*

Some of us aren't so lucky.

Chevy and I have been best friends going on eight years now, ever since his family moved in across the street. Their house is right on Lake Michigan, which means that yes, Chevy does have a beach in his backyard. Er, rather, the beach *is* his backyard. Either-or.

The two of us make for a strange pair. I'm white, he's Black. I've been to the weight room, Chevy's built like the skeleton man in *The Nightmare Before Christmas*. Girls think he's cute, girls think I'm . . . I don't know—tall? Same thing personality-wise. Chevy is relentlessly sunny. And charming. And likable. The kind of guy who ascended the STHS social ladder through sheer force of personality and an endless list of extracurriculars.

Versus me. I play basketball. And can't stand anyone. Go figure.

The Happy Couple then turn their collective attention to me. Chevy states the obvious.

"You look like shit."

Mom's focused on her screen. I take advantage, wordlessly assuring my friends that, while my leg is in ruins, my middle finger remains intact.

"He's just being dramatic," Mom chimes in.

"Thank you, Mother, for that ringing endorsement."

Chevy comes over and squats beside me. Knees *completely* bent. Show-off. "How was surgery?"

"Yeah, I'm gonna need you to close those." His crotch is right in my face. Instead, Chevy spreads them farther apart, waddles closer. I flinch at him, throwing off his balance.

"Can you guys stop flirting for like one second?" Lisa quips, stepping over her boyfriend.

"Didn't realize you were coming," I say.

"We have a team lift in an hour," Lisa explains. "I just came to make sure you weren't dead."

"So thoughtful."

"Thanks, I'm kind of an amazing friend."

Like Sandy Koufax and Amar'e Stoudemire before her, Lisa Langer follows in the rich tradition of exceptional Jewish athletes. By sophomore year, she had already committed to play volleyball at the University of Wisconsin. (Chevy's headed to Stanford.) (Can you say *safety school?*) During the school's off-season, she plays for this elite Chicago club team, so even in the summer her attendance at group functions isn't guaranteed.

Lisa offers me a hand then. "Come on, let's get you up."

I grab hold. The second Lisa begins to hoist me, my knee tenses. It's inadvertent, but the muscles in my leg don't care. They howl bloody murder. My leg twists awkwardly, slagging behind the rest of my able limbs. I yelp out and start to buckle, but Lisa's got those Division One reflexes. She cups me by the armpit and steadies us, buying Chevy the second he needs to spring into action and link his arm around my waist. Together, they haul me to my feet. Er, foot.

"That bad, huh?" Chevy asks, baring his teeth apologetically. The two of them act as my crutches, helping me over to the kitchen island. They arrange two stools—one for my foot, one for my ass. Dr. Vernon was very clear about keeping my knee elevated while it healed.

"Have any of you seen Rose Hollander around school recently?" Mom asks once I'm settled. "She was supposed to come in for a follow-up appointment, but I haven't had any luck reaching her or her parents."

"Hmm. Not that I can think of." Chevy already has his head buried in the fridge. He starts blindly lobbing sandwich ingredients over his shoulder—bread, ham, cheese. Lisa's there to catch them.

"Yeah, no. Sorry, Dr. Garrity," she adds. "I had a class with her last semester, but she switched sections."

Mom turns my way. "Don't look at me," I say.

Once the fridge is tapped, Chevy moves to the pantry. "You want chips on yours, babe?"

"You know me so well, babe."

"I'm lucky to know you at all, babe."

Aaaaand, great, now they're kissing. Is no place safe from their boundless affection? Get a room. Preferably one that isn't my kitchen.

I shouldn't be complaining. The two of them have always been like this. Four years together and still acting like couples did back in middle school, always touching on each other, trading sappy compliments.

You're so beautiful . . . Your intellect inspires me . . . I would do anything for you . . .

Who talks like that?!

Most people still find them adorable—they ran away with the "Most Likely to Get Married" vote in the yearbook. (Oddly enough, Chevy and I came in second.) But then, most people don't have to sit through this shit every day. Most people aren't nursing a broken heart.

It takes three *"Ahems!"* to pry them apart. Blushing, Chevy gestures to the spread. "You want one?"

I shake my head. The thought of digesting even a single slice of unbuttered toast is enough to kick-start the churning below my belt.

"What's going on with Rose?" I ask Mom, hoping to change the subject.

"None of your business," she snaps. "You know I can't talk about my patients, Cameron. I could lose my medical license. Do you want me to lose my medical license?"

"Seriously, Mom? All you do is tell us about your patients! It's like your go-to party trick."

What you need to understand is there's precedent here. Mom

is always divulging the intimate details of my classmates' medical histories, especially when Chardonnay is involved. It's actually proved to be a huge problem—I had to beg her not to tell me anything about Ally after we started dating.

Mom glares at me now like I've just cursed out my grandma. "When have I ever done that?"

"What about the time you told us Piper Bell is adopted and doesn't know it?"

"Or that George Douglasson has a micropenis?" Chevy adds.

"Or how Lizzy Pope has a sentient fibroid?" Lisa piles on.

"Or how Pat Michaels has to wear an adult diaper because he has stress incontinence?"

"Jesus, that guy is falling apart."

By now, smoke's billowing from Mom's nose. "I only shared those things because I assumed you three knew better than to gossip."

Surprise—we didn't know better!

Mom slams her laptop closed and pushes away from the counter, her stool whining against the floor. "I'm not going to sit here and listen to you question my integrity."

"Aw, come on, Cin. We were just messing around," Chevy protests, but Mom waves him off.

"It's fine, it's not a big deal." Which is precisely what Mom says when she wants you to know something is a big deal. "I have to take Maizy to school anyway." She takes a second to compose herself—it's all so very dramatic—then looks down at her loose-fitting Submariner, a wedding gift from my dad she never got around to taking off. "Where is that girl? She should've been down here five minutes ago."

Mom sticks her head in the front hall and shouts up the staircase, "MAIZY! WE NEED TO GO!" She turns to me. "I left your painkillers on the windowsill," she says to me. "Dr. Vernon wants you to take two every six to eight hours. Got it?"

"Take six to eight every two hours, got it."

Mom slings her straw summer bag over her shoulder and slips her sunglasses on. "You're not as funny as you think you are. The last thing you need is a substance dependency." She considers our company. "The same goes for you two. Don't go getting any ideas."

Chevy gasps, sensationalizing his offense. "Cindy, I would *never*! You know your son and I only do drugs with needles."

Mom rolls her eyes. "Tell your sister I'm in the car."

Once she's outside, Chevy goes, "God, I love your mom."

"You don't have to live with her."

Lisa circles the island. "So what'd they give you, anyway?" she asks as she picks the bottle up.

"I forget what it's called. Something like . . . Demonmix? Datablitz?"

Chevy perks up. "Delatrix?"

"Yeah, that's it."

"No way!" Chevy snaps and Lisa passes him the bottle. "I've heard about this stuff. It's supposed to be wild."

"Really?" I frown. "My doctor told me it was safer than the painkillers they used to give out."

39

"It is. But apparently some people experience the *craziest* side effects. Like, way wilder than some hallucinogens. It's a super-small percentage, though, something like point one percent of people." He unscrews the cap and looks down the barrel. "Is this all they gave you?" I shrug. "Any refills?"

"Nah, I think they're way stricter about that stuff now."

Chevy hands me the bottle, and I dump a few capsules into my palm. Each one is cylindrical. Half-red, half-white. Coated in a chalky powder that cakes onto my skin, like white cheddar Cheeto dust. I hold one up to the light. Inside are these little beads, almost like poppy seeds. And somehow ingesting them makes the pain in my knee a little less than unbearable.

I raise two overhead—a toast to modern medicine and the chemists at Synergy Pharmaceuticals—and toss them back.

5

After Mom leaves, we retire to the living room, where my new best friend is waiting. The POLAR ICE™ 5000, or POL-I, as I now refer to her. I can't connect to her fast enough. Ours is a new relationship, one built on support, comfort, and her unique ability to numb the hellfire incessantly smoldering beneath my stitches. POL-I is the only good thing in my life right now. I would die for her.

POL-I has the look of a shredder, save the four hoses protruding from her sides. It takes me a second to get situated and link each of the hoses to its corresponding valve on my ice sleeve—the middle layer between brace and bandage. Once everything's secure, I power POL-I on and watch as she spits coolant through the tubes. A welcome chill engulfs my leg.

Sweet, sweet release.

I drape a bicep over my eyes and lie back. "You guys have got to try this when I'm finished. It's like cocaine mixed with nicotine mixed with confectioners' sugar. And more cocaine." I wait for a laugh, a response of any kind. "I said, better than the time we—" Murmuring now, urgent whispers. I lift my arm. "Guys?"

The Happy Couple stands shoulder to shoulder, facing me. Shoes off, Chevy has maybe an inch on Lisa, if that. He's a good enough sport about it when she wears heels.

"What's going on?"

They share a look. Never a good sign. Chevy and Lisa don't usually keep things from me; we were as close to a throuple as you could get without making it all the way to Paris. (That's Ally's joke, for the record. She would insist on credit.) I was the first person Lisa called after each scholarship offer she received from some brand-name school. Chevy's my emergency contact in the STHS directory. But recently, I've noticed a growing number of these knowing, privileged glances.

"Would someone just say something!"

Chevy draws a short breath. "Cam, this is an intervention."

My first instinct is to laugh. *Surely I misheard.* "Sorry, what?" I've only ever seen interventions in movies and stuff. And once with my uncle Markey, but that was a much different situation. He got caught up in something called *findom*, where you pay a woman online to say mean things to you. (I don't get it either.) Things got pretty bad. Drained his 401k along with my cousin's entire college savings account. They had to refinance their house. *That* warranted an intervention. What the hell did I do?

"Maybe it would be easier if I read from my letter," Lisa volunteers. She lifts her phone up to her face. "Dear Cameron," she recites. "Thank you for agreeing to meet with us today . . ."

"I've agreed to nothing."

"Chevy and I are here because we love you . . ."

42

"I only like you guys as friends."

"And we want our final few months in Shermer to be the best they can be."

Then it dawns on me. "This is about Ally, isn't it?" Lisa's mouth gapes open. Chevy takes an interest in his sandals. "So let me get this straight," I say, raising my voice. "You two are intervention-ing me"—*is that a verb?*—"because you want me to forget the fact that Ally is in a coma? So we, what? Can have a normal, *fun-filled* summer?"

"That's not—" Chevy grimaces. Lisa starts rubbing his back. "Cam, we'd never expect you to forget about Ally."

"We're not here to mourn-shame you," Lisa adds. "Ally was—*is!*" She quickly corrects herself. "Our friend too. I know I haven't stopped thinking about her since the accident, and I'm not the one who dated her for a year."

Chevy nods along. "This isn't about forgetting her." He pauses, nervously sliding his teeth along his bottom lip. "That said, Lisa and I have been talking, and we think it's time you got back out there. Start the process of getting over Ally."

My pulse revs up.

I am over Allison Tandy.

"Guys, you don't have to worry about me," I insist. "I'm fine!"

Again with the looks.

"How do I put this delicately?" Chevy scratches his chin. "Cam, all you do is talk about Ally."

"Last month in English, you managed to turn a class discus-sion about *The Grapes of Wrath* into a rant about Ally's love of oat milk," Lisa says. "Mr. Broderick pulled me aside after class to ask if you were feeling okay and if you, quote, 'need to talk to someone.'"

"Yeah, and when we were making plans for prom house, you suggested, in front of my parents, we bring Ally along for, and I quote, '*Weekend at Bernie's*–style hijinks.'" Chevy cringes. "My parents love you. But still. Not a great look."

"Then there was the incident the other day with—"

"Alright, I get it!"

It's impossible to argue with them when they get on a roll like this. That wasn't an issue when Ally and I were together; finally, after years of getting double-teamed, I had a partner to match up against them. Ally was great at it too, she—

Shit.

I'm doing it again, aren't I? Shoehorning her into every conversation—even the ones with myself.

Okay, so maybe they have a point. Between the breakup and the accident, Ally's been on my mind a lot lately. A one-two sucker punch sure to leave anyone flat on their ass. But that doesn't mean I'm not over her.

"Look, we wouldn't be doing this if Ally's situation hadn't improved, health-wise," Chevy says. "But she's stable, right? And her doctors think she'll wake up soon-ish. Cindy said so herself."

I frown. "When did Mom say that?"

"Yesterday."

"When did you talk to her yesterday?"

". . ."

"Dude, what did I tell you about texting her?!"

"Don't change the subject!" Chevy forges ahead. "Cindy says they're optimistic about Ally's chances. She's gonna be okay, man. It's just a matter of time. Soon she'll wake up, and this will all amount to a three-month nap."

Lisa whistles, laughing to herself. "God, I'd cut off my left hand for a three-month nap."

Chevy extends his bottom lip. "Aw, babe. Your spiking hand."

We interrupt this intervention to bring you ten uninterrupted seconds of The Happy Couple gazing longingly into each other's eyes, a subtle reminder to anyone in close proximity (i.e., me) that he is violently alone. Thanks, guys.

I am pretty lonely. After Ally's accident, I took to isolation like dust to electronics. The steady stream of daily messages slowed to a trickle. Eventually they dried up altogether. Not so fun hanging out with a guy who's heartbroken and in mourning. Can't say I blame them. I wouldn't want to spend time with me either.

Maybe The Happy Couple is right. Strictly speaking, Ally is "okay." Er, as okay as anyone attached to a ventilator can be. And she did break my heart. That happened—no denying it.

"Let's say I was interested in getting back out there— *hypothetically*," I'm quick to clarify. "Who's gonna want to hook up with me like *this*?" I gesture up and down my leg.

Chevy breaks into a smile. "I'm so glad you asked." Lisa reaches into her bag and pulls out her laptop. "Behold!" Chevy shouts, and she places it on the coffee table in front of me. "The Cam Rebound Project!"

The words *The Cam Rebound Project* appear on-screen under a red-faced photo of me from some party last year.

"We approached this endeavor with one simple challenge." Chevy clicks to the first slide. "How could we find a suitable rebound for a subject as stubborn . . ."

"Grumpy," Lisa adds.

"Lazy."

"Irritable—"

I cut them off. "I get it!"

"Our methodology had to be airtight," Chevy continues. "Data driven. Otherwise you'd dismiss us right away."

Lisa takes over with the next slide. I feel like I'm at a TED Talk. "This process began back in January, days after you and Ally broke up—*well* before her accident. Back then, it was all very basic, just some light, informal polling to help us better understand your desirability index within the greater STHS student body at large."

I frown. "My what?"

"How much people want to hook up with you," Chevy explains. "These results proved essential when it came time to develop the questionnaire."

My chest tightens. "What questionnaire?"

"This one." Next slide. A half-dozen bullet-pointed questions, each one more embarrassing than the last.

On a scale of 1 to 10 . . .

- How would you rate your level of interest in hooking up with Cameron Garrity?
- Do you find Cameron Garrity funny? If not, are you willing to laugh at his jokes anyway?
- Are you a patient of Dr. Cindy Garrity?

I feel my face getting hot. "You guys gave this out to every girl in our grade?"

"God, no," Lisa says with a laugh. I breathe a sigh of relief. "Not our entire grade. That would be *crazy*. Just like two hundred. Give or take."

"*Two hundred?*" My muscles tense—a mistake. The pain racing up my thigh supersedes any embarrassment.

"We needed to be thorough!" Chevy argues. "Otherwise it would've thrown off our entire algorithm." Next slide: a dizzying array of numbers and equations. "We created it using factors specifically tailored to your wants and needs. Things like sense of humor, height . . ."

Lisa picks up. "Attractiveness, what they're looking for out of a physical relationship. But most important." She grasps Chevy's hand. "Whether or not *we'd* be willing to hang out with them for the next four months."

I roll my eyes. "Why would I care whether you guys want to hang with who I'm hooking up with?"

Twin blank stares. Twin bursts of laughter.

"That's a good one, Cam," Lisa says, wiping away tears. "But seriously, we're just as much a part of this as you are."

"This is our last summer in Shermer," Chevy says. "Did you really think we'd leave this decision entirely up to you?"

And here I thought I had a say in who gets to stick their tongue down my throat.

"To that point," Chevy continues, "we did apply editorial discretion in some instances. Like Avery Prewitt—she ranked pretty high initially. But then she announced she's going to Ole Miss next year, and we don't trust someone voluntarily moving south of the Mason-Dixon."

"Or Camryn Walters," Lisa says. "Since she has the same name as you. Which, gross."

"Phoebe Lin wears transition lenses."

"Sophie Zachs is an anti-vaxxer, and Cindy says you're due for your boosters next month."

"Aisha Yarborough has a new boyfriend."

"Mae Raddison has a new girlfriend."

"Britnee Bailey started wearing her hair in a side ponytail . . ."

They continue on like this for a while, rattling off discarded candidates. Finally, I'm like, "Is there anyone left, or have you guys ruled out the whole school?"

Lisa reaches into her backpack, producing a black leather folio—the kind I imagine businesspeople carry into boardroom meetings. "Presenting the official dossier of the Cam Rebound Project." She places it delicately on the coffee table in front of me. "Inside you'll find the final list—your top twenty potential matches, ranked according to the algorithm."

"We took the liberty of drawing up profiles for each of them," Chevy says. "Including their scores from the questionnaire. In case you had doubts about their interest."

There was this brief period a few years ago when my mother decided to try her hand at cooking. I can still remember the look of anticipation on her face as she watched me bite into whatever she'd prepared, followed by sheer disappointment when I spit it into my napkin.

That's how The Happy Couple is looking at me now. I don't want to spit their project in my napkin.

So I pick up the dossier. Flip through the first couple pages. "Let me think about it." They go to celebrate, but I shut it down. "No promises, okay? This is still weird for me. It's just— with everything else going on . . ." I trail off. "I don't know. I still feel bad."

Chevy's expression turns serious. "We all want Ally to wake up, man." He glances at Lisa, who nods hastily. "But Ally broke your heart. She started seeing someone else. So while she may be our friend too, you were our friend first. And this?" He taps the dossier's cover. "*This* is your fresh start. *This* is how you get over her. You do want to get over her, right?"

I am over Allison Tandy. Of course I want to.

I think.

———

LAST TIME, I didn't have to work quite as hard. Last time, I wasn't nursing a broken heart or a busted kneecap. Last time, well, frankly, Ally did most of the heavy lifting. Starting with asking me out. About a week after the Eczema Incident, she cornered me at my locker.

"Cam?"

I spun around.

"I almost didn't recognize you with a shirt on." Ally's the kind of person who can't help snorting at her own joke before she's even reached the punch line. Very cute.

"You know, I tried taking it off earlier, but apparently it's against the rules," I said, playing along. "Something about a dress code violation."

"It's so unfair of them to censor your body like that. It must be so tough being a tall, attractive, white guy."

My ears perked up. "You think I'm attractive?"

Ally cheeks flushed. Her one tell. The ginger's curse. "Mmm, don't think so. I remember saying white. Because you are very, *very* white."

"Wow, high praise coming from a ginger."

"Hey, only we can say that word!"

The one-minute bell poured cold water on us.

Ally looked at her phone, then went, "When's your lunch period?"

"Right now. You?"

"Same. We should grab food sometime."

"Yeah!" *Too thirsty.* "Yeah . . . ?" *Too uncertain.* "I mean, yeah. Sounds like fun."

"Great." I expected her to leave, but she just kept standing there eyeballing me. "How about now?"

I drove. Ally picked the restaurant. Walker Bros. Pancake House, a Shermer institution. We split a stack of chocolate chip pancakes and drank bottomless OJs.

Right off the bat, Ally set the tone.

"No pop-culture talk. My one rule."

I gave her a look. "That's a weird rule."

"Not forever—just right now. I feel like people always use whatever show they're watching or music they like as a substitute for having an actual personality, you know? Like, we all watch the same stuff on Netflix. We all listen to Kid Xannabis."

I perked up. "You listen to Kid Xannabis?"

She shot me a playful look. "We'll have plenty of time to talk about it eventually. Just not yet. Not until I've decided what I'm gonna do with you."

My stomach twisted. I could think of a lot of things I wanted her to do with me. From that day, we started talking. And when I say talking I don't mean the physical act of conversing, I mean it in the modern context, i.e., texting constantly between hookups. A couple months later, at Chevy's Halloween party, we made it official. Ally was pretty drunk when she and her friends rolled in; I remember her stumbling into my arms when they arrived.

"Hey!" she shouted over the music.

"Hey!" I did the same.

Then she booped me on the nose. But, like, in a romantic way. "I don't want you to hook up with anyone else."

"Oh. Okay. I don't want you to hook up with anyone else," I shouted back.

"Good, then it's settled."

"What is?"

She hit me square in the sternum with the heel of her hand. Hard. Twice. "We're dating."

I never considered falling in love with Ally a mistake. An inevitability, maybe, but not a mistake. The mistake came in assuming she'd feel the same way.

6

I've sweat the bed.

Er, couch. The cushions squelch as I sit up. My shirt's sticking to me like it's mile day in gym class. Falling asleep in the afternoon is always so goddamn disorienting, especially when the sun sets while you're KO'd. It takes me a second to get my bearings. My knee wastes no time making its objections known. Time to re-up.

The Delatrix bottle is right where I left it, on the windowsill above the kitchen sink, shaded by Mom's wilting Christmas cactus. I take two, chase the capsules with water, and pour the rest of the glass in the cactus's pot. The pills taste bitter. Maybe that's just my mouth. God, when was the last time I brushed my teeth? The fact that I even have to ask isn't a great sign.

That's when I notice the dossier sitting on the counter, stacked atop a pile of week-old *Chicago Tribune*s. A peach-colored Post-it note stuck to the cover, slightly off center.

You're Welcome—C+L. Charming.

Curiosity gets the better of me. It couldn't hurt to see who's interested, you know? I'd be lying if I said part of me wasn't a little intrigued by the idea of getting back out there. I'm just not sure it's the part of me I should be listening to.

The mere fact there are girls willing to admit their interest in me on record sparks a fuse in my chest. And I've gotta hand it to Chevy and Lisa, they really went all out on this thing. Each candidate has their own page, complete with yearbook photo, known dating history, fun facts, and the results from their questionnaire. Not something you throw together over a weekend.

Assuming they really did start assembling this dossier before Ally's accident, maybe it isn't as tasteless as I originally thought. After all, Ally was the one who ruined my life. She got to move on. Why shouldn't I?

My tummy rumbles. The dossier will have to wait.

I find some leftover wagon wheel pasta from the fridge, blanket it in shredded cheese, and pop it in the microwave. Peering through the filmy mesh window, I start to zone out as the bowl makes its orbit, oblivious to everything but my impending carbs, until a haunting voice cuts through the abyss, severing the microwave's spell.

"Why in the world is Jackie Olsen on here?"

I snicker. I'd had the same thought when I saw her name in the table of contents. Jackie's attractive and all, but there was this whole thing last year where she tried convincing everyone she was hooking up with one of the Chicago Blackhawks. Total lie, eventually she copped to it. Not exactly someone I'd expect an algorithm to pair me with. Glad someone said it.

Wait—who said it?

"Remember when she told everyone she was hooking up with that hockey player?"

I seize up, muscle fibers zippering until my shoulders touch my ears. Every hair on my body stands at the ready, as though I've gone swimming in Lake Michigan in January.

"Were we too hard on her when it came out she'd made it up?"

Maybe if I don't turn around it'll just go away.

"It must be hard being tall and blond and having perfect boobs and zero percent body fat and—actually, you know what, I take it back, we should've been way meaner to her about it, what a weird fuckin' thing to do."

This can't be happening . . . The other night was a dream . . . A nightmare . . .

Carefully, cautiously, I pivot on my good leg and about-face. The moment she enters my field of vision, logic, as ocularly presented, ceases to exist.

Ally's folded over the island, balancing on her elbows, nose glued to the dossier.

I'm not prepared for her to look up.

Sweep her auburn hair behind her ear.

Meet my gaze.

Smile.

If not for the microwave, we might've remained there in perpetuity—me, paralyzed by a mix of horror, confusion, and a smidge of arousal, and Ally, relishing every second of my reaction to her surprise reincarnation. Only the buzzer blares, ending our brief stalemate and my verticality.

I hear her cackling before I've even hit the floor. "You good?" she asks halfheartedly, moving away from the island and stepping into full view.

No, Ally. The answer is no.

Something's different about her. Not different. *Changed*. New outfit. The candy-cane-striped pocket tee she had on last night is gone, replaced by a pair of black corduroy overalls I've seen her wear a thousand times, layered over a cream-colored cable-knit sweater I've never seen before. Must be new. A post-Cam purchase. Retail therapy? A fleeting moment of optimism. More likely a purchase for HIS benefit.

Her hair is shorter too; didn't even occur to me last night. It was long when we were together, dribbling to her shoulder blades. She chopped it off after our breakup, opting instead for a style known as a *bob*. (Had to google that one.) It's the first time I've seen her up close since she cut it, I realize. Since she ended things. Not counting last night, of course. It's wavier than it looked in pictures. Lighter too, at least at the ends. Her roots betray her.

"You alright there, Cammie?" I startle at the sound of her voice. "You look like you've seen a ghost." Her expression drips with faux sincerity.

Tenderly, I push myself into a seated position. Inhale a breath, release it quickly. The words come easier than they did last night. "But . . . but . . . but . . ."

Okay, one word.

"Spit it out, Cammie!"

"You're in a coma! You're . . . you . . . you can't be *here*!"

Ally looks straight down, pinning her chin against her clavicle, and tugs at her crewneck's chunky collar.

"Doesn't look that way, does it?"

"Ghost," I murmur, tentatively at first, my voice growing stronger as the idea gains traction in my head. "You're a ghost."

"I'm not a ghost, Cammie." Her eyes fly sideways, reconsidering. "Not yet, anyway. We'll see how the next couple of weeks go."

Her attention turns to her surroundings. She scours the kitchen, soaking it all in. "Been a while since I was here last."

The place where it all started, I think. I wonder if she's thinking the same.

Something catches her eye then—suddenly she's on the move, rounding the island. The Delatrix. She reaches for the bottle, stopping just short, arm outstretched, fingertips hovering inches above the cap. *What's she doing?* She looks tentative, almost afraid. It doesn't last. The next thing I know, Ally's beaming, the pill bottle secure in her hand. Her nonexistent hand. Someone please wake me the fuck up.

"Cam, look!" She gives the bottle a shake. The pills rattle accordingly. "Two months! For two goddamn months I haven't been able to touch anything. And now look!"

She tosses the bottle to herself, marvels when she catches it.

"Un-fuckin'-real. And all I had to do was find somebody high off their ass. No offense."

Tough to be offended when it feels as though your brain's been unclipped from its stem. Ally returns the bottle, then sidles back over to the island. To the dossier.

"So what exactly am I looking at here?"

Blood rushes to my cheeks. "That's not mine!" *Well, well, well, look who finally found his voice.*

Ally flips the dossier closed and reads the glossy gold lettering emblazoned across the cover. "'The Cam Rebound Project.'" She looks to me. "Kinda sounds like it is yours."

My palms are slick and greasy, my mouth dry. "Probably Maizy's."

"I highly doubt that."

"Or Mom's."

"Your dad left seven years ago."

"Or Chevy's."

"He and Lisa are still together."

"Someone broke in."

If there's one thing I've learned in my eighteen years on this planet, it's that whenever you've dug yourself into a seemingly bottomless hole you have no hope of climbing out of, there's really only one thing to do: Keep digging.

"Why would I even need a Rebound Project . . . Like, I can find a booty call all on my own . . . and I have, for the record . . . been hooking up left and right . . . front and back . . . not back as in—you know what I mean. Because I'm over—I mean, I'm not sad anymore . . . I mean, I am sad, but that's because of the whole coma thing . . . What I meant to say was, I'm happy to hear you didn't die or whatever . . ."

Nailed it.

"Uh-huh" is all Ally contributes. "Well, I guess you won't mind if I borrow it? Since it's not yours?"

"Uh . . ." *Keep digging.* "Yeah, that's fine."

"Great!" Ally unclips the kangaroo pouch on the front of her overalls and tucks the dossier away. The pouch isn't quite wide enough; she has to force it in crooked to get it to stay. "So, you're really all the way over me?"

"Y-yeah. Yes. Mhm." Worst time for my voice to crack.

"Really?"

"Really."

"Then say it."

"Huh?"

"You heard me." She's edging closer, I realize. On instinct, I scuttle backward until I run out of room, my spine flush against the dishwasher door.

"Say you're over me," she instructs me—*dares* me—looking far too pleased with herself.

"I . . . I just did."

Ally hinges forward, tilting at the hip, sliding her hands to her knees. Close enough for me to catch a whiff of her shampoo. Cucumber and eucalyptus. (Whatever that is.)

"Look, I get it. You're a little freaked out. I would be too, if I were you. I mean, twenty-four hours ago you thought I was holed up in my hospital room. Which, by the way, I still am. Part of me, anyway. And now . . ."

Right. *And now.*

"Don't you worry, though," she says. "This'll all be over soon."

My heart slows. *Over?* That could only mean one thing. "You're dying?"

Ally makes a face. "What? No! What makes you—" It takes her a second. "Oh, you thought— Okay, I hear it now. That one's on me. No, I am not dying. What I meant to say is I won't be in a coma much longer. In fact, I've decided to end my leave from consciousness. Just in time for graduation."

"Bullshit," I snap, without missing a beat. "You can't just *decide* to wake up from a coma. That's not how comas work!"

Ally sets her hands on her hips. "Sure you can. Just like a man to speak with complete certainty about something he has zero experience with."

"If you were about to wake up, my mom would've told me."

"Believe it or not, Cam, but there are some things in Shermer even the great Dr. Garrity isn't the first to hear about."

Mom would beg to differ. She's right upstairs; I could just ask her. *We* could ask her.

"MOM!" I'm five again. "MOM!" Awoken by a nightmare. "MOOOOOM!" Begging my mommy to come and make it go away.

Ally clucks her tongue. Flashes another shit-eating grin. The same look she always used to deploy whenever she got a rise out of me. "Relax, *babe.* You're starting to sound crazy." She squats down to my level. For a moment, I think she means to kiss me, but it's merely a flyby, her lips destined for my ear.

"You don't want to sound crazy, do you?"

With a wink, Ally gets to her feet. Then she—how do I put this? *Vanishes.*

Just fuckin' dissolves into thin air. The dossier along with her.

On cue, Mom comes bursting into the kitchen, Maizy nipping at her heels. "What the hell is going on?" Mom's in her monogrammed bathrobe, her sleep mask resting atop her head. My sister's wearing one of my old STHS basketball T-shirts. It comes down to her knees. "For Christ's sakes, Cameron. Why in the world are you hollering like that?"

Why am I hollering? How should I put this . . . ?

I know how this must look to her: me, manic, sweaty, floor-bound again. Can she tell I've lost my mind just by staring at me? Is that something they teach in med school?

Apparently not, because Mom reaches another conclusion.

"Have you been drinking?" An accusation in the form of a question. "Jesus Christ, Cameron. You're not supposed to drink while you're taking Delatrix."

"I haven't been drinking," I offer meekly.

"Well, what do you have to say for yourself?"

Ally's disembodied spirit was right where you're standing thirty seconds ago. That'll go over well. No, I can't tell Mom what I've just witnessed. Because I already know her response. Pills. Pills. And more pills. If Mom thought for a second I might actually be losing my mind, I'd be tethered to a lithium drip before sunrise.

So I just shrug. Avoid eye contact.

Mom presses her thumb and ring finger to the bridge of her nose. "I'm at a loss, Cameron. Truly. I cannot for the life of me understand why you think it's okay to behave like this. You're acting like more of a child than Maizy."

"I am not acting like a child!" I yelp back, like a child.

"Enough! We will deal with this in the morning! Come on, Maizy. You should be in bed." With that, Mom storms off. My sister hangs back.

"Hey, Cam, guess what?" she whispers so Mom can't hear.

I let my head flop back against the dishwasher. "What, Maizy?"

"I'm Mom's favorite."

"Oh yeah? How do you figure?"

"In the car, on the way home from school, Mom said, 'Maizy, you're my favorite.'"

I sigh. "Sounds about right."

7

Well, this sucks.

Ally's impromptu rendezvous earlier confirmed one thing: This isn't a dream. It can't be. Dreams are a side effect of sleep, and it's pretty clear I'm never sleeping again. Even with the blinds closed and our home security system switched on, I still can't escape the uneasy feeling of being watched. That I'm not alone. ADT doesn't account for the paranormal.

I keep replaying something Ally said, the part about finding someone "high off their ass." It's true, in the two months since her accident, I haven't experienced anything like this. Not until early yesterday, once I started on the Delatrix.

I try googling my symptoms. Hallucinations, fantastical delusions, insomnia. The results read like a late-night infomercial.

Are you . . .

  1) Seeing and/or hearing things that aren't there?

  2) Dwelling unreasonably on the past?

  3) Confusing dreams with reality?

If you answered yes to any of the above questions, then
do I have a special diagnosis for you! Introducing . . .
schizophrenia! The fun and exciting new—

I close the tab, along with the seventeen others I opened in a fit of nervous link-hopping. If my REM cycle isn't responsible for her presence, two possible explanations remain: (1) inter-dimensional beings exist, which is fucking terrifying, or (2) I'm losing my mind irrespective of the narcotics, and Ally's aberration is acting as the canary in the coal mine, signaling my imminent and full-blown mental breakdown, which is somehow even more terrifying than Option 1.

I'm deep in the r/halluciNATION subreddit when another explanation hits me, possibly even crazier than the first two.

What if that actually was Ally? Not a supernatural projection; her real-life physical self. For that to be true, it would mean she woke up from a two-month coma without my knowledge, revamped her motor skills to the point she could leave the hospital under her own supervision, and trekked to my house in the dead of night—*twice!*—all in the name of an elaborate prank.

It defies reason. Which is exactly what I keep reminding myself as I dial the Shermer General ICU. On the second ring, a voice far too chipper for the graveyard shift answers.

"Shermer General Intensive Care Unit, how can I assist you?"

"Hi," I default. "I'm, uh . . . I'm looking for somebody." Really should've scripted my questions beforehand.

"And who might that be?"

"A patient. Al—" Her name sours on my tongue. "Allison Tandy."

"Oh." A long pause. "Sir, I'm sorry to have to be the one to tell you this, but Allison Tandy is in a coma."

"Oh thank God!" I heave a sigh of relief.

"I'm sorry?" Horror fills her voice now.

"No, it's not . . . I didn't mean it like that! I knew she was in a coma . . . I was just double-checking that, uh . . . nothing had changed . . . with her situation."

Another long pause. "Sir, how exactly do you know Ms. Tandy?"

"I'm, uh, I'm her . . ." *Fuck, what am I again?* "Dad?" *CHRIST!* "No, her boyfriend!" *WHY?!* "No! I'm her . . . Sorry, wrong number!" I end the call. Pitch my phone to the other end of the couch. Where it can't do any more damage.

So. Ally isn't awake. She's still laid up at Shermer General. *Physically*, anyway. As for her metaphysical status?

Currently unknown.

SUNRISE ROLLS AROUND a couple hours later, and before long I hear Mom's slippered footfalls coming down the stairs. She won't come for me just yet, not until she's had her morning coffee. If my nerves weren't already shot to hell, I'd be more worried. Understand: Dr. Garrity does not believe in proportional responses. One time I missed curfew, and she threatened to put me up for adoption. For waking her up on a weeknight? She might disown me.

"Cameron Alan Garrity."

Full name. *Fuck*. I sink deeper into the couch cushions. "Morning, Mom."

She sips from her metallic, hospital-branded thermos, her electric green eyes unblinking. Zeroed in on her target. Me. "Set aside some time this afternoon. There's something we need to discuss."

I brace for more, but Mom just turns and walks away. A stay of execution. Better than I'd hoped for. Just to be safe, I pretend to sleep the rest of the morning until I hear her leave with Maizy.

I need a break from my brain. Something to take my mind off Ally.

The problem with dating someone for a full year is you end up sharing *everything*. From germs (I got Ally's seasonal flu last year) to test answers (she got my AP Psych Scantrons). As a result, when Ally dumped me, I also lost the one thing I cherish in this world most of all.

I lost my shows. Our shows. *What's mine is yours, babe!*

Bingeing together was our pastime. True crime docs, prestige dramas, old sitcoms, you name it. After the split, it quickly became clear I couldn't sit through any of my old comfort shows without being reminded of her. Even new stuff, if it sort of resembled something we would've watched together. Which really sucked at a time I was in desperate need of distraction.

I had to get creative. Embrace the one type of show I knew for a fact Ally hated.

Network procedurals. You know, those formulaic murder

shows everyone's parents are really into? Stuff like *CSI, Law & Order: Public Relations, Chicago Fire, Chicago DMV, Criminal Minds, Criminal Mimes, Criminal Mines, 9-1-Fun, Seal Team 69,* and, most recently, *NCIS Boise,* a show centered on the special agents investigating naval crimes on the high seas of southwest Idaho.

Were any of these shows good? Who's to say. I mean, no, they're really not. But Ally refused to watch them, so for my purposes they did the trick.

I take my morning dose of Delatrix and sidle up to POL-I, then mow through two episodes of *Boise.* Right as I fire up a third, my phone dings.

CHEVY

Skipping school. Impromptu beach day.
Scooping you in 10

He's here in seven.

"Why aren't you ready?" Chevy scolds me upon entry. "Swimsuit, towel, sunscreen, let's go!"

I grunt. "Do I look like someone capable of leaving the house?"

"No, you look like a guy who just woke up in the desert twenty miles outside Vegas and can't remember how he got there."

Oddly specific, but okay.

"I'm not going anywhere. You have no idea the night I've had." I turn to the TV. A second later, the screen goes black.

"Dude!"

Chevy dangles the remote beyond my reach. "What happened last night? Not sleeping again?"

I shudder. "Not exactly." Wait, what am I doing? If there's one person I can explain this to, it's Chevy. He's the one who'd actually heard of Delatrix—he even mentioned this side effect. Yet one thing gives me pause. Not the absurdity of the situation—Chevy could handle that. Something else he said yesterday.

All you do is talk about Ally.

When you're heartbroken, you run the risk of alienating the people in your life. For you, it's like the breakup is permanently etched into the side of your skull, the only thought thrumming through your brain, percolating on your tongue. Good friends will listen. They'll be supportive. But only to a point.

I saw it happen last year with Logan Weaver, one of my basketball teammates, after Brie Tisch left him for Maggie Wasserman. Me and the other guys had his back for the first couple weeks. Gave him space when he needed. Listened when he bitched about Maggie and Brie. But we weren't quite so forgiving after he burst into tears at the foul line in the middle of a game. (The refs had to call an injury time-out.)

I'm lucky. Chevy and Lisa have stuck with me. Still, everyone reaches a breaking point. I guess I can't blame them. Five months is a long time to remain invested in a relationship you weren't a part of.

"Do you believe in ghosts?" I ask, couching the Ally piece of the story for now.

Chevy tenses, his eyes suddenly wide and frenzied. A phony newscaster smile creeps across his face. "Of course I don't believe in ghosts!" he half shouts, hands cupped around his mouth so his voice carries through the house. "What a ridiculous question!"

"The fuck are yo—"

"Shh!" Chevy slaps his hand over my mouth. "They'll hear you!"

I lick his palm until he yanks away. "Who?"

"The ghosts!"

"So you *do* believe in them?"

"No, Cam. I think we just become worm food after we die." I honestly can't tell if he's kidding. "Of course I believe in ghosts!" Huh. You think you know a guy. "Why do you ask? Did you experience an encounter?"

The memories from last night come flooding back. Ally. Talking, bouncing, smiling that goddamn adorable lopsided smile. Picking up tangible matter.

Something like that.

"Of course not," I play it off. "Forget I said anything."

"You sure?"

Not even a little.

"Yeah, all good. My head's just all over the place this morning."

Chevy nods. "You'll feel better once you get a little vitamin D."

Fighting him on this is a losing battle, so I begrudgingly start uncoupling from POL-I. *Be back soon, girl.*

As Chevy helps me to my feet, he goes, "Actually, there is something I've been meaning to talk to you about. Remember at the end of summer, like, right after classes started, when you, me, and Ally went golfing up on my roof?"

I nod. Smile. I remember it well.

"And we got to talking about dating after high school. Long-distance relationships. That sort of thing?" Chevy stops to gather himself. He's building to something, I'm just not sure what. "How Lisa and I were considering an open relationship?"

"Oh yeah, I remember that!" I find myself laughing at the thought. "Jesus, what a terrible idea. Thank God you guys didn't go through with it. Can you even imagine trying to pull off an open relationship? Constantly worrying about what Lisa's doing, who she's with. Knowing that, at any moment, she could be getting dicked down by some random frat guy, and you couldn't say shit because you gave her the green light. Sounds like a fucking nightmare. Why do you ask?"

Chevy's eyes won't meet mine. "Chev?" He lifts his pinky nail to his lips. "No way . . ." Sinks his teeth into it. "Tell me you didn't—tell me you didn't agree to try an open relationship."

"I think it could work."

"It can't!"

"Our relationship is solid enough to withstand the complications."

"It's not!"

"Lisa and I are just trying to make the best of a bad situation, okay?" He's talking like he's still trying to convince himself. "We love each other and we both want to make this work next year. Long distance is hard as it is, so we're taking the 'progressive approach.'"

"Yeah, okay," I sneer. "Talk to me after Lisa starts pulling other D1 athletes. We'll see if you still prefer the 'progressive approach.'"

Chevy kisses his teeth, shifts his weight. Whips out his phone. Just to do something with his hands. "Even if she did, it's not like I'm gonna find out anyway. We both agreed *if* one of us hooks up with someone else, we'll keep it to ourselves. Everything's operating under a strict 'don't ask, don't tell' policy."

"Chev," I say, lacing my voice with as much derision as I can muster. "If the United States military considers a policy to be archaic, then you probably shouldn't apply it to your romantic relationship."

"Right, because you're the expert." Chevy must realize how dickish he sounds, because he immediately backpedals. "Sorry, that's not fair. But you're only seeing the negatives. Think about it from my perspective; what if there's some sexy-ass California chick—"

"Did you just say 'California chick'?"

"Begging for the D—"

"Who are you?"

"I can go home with her without resenting Lisa."

"Right . . ." I squint at him. "But by that same logic, can't Lisa do the exact same thing?"

"Why would you even say that?" Chevy's scowling now, his cedar-colored eyes reduced to kindling. "Lisa's not like that." Another nail hits the chopping block. A little voice in my head pipes up. If I didn't know any better, I'd wager Chevy isn't exactly comfortable with The Happy Couple's new arrangement. On the fence, at the very least. But I'm not trusting of the voices in my head at the moment, so I keep it to myself. He knows where I stand. An open relationship is destined to fail.

Just like Ally told him.

"A HUSH FALLS over the crowd as Chevy Wyatt lines up his next shot."

I don't golf. (Too white.) Neither does Chevy. We do, however, enjoy taking his dad's clubs up to the level portion of his roof and launching golf balls into the lake.

Welcome to Wyatt Family National: Shermer's best (and only) aquatic-based golf course. Fingers crossed the Coast Guard never does a sweep of the lake bed along the shoreline, otherwise the Wyatts are facing a pretty hefty littering fine. Probably looks like someone murdered a country club down there.

It was an unseasonably warm day, right before the leaves changed. We decided to play hooky and squeeze in one final round before the end of the season. Normally Lisa would join in, but she was in-season and therefore out-of-commission. In her place, Ally stepped in, despite her insistence (due to certain physical attributes) she wouldn't be any good.

"Wyatt's two shots off the lead, three up on Garrity's waffle-head ass . . ." Chevy hovered over his tee, muttering in his best golf announcer voice.

"Just take the shot!" I hollered at him.

He jerked out of his stance. "Quiet on the course!"

"We're gonna be here all day if you keep—"

"QUIET ON THE COURSE!"

Ally turned to me. "Does he always take this long?"

"Every single time."

There was enough space on the Wyatts' roof for a whole tailgate setup: folding chairs, a cooler, speakers blasting the Kid Xannabis and Xanz FerdiXanz new collab EP, *The Duality of Xan.*

Finally—*mercifully*—Chevy lurched into his backswing, and followed through with aplomb. His ball dribbled across the shingles and shot straight up, directly overhead, before touching down somewhere in his dad's garden.

"Fuck."

"Great shot, Chev. Completely worth the buildup." Chevy downed the rest of his tall boy and thrust it at me. Wielding a five iron, I swatted it out of the air, over the ledge.

"If either one of you hits me, there will be dire consequences," Ally warned us.

Chevy grabbed another can from the cooler and plopped in his chair. After a *looooong* pull, he was like, "Can I run something by you guys? About me and Lisa."

"Are you guys getting married?" I half joked.

"Don't be silly, Cam," Ally joined in. "It's way too early for that. I'm guessing Chevy bought her a promise ring."

"Dude, I swear to God, if you got Lisa a promise ring, we can't be friends anymore."

"Seconded."

Ally and I broke down giggling then, cheesing at each other like a couple quokkas. Chevy wasn't amused.

"What is this?" He motioned between us. "I don't like this."

"Oh really?" I shot back. "You don't like being the third wheel? Gee, I can't imagine what that's like."

"Now, Cam, we shouldn't be childish. Let's be the bigger"—Ally feigned a whisper—"and better couple and help Chevy out with his relationship troubles." She turned to Chevy. "Apologies, Chevrone. You were saying."

I remember Chevy going to town on his nails back then too. We had to ask him to stop; we couldn't understand him. "It's nothing. We've just been talking about what's gonna happen next year. With us."

Oh. That conversation. The elephant in the room with every high school couple—me and Ally included. By then, we'd been together almost a year. We'd said I love you. Lost our virginities to each other. Ally was my best friend (don't tell Chevy). My favorite person. I didn't want to lose any of that just because our time at STHS was almost up.

Shermer wasn't exactly the kind of place where people wound up with their high school sweethearts (you're thinking of *literally* anywhere else in the Midwest). But that didn't mean it wasn't worth trying. Hell, for Ally, I would've tried anything.

As Chevy laid out Lisa's "open relationship" suggestion, I tracked Ally's expression from the corner of my eye, trying to get a sense of where her head was at. Once Chevy opened the floor to comments, I got my answer.

"Look, if you and Lisa really think you can make an open relationship work, then more power to you," Ally said. "But I think it's a terrible idea. I sure as shit couldn't do it. One picture of Cam at a concert with some girl on his shoulders and I'd be ready to smash his windshield in."

I let out a sigh of relief. That felt like an answer. Jealousy, if nothing else, would keep us together next year. Content, I picked up my club and strolled over to the tee. We'd been up there a couple hours; I could feel the sun stripping away my SPF 30 as I positioned myself over the drain.

Behind me, the conversation continued. From the sound of it, Ally'd pivoted from poking fun at Chevy to trying to lift his spirits.

"Maybe it won't be so bad. If any couple can pull off that sort of arrangement, it's you and Lisa. Plus, anything beats long distance, you know? So if this is your best-case alternative, I say go for it."

I took aim at my target—a sunbathing buoy loafing in the surf. Zeroed in on the ball. It was only after I reared back that I heard it.

Anything beats long distance.

Ally wasn't just against open relationships; she didn't want a long-distance relationship of any kind. And if she was completely against long-distance relationships, that meant—

My club missed the ball. My hands missed the club. It hovered a moment, sun glinting off the titanium finish, as surprised as I was to find itself airborne, then fluttered to the ground, landing in the Wyatts' pool below.

Right in the deep end.

8

By the time Chevy and I arrive at the beach, Lisa's already set up shop near the south jetty. She's got her nose buried in some athlete's memoir (because the world needs more of those), and is absentmindedly chewing on the end of a green Starbucks straw.

"Took you guys long enough," she needles, peering over the spine.

"Cam's fault," Chevy goes, bending over to peck her on the cheek. "Took forever to get ready."

I shrug. "Couldn't find any clean underwear. Had to make do."

Lisa shudders. "I don't wanna know."

On the drive over, Chevy asked me not to mention their open relationship. Fine by me. I want as little to do with that disaster-in-waiting as possible.

The lake looks less than inviting today, the waves slate gray and choppy. The wind's in a shitty mood. About what you'd expect for a random Wednesday in May. No wonder we're the only ones out here, save for a few hazy shapes bopping around closer to the shoreline.

Chevy's brought along a six-pack. He and Lisa are quick to help themselves. I have to settle for Smartwater. I take a swig, then set the bottle in the sand. When I look up, The Happy Couple is staring at me.

"What?"

"Cam, we wanted to apologize for what happened yesterday," Lisa says. "It was a mistake to spring the dossier on you right after surgery. Especially with everything else going on."

"Our timing could've been better," Chevy adds. "We see that now."

"Guys, it's fine," I say quickly, hoping they'll drop it. "I know you didn't mean anything by it." I take another sip, just so I have something to do with my hands. They're still gawking at me.

Chevy. "So?"

Me. "So what?"

Lisa. "Have you looked through the dossier?"

So much for their apology.

"I may have glanced at it."

"And?" Chevy adjusts his chair so it's directly facing mine. "Any thoughts? Questions? Concerns? Front-runners?"

Lisa does the same. "Why don't we go through it right now? We can review each prospect, one by one. Discuss their pros and cons."

"You know, I would love to . . ." That's a damn lie. "But I forgot to bring it."

For a split second I'm actually grateful Ally took it off my hands, until I see Lisa riffling through her bag. "Aha!" she cheers, producing *a second* leather-bound dossier, identical to the first.

"You made copies?!" Goddamn my friends and their commitment to a bit.

"Of course," Lisa says, flinging it to me. "We're proud of the work we did here."

"We're thinking about submitting it to some academic journals," Chevy adds excitedly. Great, just what I need: my heartbreak immortalized for a bunch of nerds.

I balk for a moment. It's not that I don't appreciate the gesture. I'm just not sure my head is in the right place for this. But I can tell from their expressions they aren't letting this go. Better to capitulate than fight them. "I'll take a look," I promise them. "For real this time."

Before either of them can press the issue further, I turn away, scanning the beach for a reason to change the subject. My out materializes; one of the shadows near the water is headed our way. He's close enough now I can make out Robby Donovan, the now-former starting quarterback of the STHS Wasps football team. Robby is . . . How should I put this? Clueless? Spacey? The guy has resting puzzled face.

Oh, and he's dating my ex-girlfriend. Sorry, my *other* ex-girlfriend. BA—Before Ally. Steff Ambrose. We dated for like six months sophomore year.

I bat Chevy on the arm. "Looks like we've got company."

Chevy swivels his chair. "Is that QB1? Dude, what's good with his swimsuit?"

Robby's wearing some sort of skintight boxer-brief-style swimsuit. A weird choice, even if it wasn't this cloudy out. "Maybe his normal swimsuit is in the wash and he had to get one out of his little brother's closet."

"That thing's a size extra sh-medium," I crack.

"There's nothing sh-medium about what he's got under his swimsuit," Lisa pipes in, lowering her aviators for a better look. "Hello, sailor."

"Babe!" Chevy snaps. "What the hell?"

"What? You two talk about girls all the time—why can't I make comments like that? It's chilly out here; I'm impressed." Lisa's smiling. Chevy's not. He turns his head so she can't see the scowl rippling across his face.

"Babe, come on." Lisa jostles him on the shoulder. "You're not even the one who should be worried right now. Maybe Robby's on his way over to finish Cam off once and for all."

A lump clots my throat. "Ha ha, very funny!" Lisa's kidding. At least, I think she is. It can be hard to tell with Robby. See, Steff and I were the rare exception, a couple that split pretty amicably. I wouldn't say we're still close necessarily, but I enjoy catching up with her every once in a while. To Ally, that meant one thing.

"You're still into her."

Ally's jealousy was unwarranted and could get annoying fast, but at least it made sense, you know? *Boyfriend's ex-girlfriend = ENEMY.* Robby took a different approach. Overly friendly, to the point that it can get uncomfortable. I guess it's preferable to him wanting to fight me or something. To that point:

"Robby and I are boys, remember? See, watch." I shoot my hand into the air. "QB1! What's up, buddy?"

Robby's jogging now, flagging us down as he nears our campsite. Thanks to Lisa, I can't help but sneak a peek below his beltline. Fuckin' thing keeps making eye contact with me. I glance at Chevy. He's struggling to keep his gaze above sea level too.

"Hey, guys." Robby's out of breath when he reaches us. "You know you don't have to call me QB1 anymore? I'm not even playing football next year."

"Sure we do, QB1," I go. "You were the starting quarterback! Big man on campus. That shit lasts forever! Nothing you do will ever be more important!"

"Don't listen to him, *Robby*," Lisa clucks in a playful tone she usually reserves for Chevy. "What can we do for you?"

Robby gestures the way he came. "They just restrung the beach volleyball nets for the summer. Me and some of the guys were gonna run threes." To Lisa. "We wanted to see if you were down?"

Lisa beams. "You boys have just made a terrible mistake." She jolts out of her chair and slips off her Dri-FIT long sleeve, revealing a stomach Photoshop wouldn't touch. She circles around to Chevy's chair. "Be back in a little," she says, bending down for a quick kiss. "Don't wait up."

With that, she takes off. Robby dawdles, savoring the view. The vein in Chevy's neck is going haywire.

"Run along now, QB1," he spits, shooing him. Busted. Robby

offers an apologetic nod, then hightails it after Lisa, gifting us a full view of the man-crack peeping from his waistband. Better than the view from the front.

"Who else is over there?" Chevy asks.

I squint. "Looks like Teddy Hall, Braden Campbell, John Katz, John Livingston—God, we sure know a lot of Johns."

Chevy's gaze stays keyed on Lisa as she stops to offer each of the guys a hug. The last one—Teddy—leaves his arm draped around her shoulder.

"Teddy's going to Wisconsin next year," Chevy says out of the blue.

"Is he?"

Chevy nods. "Playing soccer."

"Huh. Good for him."

"Yeah. *Good for him.*" Chevy's voice is laced with venom. "I hate when Lisa does shit like that."

"Shit like what?"

"Talk about other guys in front of me." Chevy clears the gunk in his throat, turns, and fires it into the sand. "Right now, every one of them is thinking about what's underneath Lisa's bikini."

"True. But, Chev, have you considered this: What if she has a second bikini on underneath that one?" I clamp my hands over my cheeks. "Whoa. Didn't see that twist coming, did you?"

"This isn't funny, man."

I mean, it's a little funny. Chevy and Lisa are the most rock-solid couple in Shermer—including the married adults.

"Cheer up, bud." I clap him on the back of the neck. "I've wanted to sleep with Lisa for years."

"Is that supposed to make me feel better?"

"Nah. I'm just letting you know." He shrugs me off and slumps further in his chair. Over on the court, they've split into teams. Lisa sides with Teddy and one of the Johns. A devastating development for Chevy.

I try again. "Who cares if they wanna sleep with her? It's not like Lisa would ever hook up with any of them."

"That's not the point. You should know better than anyone what I'm talking about."

I frown. "What's that supposed to mean?"

"Tell me you didn't freak out when you saw Ally talking to other guys? Or am I imagining the time you tried to fight Del Dwyer because he dared to be Ally's beer pong partner?"

Actually, I challenged Del to a trial by combat. And I was kidding. Mostly.

"I have no idea what you're referring to," I deadpan.

For a few minutes we sit in silence, watching the game unfold. Even from a distance it's evident Lisa is having her way with them, her limbs succinct in their quest to drill the ball past her opponents' outstretched arms. She's a force. And she's in love with Chevy. More importantly, she cared enough about him to address their college plans a full year before the bill came due. Because she *wanted* to be with him. I'd have sacrificed my left pinky toe for Ally to care that deeply for me.

"So, how's the open relationship going again?" I ask, coating my tone in spite.

"It's a dream," Chevy mutters. "Sometimes I kinda wish she was only attracted to me, you know? Does that sound bad?"

I swallow an *I told you so.* "Kinda. But I get what you mean."

Chevy crushes his wounded soldier and flings it into the cooler. "Let's just go. I can get drunk on my own beach."

9

Chevy's still whining about Lisa on the drive home.

"Those guys are allegedly my friends, you know? Where do they get off?"

"Teddy isn't even her type."

"Should I start lifting when I get to Stanford?"

I tune him out and set my mind adrift, idly watching glimpses of shoreline flash between the houses whizzing in and out of frame. Under different circumstances, I might actually feel for him. But not right now. Chevy got four good years out of his relationship before jealousy reared its ugly head; most of us are stuck fighting it from day one.

As we approach our shared slice of block, I notice an unfamiliar car parked in my driveway. A gold Audi convertible, top down. Random cars mean one thing: one of Mom's patients is here. The *I Have an Honor Roll Student at STHS* bumper sticker is a dead giveaway.

"That's Jake Cooper's car," Chevy says when he lets me out. "See if you can find out what he's here for."

"I'm not doing that."

"Fine, I'll just text Cindy and ask her myself."

"STOP TEXTING MY—" But Chevy's already reversing, scooting across the street and into his roundabout.

I bump into Jake on my back porch just as he's sliding the patio door closed.

"Cam! What's up, buddy?"

Much as I hate making small talk with my mom's patients, you could do a lot worse than Jake Cooper. Jake's a quasi-friend, your run-of-the-mill Shermer bro. Plays a couple sports, smokes a bit of weed. State-school catnip. His friend group started going out around the same time we did freshman year, so we've been attending the same social functions for a while.

"Sucks about your leg, bro," he says, all glum-like. "Right before Senior Olympics too. Huge blow for you guys. Not sure Team Australia will be able to recover."

"That's where you're wrong, Jakey," I go. "Chevy's replacing me in all the athletic competitions, so we're in great shape."

That draws a laugh. "You can't drink either?" I shake my head. "They probably gave you some pretty *wild* painkillers, though, huh?"

Oh, Jake. You have no idea.

We give it another minute before Jake signals he has to run. Two steps down the driveway, he turns back.

"Oh, before I forget, my parents are leaving for our lake house in the morning, so I'm having people over for a little Thursday night, Opening Ceremonies thing tomorrow." He gestures across the street. "I'll tell Chevy too."

He doesn't have to. Jake's still backing his car out of my drive-way when my phone buzzes.

CHEVY

Party at Jake's tomorrow. YOU'RE GOING

INSIDE, MOM'S STILL cleaning up from Jake's appointment. Maizy's parked at the kitchen counter, elbow deep in a bowl of Kraft macaroni. She spots me first.

"Cam's home!"

Mom glances up. It's a reflex; my mere presence brings a frown to her face. She picks up the remote and switches off whatever show Maizy was watching.

"Mooooooooooooom."

"Upstairs, Maizy. You have homework, and I have to talk to your brother."

Uh-oh. Never a good sign when Mom sends Maizy out of the room. Mom makes a point to avoid chewing me out in front of her. Claims it's harmful to her development. That adorable little menace is the closest thing I have to a human shield. She knows it too.

"But I wanna see you yell at Cameron!"

"Now, Maizy! Once I finish Cameron, he'll come up and help you with your times tables."

She meant once she's finished *with* me, right? You guys heard that too?

Maizy huffs but does as she's told, stomping down the hall and up the stairs. Mom waits until her footsteps fade before closing her laptop and turning to me.

There are two rules in our house:

1) No mentioning Dad. (More than fair.)

2) No waking Mom up unless "you're dead or on fire."

One time I actually was on fire, and she still took away my Wi-Fi privileges for a month. I haven't broken Rule #2 since. Until last night.

I try to get in front of it. "I know, I know. Last night is on me. I—"

Mom holds a finger to her lips. I fall silent. For a few moments she just stares at me. The silence is unsettling.

"Something's happened," she says finally. "With Ally."

"Oh." My stomach sinks to my toes.

"She's alright," Mom's quick to clarify, before my mini heart attack can evolve into the real thing. "There's been an update of sorts to her trajectory. I thought it best you hear it from me. So you can process it properly."

Process it properly? Mom's never offered to let me process any-thing. Who is this, and what has she done with my mother? Bedside manner is reserved for her patients, not her eldest. She looks physically uncomfortable, compassion pasted on her face like a bad Photoshop. It's like seeing a dog try on silly outfits. *Aw, it thinks it's people!*

"When a person falls into a coma, they lose all control of their motor functions." I nod. "However, while a comatose person can't control their movements, they're still capable of involuntary motion. Usually we see some eye movement, limbs twitching, that sort of thing."

"Really?" This is news to me. "How does that even work?"

"It's random. And not necessarily indicative of a patient's timetable—or even the likelihood they'll wake up." Mom hesitates briefly. "That said, there is a portion of the medical community—a minority—who believe that movements of this nature can be a sign of potential recovery."

"Uh-huh . . ." What is this feeling brewing in my chest? Is it—*hope*? No, it can't be. Hope and I haven't been on speaking terms in months.

"So, what?" My voice is shaky. "Did Ally move or something?"

"Not exactly." I can't remember ever seeing Mom this nervous before. She buys herself time by gazing up at the ceiling, muttering to herself about needing to dust the light fixtures. They're new, the light fixtures. Mom had them installed last year. She asked Ally for her opinion on them. Publicly, Ally gave her an enthusiastic endorsement. Privately, she told me they looked like "light-titties."

"Mom?"

"She screamed."

"Screamed?"

"Yes, Cameron. Screamed."

"Screamed like . . ." I raise my arms like I'm on a roller coaster. *"Ahhhhhhh."*

"That's one way to do it."

"Is screaming common in coma patients?"

"It's highly unusual, but not unheard-of." Mom waffles, then relents. "It's likely nothing; I'm only telling you this in case you hear it from someone else. Don't go getting your hopes up, though."

Too late.

"One of the nurses claimed they heard her scream . . . *something*." A beat. "A name." One more, for good measure. "Your name."

"My name?"

"Yes, Cameron. Your name."

"Cameron Alan Garrity?"

Mom rolls her eyes. "You know, I've always hated the name Alan. I never should've let your father choose it."

"Mom!"

"To my knowledge, it was just a single word. *Cam.*"

"*Cam?*" I repeat it back. Then again: "*Cam.*"

"It was probably nothing," Mom reiterates. "For all we know, the nurse misheard her."

"Uh-huh." I don't buy it. "When was this?"

"A couple of nights ago, during the graveyard shift. And again last night."

"*Twice?* It's happened twice?" I'm fighting a smile.

Mom nods. "Different nurses. I wouldn't have told you about it otherwise."

"Does that mean . . . ?" I'm not even sure I know what I'm asking. Mom picks up the thread.

"Her vitals are solid, and her doctors remain hopeful. But when it comes to coma patients, there's still a lot we don't know. Does it mean anything that she said your name?" Mom grimaces. "It's possible. But highly unlikely. We're all better off keeping our expectations in check."

Yeah, no. That ship has sailed. My brain launches into overdrive, processing the onslaught of new information. Amid the noise, it manages to summon a memory. From yesterday. Something Ally said.

"Graduation," I blurt. "Do they think she'll be awake by graduation?"

"I can't say for sure."

"But if you had to guess."

"I wouldn't."

"Mom!"

"We don't usually like to put timetables on this sort of thing!" Mom removes her glasses, rubs them on her scrub top. Buying time. "But if I had to. Guess, that is. Taking into account these new developments. I'd say it's more than likely that Ally will wake up in the next week or so."

Mom keeps talking—probably adding more qualifiers—but I'm not listening. My mind's racing at warp speed.

"Does anyone else know about this?" I ask.

Mom shakes her head. "Just her doctors and some of the ICU staff. And her mom, of course."

So HE doesn't know yet. God, I would honestly forfeit my

entire college savings account just to see the look on HIS face when HE finds out that Ally called my name. Not HIS. Mine. *Cam.*

Mom continues, "I also wanted to give you a heads-up in case Brenda reaches out."

Brenda? It takes me a second to place the name. Brenda Tandy. Ally's mom. Why would she wanna talk to me?

"You know she's hardly left Ally's bedside," Mom adds. I had heard that, actually. Broke my goddamn heart. "After what happened to her husband, I'm sure you can imagine how hard this is."

Mom stops short. That's when I notice a single tear loitering in the corner of her eye. Blink and you'd miss it. She brushes it with her sleeve.

"You're okay, then? Do you need a hug? I can get your sister back down here if you do."

I shake my head and tell her, "That's okay."

"Alright." Mom makes it a whole ten seconds before regressing to the mean. "Jesus, Cameron, you smell like my middle-school boys. Rubbing Old Spice under your arms once a day won't cut it."

10

Fresh off the heels of the earth-shattering, paradigm-shifting, reality-altering revelation that Ally—yes, comatose, laid-up Allison Tandy—appeared in my home not once, but twice, you'd think I'd have better things to do than, say, oh, I don't know, run times tables with Maizy. Alas, big-brother duty calls.

She's written them on color-coded flash cards; I read each, tell her if she's right. Which I do. Sort of.

"Seven times six?"

"Uh . . . forty-two?"

". . ."

"Cameron?"

". . ."

"Cameron!"

"Do you know what an astral plane is, Maiz?"

"Just tell me the answer!"

"It's a layer of existence that supposedly exists between our world and . . ." I stop. "Huh. I guess I don't know. Maybe the afterlife? And here I am, minding my own business, having discovered its all-but-certain existence. All because of these."

I rattle the Delatrix bottle. I've taken to carrying it on my person. For safekeeping.

Maizy isn't interested in the existential. She climbs over me and wrests the card from my hand.

"Forty-two! I told you!"

Later, once Mom has corralled Maizy upstairs for bed, she tells me, "We need to change the gauze on your knee. Go clean yourself up; I'll be down after I tuck Maizy in."

Showering is out of the question—the sutures holding my leg together can't get wet. Instead, Mom's positioned two dining room chairs in front of the sink—one for sitting, one for propping my tenderized leg—along with a washcloth, one of Dad's old monogrammed beach towels, a single-use razor, and an unused, unscented bar of soap. The height of luxury.

I unclip my brace and peel away the disfigured ice pack, morphed after consecutive days spent wedged beneath the cast's heavy buckles. My left leg—what's left of it—is unrecognizable. Malnourished. Half the size of my right. In just a few days' time, it's siphoned off an alarming amount of muscle. I can almost fit my thumb and middle finger completely around my thigh. Maybe the unsexiest thigh gap in history.

I shift my gaze to the mirror, my hollowed-out reflection. Not keen on the guy staring back. Visine would come in handy right now. Static's coursing through my hair, cowlicks erected at random. Worse is my rapidly expanding neckbeard. According to Ally, it starts to look pubey when it gets this long. Unfortunately, I have to agree.

In lieu of speakers, I slide my phone against the wall so the tiles can sing along. The opening track off Kid Xannabis's latest project, *Good Kid, Xan City*, fills the bathroom with his distinct flavor of oversaturated 808s. The opening track, "Xan You Dig It," was last year's runaway choice for song of the summer in our friend group.

I set the drain stopper. Watch as the sinks fills with warm water. Squeeze a dollop of shaving cream onto my fingers. Massage it around my Adam's apple. Lift the razor to my neck just as Xannabis utters his signature ad-lib—

"*XANNY!*"

You'd think I'd be used to Ally's sudden apparitions by now, and yet I flinch all the same. The razor slips through my fingers and splashes into the sink, stealing a chunk of my jugular in the process. By the time I fashion the towel into a de facto tourniquet and stanch the wound, the sink looks like a crime scene.

"*Ugh*, this song is so good!" Ally's still on about Kid Xannabis. "How is he so talented and *so hot*?! Like, excuse me, sir, what gives you the right?"

"Goddamnit, Allison!" In the mirror, I clock her at my six, reclining in the bathtub like she owns the place.

"Jeez, Cammie, what happened to you? First time shaving?" She cracks herself up.

"Stop sneaking up on me! It's not funny."

Out goes her bottom lip. "Aw, did I scare you? Poor baby."

"No more bathrooms!"

"Don't be silly. Bathrooms are the safest place for us to meet. Plus, scaring you is, like, half the fun."

She flourishes another grin. I meet it with a scowl. It takes a couple minutes for the bleeding to subside. I ball up the blood-soaked towel and launch it at the laundry hamper, missing badly.

Ally's rapping along to the music now, off the beat, overenunciated. Never thought I could hate a Kid Xannabis song, but here we are. There's nothing more torturous than listening to Ally rap. I mute my phone.

"Hey, put that back on!"

"Do you really have to be in here right now?"

"Okay, wow. First of all, rude. How about, 'Hey, Ally, nice to see you again. Fancy meeting you here.'"

"You know that's not true."

"Second of all, hurtful. That's what you are. But we already knew that." She winks. I simmer. "Don't act like you're surprised to see me. If you wanted me gone, all you had to do was stop taking your pills."

I swallow the mass building in my throat. "You don't know that. They're prescribed," I say shakily. "I don't take them for you."

"True. But you could switch meds. I'm sure your doctor would be happy to change things up if you told him about our little encounters."

Encounters. One way to put it.

"So it's the pills, then?" My voice is shaky. "That's why I keep seeing you?"

Ally clucks her tongue and shrugs. "Maybe. Maybe not."

"What happens if I stop taking them?"

"We both know that's not gonna happen."

She's right. Now that I know she's out there—*right here*—there's no going back. I can't even stop looking at her reflection in the mirror right now. Auburn hair. Lightly freckled cheeks. Heart-shaped face. A sudden wave of relief crashes over me. *This* is how I like picturing Ally, the volume turned all the way up. Not plugged into a ventilator like a vegetable. I've thought about Allison Tandy at least once an hour, every day, for two long years. Sitting here cross-legged, she looks exactly as I remembered. Except one thing.

"You got a nose ring."

"I did." She touches the silver band impaling her nostril. "In February."

"Looks good."

Ally cocks an eyebrow. "My Cam Bullshit Detector remains in perfect working condition."

"You look like every suburban white girl going through their 'rebellious' phase."

"Thank you."

"You look like the 'before' photo for someone who got clean and turned their life around."

"You done?"

"Yes."

"Okay, well, I—"

"Wait, I've got it! You look like this girl who broke my heart, except with a stupid piece of metal in her nose."

Ally steels her expression. It isn't much, but finally I've landed a counterpunch. She resets. "Clever. Anything else you want to get off your chest?"

What kind of question is that? Of course there's more—nearly six months of pent-up animosity, frustration, and pettiness. Put on the spot, though, my brain plays dead. I got nothing.

Ally fills the void. "You know, don't you?"

"Huh?"

"Yeah, you know." A smile creeps up the side of her face. "How'd you find out? Wait—let me guess! Your mom? Of course Dr. Garrity found out. I know we used to joke about how every divorced guy in Shermer hits on her, but it's true. But seeing first-hand the way the male doctors creep on her is just . . ." Ally visibly shivers. "I mean, on some level I get it; Dr. Garrity is super hot. Anyone with a pulse can see that. I hope I look that good when I'm her age."

This is Hell. I'm in Hell.

"You've gotta admit it's a good party trick—shouting your name like that. Stroke of genius. You should've seen the look on the nurse's face. I knew your ego couldn't let that one go."

"So you did call out my name!"

Ally nods. "Mhm."

"But . . . how?" My brain is swimming. "How is any of this possible?"

"Don't focus on that. The longer you think about it, the less sense it makes. Learned that lesson on day one when I came to at the bottom of the ravines. Standing over my own body." Her impenetrable smile falters momentarily. Shit, now I'm picturing it. When photos of the accident wound up online, I made a point to steer clear.

Ally continues: "Forget the *how*; what matters now is the *what*. As in, now that you can see me, *what* exactly are we going to do about it?"

With the grace of a seasoned gymnast, Ally hoists herself into the air and vaults over the side of the tub. She's wearing a home-made tie-dyed crop top from some school fundraiser last year and her favorite cutoffs. My favorite cutoffs. I don't realize I'm gawk-ing until—*CLAP!*—she snaps me out of it.

"So here's the thing. I still feel pretty bad about the way things ended between us."

The way *you* ended things, I think. She can't even admit it.

She's on her feet now, doing little three-step laps around the bathroom. "I've spent a lot of time observing you recently—"

"Wait, what?" I cut her off. "What do you mean, *observing*? Have you been secretly watching me this whole time?"

Ally flips her hand dismissively, as though swatting my ques-tion out of the air. "Okay, cocky. Don't go getting a big head about it. Sure, I may be somewhat of an amateur Peeping Tom. But you're not special, I do it to everybody." She pauses. "On a completely unrelated note, you know you're supposed to actually work the shampoo into your scalp? You can't just glob it on and let it sit. That defeats the whole purpose."

"IN THE SHOWER?!"

"What else am I supposed to do with myself all day? Be alone with my thoughts? Like a crazy person? Do you even hear yourself?"

I honestly can't tell if she's kidding.

She's on the move again. "As I was saying, I've been watching you. And the more I watch, the more one thing becomes clear. Your life is a mess."

"Gee, thanks."

"Hey, that's okay. The good news is, I think I figured out what's keeping you down." She sidles in close. "You're still in love with me."

"Am not!" My cheeks feel like the surface of the sun.

"Hey, no need to get defensive," Ally says, throwing up her hands. "Some people just take longer to get over a relationship. Nothing to be ashamed of."

I am over Allison Tandy.

It's right there, on the tip of my tongue. So why can't I bring myself to say it?

THE THING YOU have to understand about me and Ally is we argued. A lot. It came naturally to us. Part of our charm as a couple. (NOTE: Nobody else found it charming.)

I say this to give you a sense of my mindset in the aftermath of our golf outing on Chevy's roof. Mentally, I began preparing for a fight. Ally'd admitted she didn't want to date long distance. We hadn't had that conversation—or more likely, that *fight*—yet.

So Ally thought long distance was dumb. Big deal. It's not like I'd given the subject much thought. When it came to next year, I just assumed we'd stay together. We were in love, you know? People who are in love don't break up. Besides, Ally was my favorite person in the whole wide world—*full stop*. That's a pretty big sample size.

Only, that fight never came. The one subject neither one of us wanted to touch. If Ally didn't mention it, I sure as hell wasn't gonna bring it up. If anything, the stalemate bought me some time. Gave me a chance to sway her, you know? Illustrate what an ideal match we were, regardless of the potential distance between us.

I went to every debate team competition, sat in the front row, heckled her opponents. On nights we stayed in, I always let her pick out what we watched. I even stopped mentioning HIM. For the most part. (Hey, nobody's perfect.) By all accounts, my plan seemed to be working.

But then I slipped up. Late December. Harsh winter. Jake Cooper (the same one leaving my house earlier) had people over to celebrate New Year's. I pregamed with The Happy Couple. Lisa had swiped a fifth of Malört from her parents' liquor cabinet. By the time Ally and her friends showed up to Jake's, I was . . . let's say, feeling loose.

The last thing I remember is shotgunning in the snow with some of my basketball teammates. From there, it's all a bit hazy. I do remember one part: corralling Ally into my embrace, dancing poorly to some song by Charles Xanson & the Xanson Family, then shouting over the music, "FUKKIT, LET'S DO LONG DISTANCE NEXT YEAR!"

I woke up the next morning on Chevy's bedroom floor. The Happy Couple never even made it upstairs. I found Lisa in the laundry room and Chevy nestled beneath his dining room table, clutching an empty bottle of Malört like a stuffed animal. Thank God his parents were out of town.

My phone was dead, so I didn't see Ally's message until I got home. A single line. Four words.

Ally:

We need to talk.

11

Ally allows me to finish my makeshift bath in peace. When I limp out of the bathroom, she's hunched over the kitchen island, the dossier spread out in front of her.

"I'm kinda offended you went to Chevy and Lisa for help," she says. "If you were serious about moving on, I should've been your first call."

"I never asked them to make that," I clarify. "And in case you forgot, we are not friends. *We* are exes. Which makes you the last person I'd call." Mom had a washing machine installed in our kitchen pantry a couple years back. I pop the bloodstained towel in along with the rest of my rancid clothes and start the load before sliding the pantry door closed. "Also, you're in a coma!"

Probably should've led with that.

"A minor setback." I can hear her flipping through pages—some of them dog-eared, I notice. She's even scribbled little notes in the margins of their bios. "What did they call it again?"

"A dossier."

"Of course they did," Ally says, rolling her eyes. "Well, their dossier is highly flawed. Chevy and Lisa have known you longer, but I know you better." I make a face. A lofty claim. "You don't think so?"

"A week ago, I wasn't talking to an astral projection. Not sure it matters what I think right now."

Ally has this look in her eye; she lives for a challenge. "Here, I'll prove it." She spins the dossier around so I can see it right side up.

"Sloane Porter. Candidate #17. She's hot. Nice teeth. Good posture. Seems like a reasonable ranking for her, right?"

I start to nod.

"Wrong! Little-known fact about Sloane: She goes by another name—Norma L. Gurley. And Norma hosts a podcast called *Teen Talk* in her spare time focused on"—Ally's eyes widen—"being a *modern teen.*"

I shudder. "Gross! What if she tries to get me to come on as a guest?"

"Or worse . . ." Ally purses her lips. "Her *co-host.*"

My stomach clenches. The horror.

Ally's flipping again. "Candidate #8: Adriana Cisneros. Great ass. Would kill for her eyebrows. Decent ranking, yes?"

I fall for it *again.*

"Nope! Adriana is allergic to peanuts. And I know for a fact your diet consists of like ninety percent peanut butter."

It's true. Choosy Cams choose Jif.

"One kiss with you, and it's bye-bye, Adriana." Ally slides a finger across her throat.

That does sound less than ideal.

"But worst of all is their top pick." Ally flips to the first page. "Candidate #1. Ms. Claire Heston."

"Hey, I like Claire!" I clap back. Claire was one of the few candidates that actually piqued my interest. We'd always had a semi-flirty relationship, dating back to being lab partners in freshman year Biology.

"Really?" Ally arches an eyebrow. "Because I have it on good authority Claire can lick her elbow."

My heart sinks. *Oh no.*

"Which, to a normal person, wouldn't be cause for concern. However, I know you're a weirdo who believes women who can lick their elbows are witches."

"That's a real thing!" I'm adamant. "If they'd used the elbow-lick test in Salem, things would've gone a lot smoother!"

"We are not having the elbow-licking argument again!" Ally says. "But I think we both can agree it's a pretty big oversight on Chevy and Lisa's part."

Hm. She does have a point. I hate it when that happens. This is all just too weird. I keep scrutinizing every inch of her expression, hunting for a trace of sincerity. Ally's as sarcastic as they come; it's one of the things I love about her—er, *loved* about her. But right now, it's the last thing I need.

With her pinky, Ally flicks the dossier closed.

"Look, I know they're your friends—"

"They're your friends too," I'm quick to remind her.

Ally's eyes narrow. "*Sure.* They're great." A tacit smirk emerges.

"So, *so* great. And this?" She nods at the dossier. "Is a good start. But Chevy and Lisa don't have your best interests at heart."

I scoff. "What, and *you* do?"

"Is that so hard to believe?" I loft my eyebrows. Ally recoils, feigning hurt. "I just want you to be happy, Cammie. You think I enjoy seeing you like this? Depressed. Lonely. Bent out of shape. Pining after me."

"You're smiling."

"Am I?"

She is. "You are."

"How about now?" It's even wider. "Okay, fine. So maybe I'm enjoying this a bit. But this is a once-in-a-lifetime opportunity, Cammie. How many exes actually get a say in their replacement?"

"None."

"Exactly!" Ally's enthusiasm isn't contagious. Finally, she takes the hint. "I know it's weird. But due to recent events, I have a new outlook on life. And helping you in your time of need will bring me some much-needed peace of mind."

"And why's that?"

"I dunno." Ally breaks eye contact then, bowing her head. I watch her tangle and untangle her fingers. She never has figured out what to do with them when she isn't talking. "Maybe I don't love the way things ended between us," she says finally. "Maybe I'd feel better if we were on decent terms."

This she says without her customary sarcastic acrobatics. Almost . . . *sincerely?*

"Say I agree to let you help me—not saying I am! What would that look like?"

"Simple really," Ally says with a shrug. "I'll tell you what to say, what to wear, what to fix—"

"Yeah, okay," I scoff, cutting her off. "What do I need to *fix*?"

Ally parks her hands on her hips. "Do you really want me to do this?"

We hold each other's gaze. *One Mississippi . . . two Mississippi . . . three Mississippi . . .*

"Yes—"

"Your posture sucks, your eyebrows are an abomination, you chew with your mouth open, you have a weird patch of hair on your lower back that looks like a furry tramp stamp, you say *pellow* instead of *pillow*, you wear some variation of the same gray STHS basketball T-shirt every single day . . ."

She goes on like this for another minute. I'll save you the trouble and skip ahead.

"Had those locked and loaded, huh?" I say when she finally runs out of steam.

Ally tosses her hair over her shoulder. "Whaaaat? *Nooooo.*" She breaks into a smile. Against my better judgment, I do the same. "Graduation's what—next Saturday? Ten days?" Ally brings her hands together. "It's settled, then. Ten days from now, I'll wake up. Reenter. Ten days for us to find you a new distraction."

I'm still not sure I buy her coma claims, but I don't have the energy to push her on it right now. Upstairs, a door latches shut.

Footfalls overhead, away from Maizy's room, headed for the stairs.

My heart leaps into my throat. "Deal," I hiss. "Whatever you want. Just go!"

Ally's eyes dart toward the stairs. She hears Mom too. "Why do I have to leave?"

"I'm not fucking around, Al. You need to leave right now—"

"Who are you talking to?"

Shit. Mom walks in. Already looking suspicious.

"Nothing!" I sneak a peek at Ally, loitering in my periphery. "No one!"

Mom studies me a moment. "Have you been taking your meds?" I nod. "Good." She instructs me to get situated at the dining room table, leg elevated, then goes to wash her hands, passing between me and Ally. While her head is turned, I whip around and glare at Ally.

GO! I mouth.

WHAT? Ally mouths back.

GOOO!

Ally starts mouthing again. "Wait, why am I whispering? Your mom can't hear me," she says with a snort. I hear the faucet shut off before I can respond. I turn back to Mom, sporting a big, fake smile.

Mom positions the remaining stool beside my foot and slowly begins stripping away the mechanisms holding my leg together. First the cast, then the ice pack. As she's unwinding the gauze,

Ally appears over her shoulder, peering down at my leg. I glare at her long enough to draw her attention.

"Relax, Cammie," she says. "I just wanna see what all this fuss is about. I'm not saying you're being a baby about this." Ally gestures broadly at my leg. "But come on. It's *one* knee. I literally had a bone sticking out of my wrist when they pulled me out of my car. I seriously doubt one teensy-tiny little knee scar is worth all this trouble—"

Ally freezes. The color drains from her face. She looks like she's seen a ghost. Oh, how the tables have turned. Only, then I see it too. My knee. It's . . . it's . . .

A monstrosity. An abomination. An affront to God.

The incision is BIG—the length of a pen. An impossibly deep shade of purple. Almost black. Caked in dried blood, the surrounding skin is a sickly jaundice color. Yet the scar itself is damp, slick with pus and sweat.

That thing's been there this whole time?! I want it off me, even if I have to carve it out of me with my bare hands. Anything to get this thing off me.

"It looks good," Mom says without a trace of irony. Gently, she rolls my leg from one side to the other, examining it closer.

"*That* looks good?" Ally cries. I look up at her just as she covers her mouth with the back of her hand. Are astral projections supposed to turn green? Because she's not looking so hot. Wait . . . is she—?

"Do *NOT* throw up!" I break protocol, addressing Ally

directly. *Out loud.* Desperate times. "If you throw up, then I'll throw up."

Mom looks up at me with utter confusion. "Why would I throw up, Cameron? I've seen far worse than this."

"YOU MEAN IT COULD BE WORSE?!" Ally doubles over, clutching her stomach, retching. "That is the (*hurk*) most disgusting thing I've ever (*hurk*) seen. Every time I look at it I just—(*hurk*)"

Me: "Then stop looking at it!"

Mom: "How am I supposed to replace your bandage without looking at it?"

Ally: "I can't help it! It's like a car wreck. (*hurk*) I'm allowed to make that joke by the way because . . . (*hurk*) Oh God, what's that smell. Is—is that coming from your knee? (*hurk*)"

Jesus Christ, she's right. It smells like a decaying retainer. It's the other night all over again; I'm dry heaving too.

Mom jolts to her feet, missing Ally by inches. "I just had these floors waxed, Cameron. Don't you dare throw up in here! Cameron? Cameron!"

12

Is insomnia one of the side effects of Delatrix? I can't remember if Dr. Vernon mentioned it or not. Wouldn't surprise me. I'm in for another long night.

This is crazy, right? On, like, a million different levels. Ally, my ex-girlfriend, is offering to help me move on—*from her!* To find her "replacement," as she put it. And that's before you even factor in the paranormal element.

I need to figure my shit out. No doom-scrolling WebMD tonight. Instead, I'll be productive. Put pen to paper. Organize my thoughts.

Pros / Cons of Accepting Ally's Help
with the Cam Rebound Project

PRO: *We're talking for the first time in five months.*
CON: *It took a bottle of painkillers and a catastrophic*
  car wreck for her to talk to me.
PRO: *If we succeed, I get to mash my mouth against*
  someone else's mouth. It has been a while.

CON: *That person wouldn't be Ally.*

PRO: *There's a chance I really could move on. Meet someone I really like.*

CON: *The fact that Ally's offering to help indicates she's already moved on.*

PRO: *She isn't really giving me a choice. Tough one to ignore.*

CON: *The extent of her supernatural abilities remains unclear, and I'm a little afraid of finding out. (I've seen one too many horror movies.)*

PRO: *I'd get to make Ally jealous. Sure, she's talking a big game now. A couple months in the astral dimension and I'd probably think I was untouchable too. But trust me, I know Ally. The only person in Shermer more jealous than her is, well, me. What happens if I do strike gold? What are the odds Ally actually allows that to happen?*

PRO: *I'd get to spend time with my best friend again.*

CON: *I'd have to spend time with the girl who broke my heart.*

IT'S BEEN SEVENTY-TWO hours, give or take, since Ally unexpectedly—*inexplicably*—reinserted herself into my reality. And yet, my mother expects me to return to class.

"Every day of school you miss is money stolen from hard-working taxpayers," she accosts me from the kitchen. "Are you a taxpayer, Cameron?"

"No."

"Are you planning on paying the taxpayers back the money you're stealing from them?"

"No."

"Okay. Then get up, get dressed, and get going." She's halfway out the door when she remembers to add, "And drive your sister to school."

Aaaaaand there it is. The real reason she wants me back on my feet.

Last year, Mom bought me a car for my birthday. Not just any car: an aqua-colored 1991 Geo Tracker. Purple racing stripe down the side. Similar to a Jeep, except shittier in every conceivable way. Far as I could tell, Mom had two reasons for green-lighting the purchase:

Reason #1: So I could run errands for her.

Reason #2: The goodness of her heart. A distant second.

While my sister's getting ready, I pop a couple Delatrix, then stash a few more in a travel-size Advil tube.

"You're driving me this morning?" Maizy asks excitedly when she comes stampeding into the kitchen, her light-up Jordans squeaking on the hardwood.

"Mhm. Just you and me, Maiz. You know what that means."

My sister sandwiches her cheeks between her hands, a perfect shocked-emoji face. "DONUTS?" she screeches. The rumors are true; baby sisters are very cute.

See, part of the fun of being an older brother is scoring easy points with the smallest of gestures. Like taking Maizy for

Munchkins before dropping her at school. Mom can be a little strict when it comes to junk food (I'm sure that won't have lasting, lifelong effects) so this is one of the few instances where Maizy gets to indulge. I drop her off with sticky fingers and powdered sugar around her mouth.

It is a truth universally acknowledged that a second-semester senior in good academic standing isn't gonna do shit. If everyone agrees it's a universally futile exercise, then why are we forced to show up? Can someone explain that to me?

Once AP exams were out of the way, STHS essentially became a film school. I spend my morning bouncing from one showing to the next. *Inception* in Psych. *Romeo + Juliet* in English. *Moneyball* in Stats.

As I pace through my schedule, I get the same polite surgery questions from peers and teachers alike.

"How long will you be out?" Nine months—prom babies will already be born.

"Will you be able to play next season?" Looking less and less likely by the day.

"Can I sign your cast?" Not that kind of cast, guy.

My surgery is old news, anyway; everyone's talking about one thing and one thing only: tomorrow's main event, the Senior Olympics.

What started in the eighties as a simple senior ditch day event has since evolved into a massive party with some light competition-based elements. Planning begins in the fall, when the advisory committee—yes, there's an official advisory committee and yes, Chevy's on it—divides the entire senior class into four teams, or countries. On the day of, everyone gathers at nearby Ringwald Park for a full slate of individual and team-based competitions, similar to the field days we used to have in elementary school. With one small change.

Drinking. Lots and lots of drinking.

So long, tug-of-war; hello, *drunk* tug-of-war. Au revoir, sack race; welcome, *drunk* sack race.

You get the idea. People here take it extremely seriously. It's become the most popular canonical senior event, bigger than prom, homecoming—even graduation itself. Once upon a time I included myself among those most looking forward to it. Then came the breakup. Then went my knee. Now I doubt I'll even go.

Just before my fifth-period lunch, I get a text from Chevy.

CHEVY

Meet us at Taco Carne for lunch

STHS has an open-campus lunch policy for upperclassmen, so I usually end up grabbing something quick with The Happy Couple. Taco Carne, for instance, a local burrito place that Lisa's obsessed with.

I don't see either of their cars when I pull into the lot. I head in anyway. Tables can be hard to come by here. Someone's bound to take pity on the guy on crutches, right? I'm not inside for five seconds before I hear someone shouting my name.

"Cam? Hey, Cam—over here!"

I peer over the heads of the other patrons until I spot a hand flagging me down from a booth in the back. I crutch over and find Keather James—a fellow senior and another patient of Dr. Garrity's.

"Hey, Keather." I lean over the back of the booth for a one-armed hug. "You haven't seen Chevy or Lisa, have you?"

"Actually, I'm meeting them here too!" Keather says. "Lisa asked me if I wanted to get lunch this morning. Which I thought was weird, since she's never asked me to eat with you guys before, but hey—I'm glad she did!"

"Lisa invited you to lunch?" I make a face. "*With* us?"

Keather nods cheerfully. "They're running late, though. Lisa just texted me. She said they'll be here soon."

Hm. Something's up. First off, we don't invite just anybody to lunch with us. There's a whole vetting process. Ally had to get two letters of recommendation before she was approved. But beyond that, if we were to invite someone else to eat with us, Keather James would not be high on the list.

That sounds mean, doesn't it? I should explain. Is Keather nice? Yes, absolutely. Wicked smart too. Someone who's happy to shoulder the lion's share of a group project or let you copy her homework answers at the eleventh hour.

Just one problem: Keather *loves* weed.

But, Cam, you smoke weed. That's true, disembodied voice in my head, I have been known to dabble. And I'd never fault anyone for doing the same.

With Keather, it's not the loving weed that makes her unbearable; it's the *wanting* to tell you how much she loves weed. It's her defining trait—by her own design. Remember when The Happy Couple accused me of finding ways to shoehorn Ally into conversations? That's what Keather does, but with weed.

To make matters worse, her parents recently opened the Breakfast Nug, Shermer's first legal dispensary. Meaning Keather has even more reasons to tell you about how she and her friends got *soooo* high this weekend.

I know for a fact Chevy and Lisa feel the same way about her. So why would they invite her to lunch with us? Unless . . .

"Did Lisa give you a reason for why they were running late?" I ask Keather.

"An errand, I think?" Keather steals a glance at her phone—of course her case has a giant marijuana leaf on it. "I tried asking them for a ride since I'm such an awful driver when I'm high." Keather stalls, waiting for a reaction. I'm not falling for it. "But they told me to just go on ahead and look for you."

Of course they did. Because The Happy Couple isn't coming to lunch.

It's a trap. Or, rather, a *date*.

Thirty-two mind-numbing minutes later, I'm safe inside the Geo, free from Keather and her one-track mind. My head is killing me. This might sound like an overreaction, but I might never smoke again. Keather's ruined it for me. Hell, maybe those corny drug PSAs the school made us watch are right.

Suddenly, the sound of squealing brakes approaching fast. I snap to, brace for impact. The matte-black SUV whips into the lot and screeches to a halt just inches from my bumper, angled sideways, perpendicular to my hood. Boxing me in. The driver rolls his window down.

"Cam!"

I hate them.

"Don't *Cam* me." I roll my own window down, hang over the side. "You guys might have Keather fooled, but I know *exactly* what you're up to."

Chevy feigns shock. "I'm not sure what you're implying, Cameron."

A humming sound—Chevy's sunroof. Lisa's head pokes out like she's a goddamn prairie dog.

"We got here as fast as we could!" she insists. "Didn't Keather tell you?"

"Uh-huh." I rev the Geo's engine, punch the horn with the heel of my wrist. "Now move. The period's almost over; I need to get back."

"You can't leave yet," Chevy says. "Not until you tell us how it went."

"Gee, lemme see." I say, my voice all singsongy. "Keather is one of a kind. We just . . . *clicked*. I'm seeing her again this weekend. And next weekend. And every weekend after until the end of time."

Lisa beams. "Really?"

"No! It was Keather James; how do you think it went?"

Chevy looks up at Lisa. Lisa looks down at Chevy. Then, together, they look at me.

"She talked about weed, didn't she?" Chevy asks, cringing.

"Of course she talked about weed! It's all she ever talks about! She has the personality of tap water!"

"Hey, don't sleep on tap water," Lisa scolds. "There's fluoride in there!"

"Okay, fine! She has *less* personality than tap water."

Lisa makes a face, then looks between her knees. "I walked into that one, didn't I, babe?"

"Not at all. You're doing great, babe."

"Thanks, babe."

"Enough with the *babe*," I say. "I don't get it. Why Keather? She isn't even listed in your stupid dossier."

Chevy lets out a long sigh. "Cam, this will come as a shock to you, but Lisa and I weren't actually running errands. This was a ruse. We were trying to set you and Keather up."

"I know!" I snap.

"And even though you were completely fooled—"

"I *wasn't.*"

"And are only now learning of our deception—"

"I figured it out immediately."

"We're sorry for not being up front with you."

Lisa nods in agreement. "Very sorry."

"That doesn't answer my question," I grumble. "You guys are supposed to be helping me find a new hookup, right? Wasn't that the point of creating the Cam Rebound Project? So why are you setting me up with someone who your precious algorithm didn't even recommend? What—were you using me to gain access to her parents' store or something?"

For once, The Happy Couple share a look I am able to decipher.

My eyes narrow. "You have *got* to be kidding me."

"Cam, listen!" Chevy holds out his arm like he's approaching a barking dog. "Now, before you get mad, do me a favor and think of the discounts."

Lisa eagerly nods along. "The discounts, Cam!"

"We'd never have to spend a dollar on weed ever again."

"Or those little sleepy berry CBD gummies you like so much!"

"Sleepy berries, Cam!"

And to think, I actually believed they had my best interests at heart. Turns out they were in it for themselves. I guess Ally was right. Hate when that happens.

"Is that all I am to you?" I lift my shirt and cup my left pec. "Just a piece of meat you can hawk to the highest bidder?"

Lisa's defiant. "No!"

Chevy's transparent. "I mean, kinda." Lisa knees him in the back of his head. "I'm kidding! So Keather was a bust. We know that now. But let's all take a second and appreciate the fact that you just went on your first date post-Ally."

My stomach turns. He's right. I hadn't even realized it, but yeah. If my life was a *Jeopardy!* category, the $1,000 answer would be *The first girl Cam went on a date with after Allison Tandy broke his heart.*

The question: *Who is Keather James?*

Damn. That's dark. Suddenly I don't feel so well. I need to get home.

"I'm not gonna tell you again," I shout. "Move!" This time

when I lay on the horn, I don't let up. Rubberneckers are starting to stare.

Chevy tries pleading with me—"Dude, come on!"—but the horn drowns him out. "Will you at least come to Jake's with us later?"

"If I say yes, will you get out of my way?"

He consults with Lisa. "We'll allow it." He inches forward. As soon as there's enough daylight, I peel out and don't look back.

13

The odds of me actually making it to this party tonight were low to begin with, but when I get home from school and find I have the house to myself, Vegas quits taking bets.

Maizy's at a friend's and Mom is "Out," according to the note on the kitchen counter. Which just leaves me and my best girl, POL-I. We link up. I crank her dials as cold as they'll go, then start absolutely going to town on a tub of pure, uncut cookie dough.

I'm almost finished with Season 7 of *NCIS Boise*. Special Agent Bonesaw and his unit are closing in on this season's big baddie, the Admiral Assassin, so named because he—you guessed it—assassinated an admiral. Not to be confused with last season's villain, Captain Cutthroat, who—hold on to your butts—cut a captain's throat. (Yes, all the villains are nautical themed. *Obviously.*)

Bonesaw has the killer on his heels, tracking him through a sparsely populated shipping yard, off the coast of downtown Boise's Little Italy district. If you've seen as much *NCIS Boise* as I have (113 episodes and counting), you know Bonesaw's emotions will likely get the better of him, causing him to fall into the Admiral Assassin's carefully laid trap. Then, just as Bonesaw is about to meet the wrong end of a bullet (is there a right end?), he'll reveal getting captured was all part of his plan. Cut to: NCIS reinforcements parachuting in and—

The TV goes dark. Over my shoulder, Ally's reflection looms in the blank screen.

"I was watching that!"

"Let me save you the trouble. The good guys catch the bad guys. Everyone goes home happy. America wins. The end."

"Spoilers!"

"So . . ." Ally wades around the sectional. Tonight she's wearing black leggings and an old Camp Fremont T-shirt she cropped herself. So many costume changes for someone lacking object permanence. "A little birdie told me Jake Cooper is having people over tonight."

"Birds can see you too now? Quite the twist. I didn't know the astral projection community had such close ornithological ties."

"You wouldn't know anything about that, would you?"

"About ornithology?"

"About Jake Cooper having people over."

I give her a noncommittal shrug. "I may have heard some rumblings."

"And are you planning on making an appearance?"

"You know, I considered it. But then . . ." I sink my spoon into the tub and scoop out a massive mound of dough, ladling it into my mouth. "I had another thought," I say mid-chomp. "What if I didn't go (*chomp*) and instead (*chomp*) I just hung out here (*chomp-chomp-chomp*)?"

I break into a wide, open-mouth smile then, cramming dough between the slits in my teeth. Ally seems unimpressed. "I've never been more attracted to you," she deadpans.

I start to laugh, but it's tricky. The dough is thick and dense and starting to block my airway. I reach for my water bottle. Ally jerks into action suddenly, beats me to it.

"Oh, I'm sorry. Did you want this?" she taunts, dangling the bottle just out of reach.

Panic grips my throat. I try forcing the mound past my tonsils, but that only makes it worse. Dough cakes the walls of my esophagus, gumming up the back of my throat. When I try saying something, I choke.

"What was that?" Ally leans in, tips her ear. "Sorry, I didn't catch it."

"Hmmmm!"

"Bet you wish you hadn't stuffed your face, huh? Do you feel good about your life choices right now?"

The dough is at a complete standstill now. I'm running short on air. I have no choice. I shake my head.

"Do you feel silly right now?"

I nod.

"Would you like your water back?"

I nod.

Ally makes like she's about to hand it to me, but it's a fake-out. "One more thing. Do you promise to go to Jake Cooper's party tonight so you can talk to girls and find a slightly less attractive replacement for me?"

It's still surreal—and a little dispiriting—hearing Ally openly encourage me to flirt with other girls. But I'll unpack that later, when I'm not on the verge of asphyxiating. I nod.

"Pinky promise so I know you mean it."

It sounds silly, I know. But trust me; Ally takes her pinky promises extremely seriously. I'd hate to be the guy who broke one of those.

With our right hands, we join pinkies. We make the handoff with our left. I guzzle the water down in its entirety.

"The fuck, Al!" I bark when I come up for air. "You could've killed me!"

"Don't be so dramatic." She taps on the lid of the tub. "This stuff will kill you. You know you're not supposed to eat it raw like this?"

I'm still wheezing. "You're the last person I should be taking advice from on staying alive."

Ally's mouth falls open. "Okay, *wooow*."

"Yeah! *Wooow* is right!"

"Was that a coma joke?"

"Yeah! I guess it was."

"So we're going there now?"

"Yeah! I guess we are."

My throat's still coated in residual gunk. It feels like there's something lodged in my nasal cavity too. I try clearing it, to no avail. Whatever's up there doesn't want out.

"We should probably talk strategy for tonight," Ally says.

"What is there to talk about?" I grumble, unclipping from

POL-I. "It's just a party. Jake's had a hundred of them. If I remember correctly, we had some fun in his gazebo last summer."

Ally's cheeks color. She must not want me to see her blushing, because she turns and goes to grab my crutches off the wall. Using her powers for good today.

"This time's different, though," she says, chasing me into the kitchen. "It's your big coming-out party. Your chance to say, 'Hello, world, my name's Cameron Garrity and I'm here to make out!'"

I look at her sideways.

"Humor me," she says gently. "Let's start simple: What are you gonna wear?"

I swallow my afternoon Delatrix, then pull on the front of my gray STHS basketball T-shirt. "This?"

Ally covers her mouth. "Tell me you're kidding." I am not. "Are you going to shower at least?"

"I'll do what I always do—put on some deodorant, then call it a day."

Ally looks at me like I've just confessed to a double murder. "And the neckbeard?" Without asking, Ally takes hold of my chin, twisting it left to right as she inspects the gash across my jugular. "Can't we put a Band-Aid over it or something?"

"I tried last night. The adhesive wouldn't take."

"You look like if they reattached Ichabod Crane's head to his body."

I wrest my chin free. "Can you just chill? Tonight will be fine, I promise."

"Prove it." Ally steps closer. "Let's practice. You be you, and I'll be one of the names in the dossier."

Falling into character, Ally props her elbows on the kitchen island and samples an indifferent expression. Ally isn't a theater kid, but she's committing to the bit. *Fuck, why do I find that kind of adorable?*

"Fine, I'll play." I set my crutches aside and try to picture it— the scene a few hours from now. *Sandwiched in Jake's basement, disappointingly sober, when—what's this? A candidate from the dossier standing all alone in the corner of the room? Why don't I just mosey on over and say . . .*

"Why, hello there, miss—"

"Wrong." Ally immediately breaks character.

"Wrong? What do you mean *wrong*? I only said four words!"

"Yeah. And one of them was *miss*. This isn't a malt shop in 1950. What's next—you gonna call me *little lady*? Quit being so formal. It's a Jake Cooper party. There are gonna be people throwing up left and right. Spencer Buckley and her friends will be doing lines in the theater room."

"Those girls do love cocaine."

"They really do."

"So early too."

"Right? That's a drug you save for college." Ally snaps her fingers. "Again!"

I take a deep breath. *Jake's basement. Disappointingly sober. Dossier candidate standing alone . . .*

"Hey, what's up—"

"Stop."

"How!"

"Could you sound any more desperate? Think *less* thirsty."
Snap. "Again."

"Hi—"

"Nope."

I throw my arms up, exasperated. "How is this helping me?" I
demand. "All you're doing is making me doubt myself."

"Better you mess up here, with me, than get flat-out turned
down by someone in the wild. Do you really think you can handle that kind of rejection right now? In your condition?"

Gauging Ally's tone used to come easy to me. I guess I've lost
a step in the five months since we last spoke because right now,
I can't tell if she's genuinely looking out for me or just having a
laugh at my expense.

"I'm a big boy, Al. I can handle a little rejection. Plus, I've
done this before, you know? I've had plenty of other girlfriends
besides you."

"You've had exactly two girlfriends besides me. One was
Tallulah Chamberlin in sixth grade, which only lasted forty-eight
hours—"

"Whirlwind romance," I mutter.

"And the other one was Steff, who we both know you're still
madly in love with."

"I'm not—" I start to defend myself, but throttle down when
Ally breaks into a smile.

"I'm just giving you shit," Ally says. "I know you aren't into

Steff anymore. Besides, you pinky promised you'd never hook up with her again, and you know what happens if you break a pinky promise."

My eye twitches. Can Ally tell?

"I'm just gonna stick with the Cam Method," I say, changing the subject. "It worked before. It'll work again."

Ally sizes me up. "Fine. You get one chance. But when the *Cam Method*"—she can't help rolling her eyes—"fails, and it *will* fail, then we start doing things my way."

"Deal."

Just as we shake on it, I feel the pressure behind my eye suddenly dissipate. Whatever was stuck there has dislodged. And then I'm coughing, hacking like a kitten passing a hairball. The object ejects, sailing past my lips, and lands with a *splat* on the countertop.

A single chocolate chip. Slimy. Molted. Disintegrating. For a moment, Ally and I just stare at it. Soak it in. Finally, Ally says what we're both thinking.

"Yeah, don't do that."

It's pretty sweet Delatrix doesn't impair your driving the way other painkillers do. It's less cool when your friends take the opportunity to anoint you their de facto designated driver.

Looking at you, The Happy Couple.

No sooner have I picked them up in the Geo than Lisa is telling me all about Candidate #21, her latest addition to the dossier.

"Her name's Jeannie," Lisa explains. She's sitting shotgun.

Chevy's in back. "Jeannie Sprinkler. We play on the same club team. Her family lives in Shermer actually, but she goes to Lake Grove." Lake Grove Academy, the all-girls school just north of here. "I wanna say she's, like, an inch or two shorter than me. Long black hair. Incredible bone structure. Sorta ethnically ambiguous, but that's only because her family vacations a lot and she's ridiculously tan. But the best part is . . . she's going to UChicago next year!"

For a second I forget that's where I'm going too. "Oh, cool," I say when it clicks.

"You should definitely be friends with her, even if you guys don't hook up. Jeannie's a good person to know, especially if you need help meeting people."

"People who aren't us," Chevy clarifies.

Lisa nods. "Jeannie just has one of *those* personalities, you know? She draws people in."

When we brake for a red light, Lisa shoves her phone under my nose. "Here's what she looks like."

First impression: Jeannie's pretty . . . I think? It's a little hard to tell what she looks like with all the filters. Her grid has a uniform color scheme, each photo the same muted pastel preset you find in those fancy photo-editing apps. I tap on the most recent post, swipe through a few. Each is geotagged at some international destination.

"Is she an influencer?"

"Aspiring," Lisa says. "She just picked up her first sponsorship actually. For this weight loss tea that targets neck fat called JowelFit. They gave her her own promo code and everything."

The light changes.

"She's smart too, but she can be a little spacey. When she told the rest of us which colleges she was applying to, a few of us had our doubts. But apparently her dad made, like, a ridiculous donation to UC, so now she's all set."

Huh. So Jeannie's rich—even by Shermer standards. We're talking family-owns-a-doomsday-bunker-in-New-Zealand rich.

Ally despises people like that. Trust-fund kids who only get ahead because of their parents' (or their *parents'* parents') money. Not that Ally's poor necessarily. Mrs. Tandy works as an accountant at a nonprofit in the city. Decent money. Just not compared to most people who live around here. And certainly not compared to people like Jeannie.

Ally would hate it if I hooked up with someone like Jeannie. Someone with more money, who's closer to my height, who can go outside in the summer without first bathing in SPF 100. Whose waist, from the looks of it, is about the size of my wrist. Someone who's already friends with The Happy Couple.

No, Ally wouldn't like that one bit.

"Yeah, okay," I say to Lisa. "Text me her number and I'll hit her up."

Jake's street is already teeming with cars by the time we arrive. "Alright, team, game faces," Chevy instructs us as we pile out of the Geo. "You know the drill."

The hardest part of getting into a given party isn't learning of its existence; it's the act of *physically* getting inside the house once you've made it to the front porch. Can't walk right up and knock on the door; you risk getting turned away by a frazzled host. Even the order your group stands in has to be tactical. It goes (1) whoever heard about the party/knows someone inside, (2) any girls, (3) all the dudes.

We're old pros at this. But after his first two calls go unanswered, Chevy lets slip his anxiousness. "Where the hell is this kid?" Just as he redials, the hallway light flickers on. A boxy silhouette coalesces behind the blinds.

The door swings open. Out steps Del Dwyer. The very same Del Dwyer who I drunkenly challenged to a trial by combat (allegedly) for the high crime of flirting with Ally right in front of me. Just my fucking luck. The Happy Couple clock it too. Chevy plays it cool, gushing political affectation. "Del! What's up, man?!"

"Chevy!" Del lurches in for a hug, but his toe catches the threshold of the door. He tumbles into Chevy's arms. Chevy should've dropped him. That's what I would've done.

"I'm *sooooo* happy you guys are here," Del slurs as Chevy sets him upright. Del's wielding an unlit loosie in one hand, an open Natty in the other.

Lisa enters the splash zone, arms outstretched. "Hi, Del. How are you?"

"Lisa!" They embrace. "Dude, how happy are you to be done

with Mr. Bolton?" Their AP Econ teacher. Notoriously tough grader.

"*So* happy," Lisa says, throwing her head back in emphasis. "Thank God we never have to see him again."

Del raises his beer. "I'll drink to that."

"Cool if we come in?" Chevy asks, already inching toward the exposed entryway.

"What? Dude, of course!" Del says. "I'd never say no to you guys—"

Del's smile wilts when he spots me.

I nod. "Del."

He sets his jaw. "Cam."

Here's the thing about the Dels of the world: Sure, he seems like the go-along, get-along type on the surface, the happy drunk everybody loves having around. But make no mistake, Del's a rubber-stamped piece of shit.

And that's not because I see him as a threat (I don't) or anything like that. An annoyance, sure, but nothing more. I mean, not to be a dick, but he's a foot shorter than me. Fifty pounds lighter. Even on crutches, I could blow right through him, like walking through a spiderweb.

Unfortunately, as it currently stands, Del's our ticket inside. The gatekeeper. He knows it too, and as he retreats into the house, he makes a point of blocking the door frame.

"I haven't seen you around much," he says to me.

"Yeah, I've been pretty busy."

Del scoffs. "Too busy to come to Ally's vigil?"

Ah, yes. The Allison Tandy Memorial Vigil. I opted not to attend. That night, social media was overrun with carefully edited photos of the hundreds of candles spread across the STHS football field. Still weirds me out they opted to call it a memorial, considering, you know, Ally's not dead. But the organizers—Del among them—didn't ask my opinion.

"You know, Del, I thought about going. But then . . ." I can't help myself. "I realized how fucking weird it was to hold a vigil for a person who's still alive."

Del scowls. He looks primed to do something stupid, drunk enough to take a swing on me. This is it, our long-awaited show-down. I tighten the grip on the crutches. They can be weapon-ized, if need be. Before it comes to blows, a new player enters the arena.

"Chevy! Lisa! Cam!"

Tonight's host, Jake Cooper himself, here to save the day. Jake brushes Del aside. He performs the same ritual, hugging us one by one, then steps into his lawn and peeks his head up and down his street.

"You guys aren't rolling deep, are you?"

"Nah, man. Just us three," Chevy assures him.

"Good. I already let way too many people in."

"Yeah, it's pretty packed downstairs." Del hasn't stopped glar-ing at me. "I'm not sure we can fit anyone else."

"Don't listen to Del. He's just embarrassed because he hurt

his finger shotgunning earlier. Hasn't stopped bitching about it since."

"It stabbed me in the nail bed! I was bleeding!"

Jake kicks the front door the rest of the way open and waves us through. Del hovers in his shadow, glowering as we push past.

Guys like Del know exactly what they're doing. The way he cozied up to Ally after class, texting her at all hours of the night about "something funny" he saw online, casually finding ways to ask, *So how are things with Cam?* Sowing the seeds of doubt until one day—BOOM!

They make their move. *He doesn't deserve you . . . You should be with me instead . . . I'm a nice guy.* Yeah, okay, Del. You and every other "nice guy" who Ally was "just friends" with. Only, my mistake came in wasting my energy on the Dels of the world. Not when an actual threat existed.

HIM. One "just a friend" to rule them all. Lurking. Waiting for his chance.

"Cam? You good?"

I fade back to reality. The Happy Couple is already at the end of the hall, queued at the top of the basement stairs.

"Yup. All good," I say.

I lie.

14

There's this accepted version of the quintessential Americana high school party you see in shows or movies where the kegs flow freely, everyone puts out, and the night ends with a mad dash into the pool. Fully clothed, of course.

Let me assure you: Those parties are *pure* fiction. My guess is most of the people making said movies, writing said shows, and shoveling said shit never actually attended a party until they got to college. If such a party exists at the amateur level, I've yet to see it for myself. Hell, if anything remotely like that popped off in Shermer, the neighbors would call the cops in like two seconds.

The reality is most of these things are confined to basements, people are extra stingy with their alcohol, and no one's losing their virginity upstairs. (Do that at your own house, weirdo.)

It's a steep descent down Jake's basement stairs—not ideal crutching conditions. By the time I make it down, The Happy Couple is nowhere to be seen, lost among the crowd. Figures. Before long, I hear someone shout, "Cam!" and I'm swept away too.

See, this is why I didn't want to come tonight. Parties like this suck when you're sober. I end up bouncing from one soul-throttling conversation to the next.

Kelly Peters is going to Belize with her parents, but "they're chill, so it should be fun."

Peter Kelly is planning on rushing an engineering fraternity at Georgia Tech, but "they're fun, so it should be chill."

Cam Garrity is planning to blow his fucking brains out if he has to listen to one more of these, but "he's depressed, so it should be both chill and fun."

No one mentions Ally. And why would they? It's a party, after all. Once Ally's condition stabilized and the social media attention dried up, people were more than happy to avoid talking about her. Pissed me the hell off. Much as I resent Ally for trampling over my heart, I find I still feel protective of her in a way I can't totally explain. Seeing all these unremarkable people moving on with their unremarkable lives while Ally lies dormant makes my blood boil.

Tonight, though, I'm kinda relieved no one brings her up. What would I even say if they did?

Actually, I just talked to Ally this afternoon. She was in great spirits!

My knee isn't helping matters. Alone and increasingly in pain, I crutch over to the quiet side of the room, collapse on an unoccupied couch. Rest my eyes—just for a moment. What I wouldn't give to be wrapped in POL-I's embrace right now.

"What did I tell you about moping?" Chevy flops down next to me, and suddenly—magically—there's an open Coors in my hand. *How'd he do that?*

"Can't drink," I remind him, setting the can by our feet. "And I'm not moping. I'm just taking a break. As a member of the disabled community—"

"You are not member of the disabled community."

"As a temporary member of the—"

"Nope." Chevy sips from his own can. "Have you talked to anyone? There's like seven girls from the dossier here."

"I talked to Sarah Dixon. Does that count?"

"Sarah's gay. And she has a girlfriend."

"So you're saying my chances aren't great?"

"They are not." Chevy's eyes look like strawberry milk. Someone must've smoked him out. "You still mad about Keather James?"

I sigh. "No. I get why you did it. Those discounts would've been sweet."

"Thank you!" He raises his can. I oblige with an imaginary drink of my own, then watch as he devours his. The ensuing burp prompts cheers from the peanut gallery. He tips his corduroy snapback to his adoring fans. Then, with some force, he clamps his hands around my cheeks, smushing them together, and reels me in close.

"Cam, look at me."

"We are literally nose to nose. Where else would I be looking?"

"You know we love you, right? Me and Lis. No tricks. We just want you to be happy. That's it. That's why we made the dossier."

Guilt thorns at my sides. What's that saying about drunk thoughts being honest ones? Deep down, I know Chevy and Lisa are just trying to help. And in return, I've done nothing but bitch and moan.

"If no one in the dossier does it for you, that's okay," Chevy continues. "But there's gotta be someone around here you're the *slightest* bit into."

He relinquishes control of my cheeks, turning to take stock of the room.

"How about Kylie Thacker?"

I shrug. "Maybe."

"Becca Carlisle? Jocinda Chapman?"

How is Chevy not getting this? I can't just swap in any old warm body for Ally and call it a day. Chev could sit here for hours, rattling off the names of every girl on the North Shore, and never come up with one capable of making me forget about—

"Bridget Kaplan?"

On second thought.

"We have a winner!" Chevy cheers, celebrating by pulling another Coors out of thin air. "Dude, this is perfect! I heard Bridget just broke up with her boyfriend. You guys can be sad together."

In every grade, there's always one girl every senior guy is, let's say, *aware* of. For the grade below us, that's Bridget. Tall, blond, stupid hot. I'm pretty sure she was engineered in a lab by a gang of eleven-year-olds deep in the throes of puberty. And at this very moment she's milling around Jake Cooper's basement, distractedly watching six boys in Mitchell & Ness snapbacks play 21 Cup.

Chevy fastens his arm around my neck. "Go over there and say something."

"Like what?"

"Gee, Cam, I dunno. Maybe, 'Hey, Bridget, wanna go out sometime? Then maybe you can sit on my face afterward?' Just brainstorming here."

"I'm not sure that last bit will go over well."

"We won't know until you try it."

"Says the guy who's literally never asked anyone out. Remind me, was it you or Lisa that made the first move?"

"Irrelevant! Do you want to hook up with Bridget or not?"

The short answer, of course, is yes, as I am a (mostly) heterosexual fellow with two eyes and a . . . well, you know. But it's more complicated than that.

Chevy doesn't see it that way.

"Executive decision!" He jumps up before I can stop him. "Hey, Bridget!"

"Dude!" My fist connects with the back of his knee. Chevy buckles, crumpling back to the couch. But it's too late. The damage is done. Bridget is looking over here . . . Bridget is coming over here . . . Bridget is— *Shit*, Bridget's here.

"Hey, guys!"

"Bridget!" Chevy's back on his feet, pulling Bridget into a hug. "Cam here was just saying someone should save you from those guys." He gestures toward the Ping-Pong table. "And we thought, who better than us?"

"Wow, so thoughtful," Bridget says to us both. "Listening to boys argue over who sank which cup isn't how I wanted to spend my Thursday night."

"DON'T YOU HAVE SCHOOL TOMORROW?!" I blurt out. Chevy smacks himself on the forehead. The Cam Method in action, ladies and gents.

"Yeah, but I'm not drinking tonight," Bridget answers, seemingly unfazed in the face of my egregious awkwardness. "So what are you guys up to over here?"

"Actually, I was about to go track Lisa down," Chevy says. "But you guys should hang out and chat a bit."

I glare at him. *Don't leave me.* "I'm sure Lisa's just fine."

"And I'm sure she's looking for me." Chevy's already backpedaling. He gives me a final wink just before he's absorbed by the masses.

Bridget laughs lightly. "He's pretty drunk, huh?"

"Yeah."

"You're not drinking?"

"Nah."

"How come?"

"Can't."

Seriously, am I incapable of stringing more than one word together? God, it's been a long time since I've done this seriously. *Soberly.* "So are you, like, friends with Jake or . . . ?"

"With his sister, Emma." Bridget whips around and points out a girl holding court behind the wet bar. Same narrow face as Jake, same bloodshot eyes.

"I didn't even know he had a sister."

jeff bishop

Bridget nods, and I nod, and then we're both nodding because flirting is awkward and weird and dumb and WHY AM I DOING ANY OF THIS, I SHOULD BE AT HOME WITH POL-I, MY ONE TRUE LOVE!

"I don't think I could date a girl who had brothers." *Why, Cam?* "It would freak me out too much." *How are you so bad at this?* "Seeing what they would look like. You know, like, as a dude." *The lake is right there; just save us all the headache and drown yourself.*

Only, Bridget isn't running for the hills; she's smiling, sort of, making scattered attempts at eye contact when she isn't sipping from the blue concoction in her Solo cup.

"Remind me not to introduce you to any of my brothers."

"You have brothers?"

She nods. "Three. Plus two sisters."

"Jesus, there's six of you?"

"Mhm." A genuine laugh this time. Clearly she's gotten this reaction before. "I'm the oldest."

"How do you live like that?"

"Years and years of practice." She pauses. "And a lot of meditation. Yoga. Basically anything calming."

And now I'm imagining Bridget doing yoga. Not an unwelcome image. Wait—was that her goal? Is this going well? Who am I kidding, of course it isn't.

Then again . . . maybe?

"They should give out Nobel Peace Prizes to people like you," I say. "I only have one little sister, and sometimes she feels like too much."

"Maizy, right?" Bridget asks with a familiarity I've seen before. "Oh my God, I'm, like, obsessed with your sister. She's so funny; I wish my siblings were more like her."

"You know my sister?"

"Yeah, I've met her a couple times. Over at your mom's office."

"Oh." I shrink six inches. "You're one of my mom's patients."

Bridget nods. "My whole family sees Dr. Garrity. Including my mom, weirdly."

Then she's laughing again. She comes by it easily. But when she goes to talk again, it's Ally's voice I hear. The last Dr. Garrity patient I dated.

"I have to go!" I announce suddenly, retroactively as it turns out, because I'm already beelining for the exit. Bridget's response gets drowned out by the music. She doesn't deserve to get left hanging like that, but she'll be okay. Probably for the best, really. Hooking up with me won't improve her summer.

15

There's a line for the bathroom when I get upstairs. I have to wait out an overserved junior and a group filming themselves dancing in the mirror. Once they're finished, I hustle in and lock the door behind me, whipping out the neatly folded Ziploc I stashed in my back pocket before I left my house. Tonight's dose of Delatrix. I wolf down the capsules, then try chasing them with the closest drink in sight—a half-finished Red Bull I find sitting on the toilet tank lid. Just as I bring it to my lips, an unseen force wallops me on the wrist. The can clangs to the floor, spraying sticky liquid.

"Jesus, Al! You scared the shit out of me!" I run the faucet and stick my head underneath. I hadn't expected Ally to show up so quickly. Which begs the question . . .

"Are you following me?"

Cue signature eye roll. "Yeah, Cammie, because that's how I like spending my free time. Chasing you around like a lapdog, watching you grumble from place to place. Sounds like a blast. Believe it or not, my unconscious life—like the world—does not revolve entirely around you."

"Then why are you here?"

"To save you from getting mono, apparently." Ally steps out from behind me. It isn't a particularly large space; it's impossible to maneuver without bumping elbows or rubbing hips. Not that I'm complaining.

"Haven't you heard? Apparently there's an outbreak. Like half the football team already has it. And once their girlfriends get it and people break up for the summer, all hell will break loose."

"You're ducking my question," I say.

Ally bends down and retrieves the Red Bull can, dropping it in the wastebasket. "It's Jake Cooper's last high school party. You really think I'd miss this?"

I can't tell if she's messing with me. She's definitely dressed for going out, having swapped her sweats for a sleeveless white top and black jeans. She's wearing makeup too. Usually I don't notice it. I think that's supposed to be the point.

"Plus, this is an excellent place to eavesdrop," she continues. "You'd be surprised what people will say after a few drinks when they don't realize there's an astral projection in their midst, listening in on their conversations. Like, did you know that Bradley Nelson and Yousef Khan were hooking up? Because until about fifteen minutes ago, I didn't."

Ally moves between me and the mirror and consults her reflection, fluffing her hair, turning to inspect one side of her profile, then the other. "Ooh, and I saw Steff outside with QB1. Are they back together again? Aw, Cam. You must be so heartbroken."

Ally snorts at her own joke. I stare at the ceiling. There's a track meet taking place under my shirt, icy beads of sweat forming on the back of my neck, taking turns racing for my waistband. I cinch my elbows tight to my sides. Pray Ally won't notice the damp spots cropping up on my T-shirt. Or keep talking about Steff.

"So why exactly are you hiding out in the bathroom?" Ally asks, running a tube of lip balm around her mouth. "Cam Method not working out like you'd hoped?"

"It's working!" I say, growing defensive. "I'm just taking my time with the process."

"The thing is . . ." Ally caps the balm. "You don't have time. Graduation's one day closer. We need to speed this along, especially if you want to have something locked up by the time I'm back on my feet. That *is* what you want, right?"

Our eyes meet in the mirror.

"Yeah."

"Good. Starting tomorrow, I'll officially be taking over as point person on the Cam Rebound Project. The Senior Olympics are the perfect place to get started. And before you say anything, *yes*, you're going."

"And the dossier?"

"We can use it," Ally concedes. "But I reserve the right to make changes as I see fit."

Looking more than a little pleased with herself, Ally turns to leave. "Enjoy your night, Cammie. Tomorrow we get to work."

"Al, wait." There's something else I need to get off my chest. "I had a little chat with your buddy Del earlier."

Ally stops short of the door. Turns around. "Did you?" I nod. "You guys talk about anything interesting? Music? Politics? Quantum theory?"

"Not exactly."

"Okay? So why are you telling me?"

"Just thought you should know."

"That you talked to one of my friends at a party?" Her jaw hangs in mock awe. "Riveting, Cammie. Thanks so much for the update. Hey, remember the time you almost got in a fight with him when he dared to be my beer pong partner? That was *so* fun for me, thanks again."

"He wanted a lot more than that."

"Like what, Cam?" Ally crosses her arms. "What did Del really want? I just love it when you tell me I only have guy friends because they want to hook up with me. Makes me feel really great about myself, thanks so much."

The hurt in her eyes betrays her sarcasm-laced tone.

"That's not—" I waffle. "You brought up Steff!"

"You *dated* Steff! I never had any interest in Del!"

"Yeah, but—" Great, now I'm the one that feels bad. "I wasn't trying to say that was the only reason all those guys liked you. Of course they liked you for . . . you know . . ."

Ally cocks an eyebrow. "For me?"

"Yes, exactly! It's just, I could tell Del had a crush on you. But anytime I mentioned it, you claimed it was all in my head." I shrug. "I dunno. You were probably right. I think it just made me a little paranoid."

"Oh, Del definitely had a crush on me."

I actually gasp. "You knew?"

"Cam, I've had boobs for a while now. I can tell when a guy is staring at them." Ally snaps her fingers suddenly. My eyes lift to meet hers. "Case in point." My ears get hot. Caught in the act. "But in my defense," Ally continues, "you brought Del up a lot. Like, a lot. Obviously not as much as you brought up—"

Ally's expression sours on a dime. I feel my intestines squirm.

HIM. She was gonna say HIS name. Ally fed me the same party line she gave me about Del. Only in that case, the crush went both ways.

Someone's pounding on the bathroom door.

"*Caaaam*, are you in there?"

"*Caaaam*, we're tired!"

The Happy Couple, come to find their chauffeur. "Just a second!" I shout back. I can still hear them giggling on the other side of the door. After a moment, it dies down.

"Could they be any more obnoxious?" Ally sneers.

"Okay, what is your problem with Chevy and Lisa?" I ask. "That's, like, the third time you've taken a shot at them. I thought they were your friends."

"I thought so too. Until *we* broke up. Then it became pretty fuckin' clear whose friends they really were."

I smack my teeth. "You're overreacting."

Ally's eyes narrow. "Neither one of them has spoken to me since we broke up. I tried texting, calling, DMing. One time I ran into Chevy in the hallway, and he literally turned and sprinted the other direction."

"Okay, but—"

She cuts me off. "And that's not even the worst of it. Don't even get me started on the merch."

I frown. "Merch? What merch—"

Oh. Right. The merch.

When I told Chevy and Lisa that Ally had dumped me, they took it upon themselves to come to my defense. Which, counter-intuitively, meant going on the offense. The next day, The Happy Couple trekked over to the local print shop and put in a rush order. By the time classes resumed the following week, half the kids in our grade were wearing matching white ringer tees with blue piping, TEAM CAM screen-printed across the front.

Chevy and Lisa didn't stop there. There were dad hats, snap-backs, pens, Koozies, Croakies, noodies. Chevy even lobbied the Shermer city council to paint *Team Cam* on the town's water tower. Team Cam merch took over STHS. It was inescapable. Of course Ally'd seen it. That was the point.

"That wasn't . . ." I fumble for a defense. "They were just look-ing out for me."

"Yeah, well, for people I considered *friends*"—Ally dons air quotes—"I thought they'd at least pretend like they hadn't picked a side." A beat. "Especially Chevy. Some of my teachers wore those fucking shirts, Cam. Do you have any idea how hard it is to pay attention when you're surrounded by reminders of your ex?"

I start to answer but think better of it. Because actually, yeah, I kinda do. When they launched the Save Ally Fund, someone must've had the Team Cam merch in mind. Her shirts were almost identical, only with red piping instead of blue.

"Al, I'm . . ." *Sorry. Just tell her you're sorry.* "I didn't think you'd care, honestly."

Ally looks at me like I'm crazy. But before she can respond—"*Caaaaaaaaam*"—our visitors return.

I yell over my shoulder. "One second!"

But when I turn back, Ally's gone. And I'm alone. Completely alone.

ALLY BROKE UP with me on January 1. Helluva way to ring in the New Year.

When I try to recall the sequence of events—how things actually played out that night—my mind draws a blank. Er, not so much a blank, but it's fuzzy. Like trying to remember a dream ten minutes after waking up.

I suppose my brain did me a favor, blotting it from memory. Otherwise I probably would've spent the last few months replaying the events, retraumatizing myself in the process.

But the fallout, post-breakup? That I remember with perfect clarity.

When I woke up the next morning, my body felt different. Deficient. Inadequate. For the first time in my life, I looked in the mirror and hated the reflection staring back. Do you know what a blackhead is? Because I sure as hell didn't until I got dumped. Turns out, my nose is littered with them.

Mom was the first person I told. Naturally, she was extremely supportive.

"What did you do?"

"Nothing! Er, I don't know."

"You probably did something. What am I always telling you about doing things?"

It took me twenty-four hours to tell The Happy Couple. We were over at Chevy's, hanging out in his basement. At first they thought I was doing a bit.

"Sure you guys did," Chevy said, rolling his eyes.

"Yeah, and I'm quitting volleyball," Lisa added.

I remember watching it sink in, the way their expressions gradually deteriorated.

"Wait, seriously?"

"Jesus, Cam. What happened?"

I didn't respond—how could I when I didn't even know the answer myself? They got the hint. When you're friends with someone long enough, you learn to read between the lines. They could tell the breakup wasn't my decision. Just like they could tell I wasn't handling it well.

And so they went to work.

The merch was just the tip of the iceberg. Chevy and Lisa went into full damage control mode. We needed to control the narrative, they kept telling me, put out an official statement. Chevy pulled a few strings (the perks of being class comptroller), and the first Monday following winter break, he managed to score a slot during the morning announcements.

"My fellow Wasps. It is with a heavy heart I announce today that Cameron Garrity and Allison Tandy have decided to suspend their relationship, effective immediately. It is the couple's official position that the breakup was mutual. It should also be known that while she cried, he did not. The couple asks for privacy at this time . . ."

Complete bullshit, obviously, but boy, it sounded good over the intercom. There's no such thing as a "mutual" breakup. It's an oxymoron. Doesn't compute. MINO: Mutual In Name Only. If someone claims otherwise, then they're no doubt the poor schmuck who had their heart broken.

In this case, me.

For the record, I never asked them to do any of this. Mentally, I was on autopilot by then. A zombie. A shell of my former self. Just going through the motions.

Sleepwalking my way through classes. Thank God we

were second-semester seniors; I can't imagine how much my grades would've tanked otherwise. And don't even get me started on basketball.

Mom, in her capacity as Dr. Garrity, put me on Prozac, which only dulled things further. Prom. State playoffs. Graduation. Senior Olympics. None of it seemed important anymore. Nothing excited me.

But you know what did? The Ex Message.

A friend told me about it. Swore it was a real thing. According to the internet, the Ex Message is a phenomenon where your ex texts you completely out of the blue—you don't see it coming—often just as you're beginning to feel like you're ready to move on. The message itself is usually some version of "I miss you," or "I'm sorry," or the less-than-subtle "Hey, how are you?" That text—or some version of it—was coming. Only a matter of time.

And I know what you're thinking: You shouldn't be taking heartbreak advice from the internet. But where else was I supposed to turn for advice on breakups? The Happy Couple? My mom? She's still technically married to my dad, even though we only see him twice a year.

I waited for Ally to text me. And waited. And waited some more. Days turned to weeks, weeks to months.

And yeah, I could've texted her first. But what good would that really do? As pathetic as I felt waiting for her to reach out, the thought of texting her first felt a million times more humiliating. After all, she'd dumped me. How would I look if I came crawling, begging her to take me back? Any residual attraction she might feel toward me would've vanished on the spot.

And then, on March 7, it happened. Not the Ex Message. Something much worse.

It was a Wednesday. Chevy texted me—just me, not the group chat like usual. He came over and we smoked for a bit. Something was off. Finally, I called him on it.

"There's something I need to tell you," he said with a heavy sigh. "I wanted you to hear it from me."

Sixty-five days. That's how long it took Ally to do what she'd sworn she never would.

Start dating HIM.

16

It's a miracle Chevy and Lisa were able to stand, let alone stumble inside his house when I dropped them off last night. Completely trashed, both of them.

Even more miraculous: the fact that they're both in my kitchen bright and early the next morning, whipping up breakfast with Maizy's help.

"Look who decided to join us," Lisa deadpans. My sister giggles. The two of them are chopping veggies at the counter.

Chevy's manning the stove. "I brought you an Australia shirt." He has to raise his voice to be heard over the hissing coming from the stovetop as raw egg fans out across the blistering frying pan. "Look over by the window, next to your pills."

"We weren't sure if you'd remembered."

That's code for *we knew you'd forget*. Both of them are already in their respective country's attire: Australia for Chevy, like me, and Canada for Lisa. She's even repurposed one of those leaf-shaped maple syrup bottles into a makeshift flask.

The shirt they brought for me is bright yellow and has a giant cartoon kangaroo on the front. Little tight around the arms. I take a pair of scissors from Mom's office and shear off the sleeves.

The food's ready by the time I've changed. Scrambled eggs with a side of OJ and Delatrix. The perfect balanced breakfast.

"Why are you guys dressed up as countries?" Maizy asks, her mouth completely full. She has a milk mustache too. Fuckin' love this kid.

Lisa takes the lead. "Because the Senior Olympics are today."

"What's that?"

"It's this big event where all the graduating seniors get together to play games and drink—"

I cough. Shoot her a look.

"I was going to say *fruit punch!*" Lisa says defensively.

Maizy's eyes light up. "*Oooh*, I wanna go!" She keys in on me. She knows how to spot the weak link. "Can I come, Cameron? Please-please-please-pleeeeeease."

"Yeah, can she, Cameron?" Chevy says, egging (ha!) her on.

"Please-please-pleeeeeease?" Lisa joins in.

It's like this, three against one, the rest of the morning, right until we reach Maizy's school. I dock the Geo at the end of the drop-off line behind a string of minivans decorated in campaign stickers for the latest local elections and those COEXIST bumper stickers spelled out using the insignias of various religions.

"It's not fair!" Maizy's full-on pouting. Arms crossed. Bottom lip extended. "How come I have to go to school and you don't?"

"Because Mom would disembowel me if I took you out of school for this," I say.

"Here, Maizy. I have an idea." Lisa fishes inside her backpack and pulls out a red marker. She has Maizy lean in, then sketches the Canadian flag on her cheek. "Even though your mean brother won't let you come with us today, you can still root for the good guys."

Chevy *pshs*. "Don't listen to her, MG. Team Australia is where it's at. Even if your brother is being a fun-sucker."

Maizy giggles. "Cameron's a fun-sucker."

Behind us, an aggressive honk. The crossing guard waves us forward. As we watch Maizy charge up the front steps, Lisa quips, "I think Maizy likes us more than Cam, babe."

"Can you blame her, babe?"

I kiss my teeth. "You guys are the worst."

Ringwald Park—the location of today's events—looks pristine when we arrive, if a bit dewy. Recently mowed, judging from the striped pattern in the grass. The tennis court nets are out of hibernation. The baseball diamond is freshly chalked. And to think, in just a few short hours the entire park will be covered in empties and vomit.

The Happy Couple deposits our group's contribution—two 30-racks of Busch—into the alcohol stockpile being amassed in the middle of the field.

"Well, boys." Lisa claps us both on the shoulder. "Prepare to be dominated." She grips Chevy by the scruff of his shirt and yanks him into a deep embrace, smacking his ass when she breaks away. "And you!" She turns to me. "Do me a favor and flirt with some girls today. Please? There are a bunch of candidates from the dossier on Team Australia. Every single one of them will need a big, strong shoulder to cry on after Team Canada finishes wrecking you."

I pull a Maizy, stick my tongue out at her. "I'll try my best."

To her boyfriend she says: "Make sure he does."

"On it." Chevy offers a cheery thumbs-up. His smile evaporates as soon as Lisa's back is turned. "Remember that guy Teddy from the beach the other day?" he asks me.

I assume he's kidding. "You mean Teddy, the guy we've gone to school with for four years? Teddy from the soccer team? Teddy, the guy you're convinced Lisa is having a passionate love affair with despite zero evidence? Yeah, Chev, I remember Teddy."

"You'll never guess which team he's on."

I don't have to. Emerging from the sea of red on the Team Canada sideline is the man himself. When Teddy greets Lisa, the two of them launch into an intricate choreographed handshake. There's hip bumping, chest thumping, elite levels of patty-cake. Not something you can whip up in ten minutes.

"Okay, so maybe I see where you're coming from," I deadpan.

"Whatever," Chevy mutters, turning. He starts for the Aussie sideline. "Let's go. We have a Games to win."

When Chevy drafted me for Team Australia, he expected Cam Garrity: basketball star and Edward 40-hands virtuoso, not Cam Garrity: injured and barred from alcohol consumption, per doctor's orders. I'm basically a waste of a roster space. Which means I'm stuck with clipboard duty, aka filling out Team Australia's lineup cards for the day's various events. So far we have . . .

- **Dizzy Bat:** *Peyton Sheedy, Sectional-champion gymnast on the balance beam.*
- **Nerf Pigeon Shooting:** *Dalton Stevens, hunting expert and guy-who-loves-telling-you-he's-a-Libertarian.*
- **Drunk Spelling Bee:** *Isaiah Williams, drank a Four Loko before the SAT and still scored a 1500.*

I've almost filled out every event before the 9:00 a.m. start time when I spot QB1 ambling by.

"QB1!" I flag him down. "Quarterbacks have steady hands, right? How's about I put you down for Giant Jenga?"

"Yeahsurewhatever," QB1 mumbles. He looks like hell. Bags under his eyes. Skin sheet-white.

"You good, man?"

"Yeah, I'm okay." He coughs into his hand. Gross. "Steff and I are back together," he blurts out suddenly.

"Oh. Okay. That's cool." What's happening? QB1 has never mentioned Steff before, or our shared dating overlap. He should know by now it doesn't bother me that he's dating my ex.

"I just thought you should know," he says. "Because . . . you know."

I laugh a little. "QB1, buddy, I have no idea what you're talking about."

Another round of coughing. He spits in the dirt, grinds it in with his shoe. "Steff told me." He raises his eyebrows. "About what happened."

She did what?! I play dumb. "And what did Steff say happened?"

QB1 hesitates. "That while we were broken up, you and Steff had—"

I spring to my feet, a shot of adrenaline, barely aware of the pain radiating from my knee. My hand slaps over his mouth before he can say something he shouldn't. I glance around. A few Aussie teammates are in earshot. Any one of them could've heard. They're not my concern, not when a certain astral projection with a habit of eavesdropping could be lurking nearby.

"Hey, Robby." I give him a hard look, use his real name so he knows I'm not fucking around. "I said, I have no idea what you're talking about. But if I did, I would suggest you keep it to yourself. I'm guessing your girlfriend feels the same way. Okay?"

QB1 looks at me, confused. So, normal. The perfect cover.

The piercing squawk of an air horn mercifully ends the conversation.

The four teams converge on the makeshift podium the Olympic committee has set up near the jungle gym. The excitement in the park is palpable. Too much for me. I hang back on the outskirts of the crowd. No use crutching all the way over there just to turn around and crutch back. Onstage, the four team captains stand before the assembled nations, including Chevy. He's the one with the megaphone.

"My fellow seniors," he belts into the modulator. "It is my absolute pleasure to welcome each and every one of you to this year's Senior Olympiad!"

The park erupts in cheers. I yawn.

"For four long years, we've waited for this day," Chevy continues. "The reason so many of us got ourselves out of bed every morning, sat through period after period, lecture after lecture. It was all for this!"

More cheering. Bit dramatic, if you ask me.

"But before we begin the day's events, there is something we must address." Chevy's voice grows somber. "Our fallen comrade who could not be here with us today. Allison Tandy, your friend and mine. If you all could please bow your heads and join me in a nondenominational moment of silence. Because even though Ally isn't here physically with us on this hallowed field, I know she's here with us in spirit."

Everyone in the crowd tips their faces to the ground like the animals at the beginning of *The Lion King*. Everyone, that is, except for one near the stage.

With us here in spirit. If only Chevy knew how right he was.

Ally waves. I return the favor. And then she's gone, absorbed by a crowd much taller than her. Moments later I spot her again, picking her way through Team Brazil, her copy of the dossier tucked under her arm.

"Sorry I'm late." She sidles up beside me. "Chevy's really hamming it up, huh?"

The last thing I need is for someone to notice me chatting to myself. Time to get creative. I whip out my phone, pull open the Notes app, and poke out a message.

What did I say about public spaces?

I nudge her, tilt the screen toward her. Not exactly inconspicuous, but desperate times or whatever.

"Sorry for breaking your *precious* rules," Ally taunts. "But what am supposed to do here? We're not exactly working with a ton of inconspicuous options."

She has a point. It'll be another week before the parks service opens the public restrooms by the picnic area. For now, they remain locked. Which is why part of our senior dues goes to the Olympic advisory committee; the committee earmarks money from the budget specifically so they can rent a couple of—

Oh no.

Onstage, Chevy's speech is reaching its crescendo. "TODAY IS A DAY UNLIKE ANY IN HISTORY," he booms into the megaphone. "BECAUSE TODAY . . ."

My heart hiccups. This can't be happening.

"ALCOHOL WILL BE CONSUMED . . ."

There must be another option.

"LEGENDS WILL BE BORN . . ."

Frantically, I sweep my gaze from one end of the park to the other.

"LIFELONG FRIENDS WILL TURN BITTER ENEMIES . . ."

But there's nothing. No alternative.

"LIMBS MAY BE LOST . . ."

I'm left with only one choice.

"BUT MOST IMPORTANTLY . . ."

I erase my previous note, tap out a new one.

"ALCOHOL WILL BE CONSUMED!"

Porta Potti. 5 minutes.

———

THIS, RIGHT HERE. Squished jock-to-jock with my phantasmal ex-girlfriend in a four-foot-by-four-foot Porta Potti. *This* is my nightmare. The only silver lining: It seems like we're the first occupants of the day, so the smell isn't terrible yet.

Ally, for her part, appears unbothered by the conditions of our rendezvous. "Don't get any funny ideas," she chirps once I've locked us inside. Occupied, twice over.

"Why would I get—" Jesus, we're right on top of each other. Now that we're actually smushed in here together, it's somehow even more claustrophobic than I thought possible. I count one . . . two . . . three . . . four . . . *five* points of contact between our skin. She's come dressed on-theme, decked in an Aussie soccer jersey. Only, she's made some alterations, sliced into the collar, freeing up extra room for her . . . well, you know. It's not that I'm trying to look—I swear! But they're kinda hard to miss when I'm forced to look straight down. I cross my ankles and stare at the flimsy plastic toilet seat, rattling off basketball statistics in my head.

"Hey!" Ally corrals my chin between her thumb and first finger. "Focus up. We've got a big day ahead of us. I'm gonna need you on your A game." She spreads open the dossier, balancing it on my stomach. "Last night I went through this again and compiled a short list of candidates from Team Australia. Now, I haven't had a chance to thoroughly vet them yet, so I'll have to do recon work as we go. In case there are gaps in Chevy and Lisa's algorithm—" She stops, glances up at me. "You listening?"

Not really. "Of course!"

"Okay, what's wrong?"

"Nothing."

"Cam."

I sigh, offering a defeated shrug. "I don't think I can do this, Al. Not right now. The thought of dating was hard enough back when . . ."

You ended things. I can't bring myself to verbalize the thought. I skip ahead.

"And now I've got this cast and these crutches and you're here—which, before you get mad, I'm not saying it's a bad thing, okay? It's just one *more* thing. And I thought I was finished with 'one more things,' like, ten things ago."

Ally closes the dossier. "It's not ideal," she agrees. "But believe it or not, I do actually hate seeing you like this." She gets defensive when I arch an eyebrow. "I'm serious! I don't want you to be miserable all the time. Just most of it."

That gets me. My lips hook into a smile. Ally builds on her momentum. "Any one of the girls in the dossier would be lucky to go out with you. You're taller than should be allowed. Good bone structure. You find yourself funny, but not in a cocky or self-conscious way. More, you're delighted by your own goofiness. Which is as endearing as it is disarming."

Am I blushing or just overheated? Where has *this* Ally been the last couple days?

"Is that why you agreed to go out with me?"

Ally bites into her bottom lip. On second thought, I don't mind the cramped quarters so much.

"Nah," she says. "I just wanted to see what kind of effect Dr. Cindy had on a kid."

"Uh-huh." I'm giving her the eyes. "That's it?"

She's doing the same. "Yup."

"No other reason?"

"Nope."

I don't realize just how far I'm bent over until my forehead scrapes against hers. Even then, I don't pull up. I feel like an asteroid, powerless against the gravitational pull of Ally's lips. Her baby-blue eyes. She can sense it too. She's antsy, switching her weight from one foot to the other.

In the end, it's Ally who flinches first. "Oh, and hey!" She takes hold of my chin. Maintains our distance. "I saw Steff over on Team Finland's sideline. If the dossier doesn't work out, you could always go and hook up with her."

Aaaaand that's my cue. I straighten up and close my eyes. Inhale deep. Collect my thoughts. "I can do this," I say more to myself than Ally.

"You absolutely can," she responds anyway. "And best of all, I'll be there every step of the way. If I find any red flags, I'll be sure to let you know."

"How do you plan on doing that?"

Ally's eyes glimmer. "I'm sure I'll think of something."

17

DOSSIER CANDIDATE #5:
Peyton Sheedy

The aforementioned elite gymnast, headed to Mizzou in the fall. Under her special skills, Chevy's written "flexible" with a winky face. Not wrong. I wouldn't be surprised if she were made from the same material as rubber bands, like, on a molecular level. If a Mini Cooper was a person—that's Peyton. But in, like, a hot way.

"Hey, Cam, you here to give me a pep talk?" Her event—Dizzy Bat—is up next. She's stretching in the grass, legs pointed in opposite directions.

"Oh yeah, the guy who's exhausted just from crutching over here is gonna tell you how to win a race."

Really wish I hadn't drawn attention to just how profusely I'm sweating, but Peyton laughs. Harder than she should. No wonder she's so highly ranked.

"Okay, here's my strategy. I'm gonna spin around really fast—"

"Without getting dizzy," I play along.

"Then run faster than everyone else."

"Interesting." I feign consideration. "Solid plan. If you can execute, you've got a real chance at winning."

Peyton laughs too hard again. Is it possible I'm nailing this on the first try? See, everyone was all worried about me for nothing.

I never see it coming, yet it hits me all the same: an empty Natty, straight to the head.

Peyton spins in a half circle, in search of my assailant. "Who threw that?"

I think I have some idea.

PORTA POTTI STATUS:
Bad, but could be worse

My ears are still ringing as I lock the Porta Potti door.

"The fuck'd you do that for?"

"I needed to get your attention!"

"And concussing me was the best you could come up with?!"

"Trust me, you'll be glad I pulled you out of there when I show you this." She holds her phone so I can see. A video starts playing of a girl who looks a lot like Peyton sitting on her bed, an acoustic guitar draped across her lap. But I can't make out what she's saying over the commotion outside.

"What is this?"

Ally hits pause. "She's singing."

"Lots of people sing."

"That's true. But they don't sing acoustic covers of trap music."

My stomach clenches. "Oh no . . ."

"Straight to camera. Completely earnest. Including a

particularly cringey version of Xanne Hathaway's 'Xannes Film Festival,' that she dedicated in—wait for it—*my* honor."

"But . . . but . . . why?"

"I haven't even told you the worst part yet."

"It gets *worse*?!"

"She swaps in 'ninja' for the N-word."

Oh God, I think I'm gonna be sick.

DOSSIER CANDIDATE(S) #11/#12:
Lindsey/Lindsay Collins

Two for one. The Collins twins: LindsEy and LindsAy. Identical in every way. Same alabaster skin. Same curtain of blue-black hair. Same full lips. Same name, save one letter. They even got the same SAT score—1450. Spooky doesn't begin to cover it.

LindsEy and LindsAy transferred to STHS at the start of junior year, so I don't know them all that well. Which makes it surprising to see them light up when they notice me crutching toward them.

"Cam!" They hug me at the same time.

"Hey . . . guys."

Confession time: I can't actually tell them apart. Which I realize might cause problems if I'm gonna, you know, hook up with one of them. Better figure it out. *Fast.*

I lead with a dad joke. "Has anyone ever told you guys that you look exactly alike?"

LindsEy and LindsAy turn to each other, in sync. Cover their mouths, in sync. Giggle, in—you guessed it—sync.

"We're identical in every way," LindsAy sings.

"Our parents *still* mix us up," LindsEy adds.

"We even tricked our boyfriends once."

"Before we moved to Shermer."

"They had no idea!"

"And the funny part was . . ."

"They were twins too!"

Okay, now I definitely believe we live in a simulation.

"So how do people tell you guys apart?" I ask.

"Oh, that's easy!" LindsAy says. "I have a beauty mark on my temple."

LindsEy nods. "And I'm the one with diabetes."

PORTA POTTI STATUS:
The CDC recommends holding your nose

"Well, that was a nightmare." I shudder. "I felt like I was in— what's that famous old horror movie? You know, the one with those creepy identical twins that haunt the little dweeby kid?"

"*The Social Network*?"

"Yes, thank you."

"That's mean," Ally says, batting me on the shoulder. "I had a class with one of them last year; she was always so sweet."

"Which one?"

Ally blinks at me.

"My point exactly!"

"Okay, fine! So it's hard to tell them apart. But doesn't every guy secretly fantasize about hooking up with twins?"

"No! What guy fantasizes about incest?"

"I don't know—I saw it in a beer commercial!"

DOSSIER CANDIDATE #3:
Imani Booker

Finally, someone I know for a fact Ally likes. Because everyone likes Imani. She's the kind of nice where, if you try talking shit about someone else with her, she'll say something like "I'm sure they're just trying their best." The type of person to go sit with a new kid eating lunch by themselves, you know?

"Cam!" Imani lights up when she spots me. She has copper-colored skin and an infectious laugh. A single dimple on her left cheek. *Really* nice feet. (Oh God—do I have a foot thing?) As soon as I'm in reach, Imani throws her arms around my neck.

"How are you? How've you been feeling?"

"Hangin' in there," I say in my practiced recovery voice, slapping the side of my cast for added emphasis.

Imani's hands slide to mine. "I feel like I haven't seen you in so long. You must be all out of sorts. First your breakup with Ally, then her accident. I can't imagine what you're going through."

It dawns on me then: Imani isn't talking about my knee. "Yeah . . ." I say. "It's a bad situation."

Imani holds a hand over her chest. "You never get used to seeing her like that. Every time I've gone to visit her in the hospital, it's like—" She has to pause, compose herself.

"You visit her in the hospital?"

"Of course," Imani says. "I try to make it over at least once a week. Don't you?"

Don't say it . . . don't say it . . . don't say it . . .

"Actually, I haven't been to the hospital yet."

Imani gasps. "Cam, you have to! It's what Ally would want. In fact—why don't I take you? Then maybe afterward we can find somewhere quiet—*private*—and talk about any emotions you might be experiencing."

Hm. Don't love the idea of discussing my feelings. Still, alone time with Imani would be nice. Tough call. If only I had someone to bounce this off of . . .

"Sorry, Imani, I've gotta pee real quick. Be right back."

PORTA POTTI STATUS:
Potentially lethal

"Okay, we both know Imani Booker is a fucking saint. There's no reason to say no . . . right?"

"Seriously? Cam, you heard her. That girl is clearly a grief groupie."

I blink at her.

"Meaning, she's only into you because you're in mourning. She wants to hook up with you because I'm in a coma!"

I say, "Someone's arrogant." I think, *She did bring up Ally a lot.* "So she likes sad boys. Is that so wrong?"

Ally's eyes bulge. "Yes! Tell me you aren't seriously trying to leverage my accident to get in some girl's pants?"

I consider for a moment. Ally slugs me in the chest.

"Ow! I was thinking!"

"You took too long! The only acceptable answer is NO!"

"Alright, fine! I won't use your accident to get in Imani's pants—but *that's it*! I'm calling it for today."

"Give me one more." Great, the dossier's back. "Keely Duffy. Chevy and Lisa have her ranked pretty low, but I actually think she'd be good for you. She's cute. No red flags on her socials. No grief fetish—that we know of."

I groan. "Fine. But that's it."

"Absolutely. Just one thing before you go. When you talk to Keely, don't ask her how her brother is doing in jail."

"He is? What for?"

"I can't remember exactly, but I know she's very, very sensitive about it. Like, loses her shit if anyone asks about him. So whatever you do, do not mention the fact that Keely's brother is in jail. Got it?"

DOSSIER CANDIDATE #14:
Keely Duffy

"Hey, Keely."

"Hey, Cam."

". . ."

"You okay?"

". . ."

"Cam?"

"WHY'S YOUR BROTHER IN JAIL?"

PORTA POTTI STATUS:
I don't wanna talk about it

"Okay, that one's on me."

"YOU THINK?!"

It's too hot for this. I'm too beat for this. Everything's too . . . *much*. For this.

"Enough, Al. No more. We can try again some other time. But right now, I need to get my keys from Chevy so I can go home."

Ally wants to object—I can see it in her eyes—but she must sense how little I have left to offer right now.

"Yeah, okay, Cam. Go rest. We'll pick things up again later."

"Thank you!"

After searching the crowd for a few minutes, I finally track Chevy down on the playground. He's slumped over a swing, bothering the wood chips with his sneaker, not looking quite as chipper as he did this morning.

"Well, if it isn't the saddest boy in Shermer," I quip to crickets. "What's up your butt?"

"Fifty other guys on her team. She could've picked any of them to be her partner. And still she picks him."

I look where he's looking: the Giant Beer Pong tournament taking place on the soccer fields. Team Canada's backs are to us, but I've spent enough time watching Lisa in action to recognize the smooth grace in her movements, no matter the sport. Next to her, Teddy crouches with his hands on his knees, awaiting the next shot. Hardly romantic, though Teddy's mere status as Lisa's playing partner is enough to bunch Chevy's panties.

"This again? Dude, they're clearly just friends. How are you not seeing this?" Chevy grumbles into his lap. "It's just the Senior Olympics; if you guys were on the same team, you'd be the one over there right now."

"But she's not on my team." He sniffs. "What if I'm already losing her?"

"That's impossible. You're Chevy and Lisa! It's gonna take something a helluva lot more menacing than Teddy to break you guys up. Like a tidal wave. Or cancer. Or a cancer-filled tidal wave. If Lisa was partners with a cancer-filled tidal wave, I'd be worried."

Chevy isn't amused. Whatever. At least I can say I tried. But I can't fix The Happy Couple right now—I've got my own shit to deal with.

"So just a heads-up, I think I'm gonna head home for a little. Ice my knee, grab some food, maybe a nap."

"Olympics aren't over for another couple hours," he mutters, squarely focused on the game.

"No, right. It's just that . . ." Is he even listening to me? "Chevy?" I repeat his name a couple more times until his attention snaps to me.

"You know what, fine. Here." He leaps off his swing, unhooks the fanny pack, and slings the whole thing at me. I have to drop my crutches to catch it. "If you want to go, then go. I can't keep carrying you forever." With that, he stalks off, leaving me holding the bag. I've never seen Chevy lash out like that. Definitely not at me.

A problem for another day. I leave without even checking the scoreboard. Without consuming any alcohol. Without becoming—what was it Chevy said in his pregame speech? That's right, a *legend*. Without a single romantic prospect.

At least my limbs are still intact. Barely.

THE HOUSE IS quiet and warm when I get back. Peak napping conditions. POL-I's waiting dutifully right where I left her. I plug in, fire up *NCIS*, and relax. For once, sleep comes easily. I'm out cold until the whoosh of the patio door sliding open and then closed breaks the spell.

I open my eyes. Chevy looms over me, still wearing his Aussie kit. He must've come straight here.

"Hey."

"Hey."

"We lost."

"Damn."

"Yeah." Chevy looks dead-eyed. Like he's not all the way here. "Lisa just left for Madison."

"Volleyball thing?"

"Yeah."

I gesture toward the kitchen and say, "Your fanny pack is on the counter," assuming it's the reason he's here.

Chevy gives a nod of acknowledgment, then reaches into his pocket and pulls out his pen. Not the kind you write with.

"Can you open a window if you're gonna do that in here?" I say. "Mom's gonna be home soon, and we can't use the 'a skunk snuck in' defense again."

"Already checked in with her. She's running late tonight." Chevy obliges anyway, cranking open the wall of storm windows overlooking the backyard. "What're you watching?"

"*NCIS Boise*. I can change it if you want."

Chevy takes another hit. "This is fine."

Okay, now I know something's wrong. As his best friend, I should engage him, see if I can get at the root of the problem poisoning his mind. That would be the mature, responsible thing to do.

But then he passes me the pen.

Dr. Vernon was very clear when he gave me the Delatrix—absolutely no alcohol. He never said anything about weed. The smoke greets me like an old friend, and soon I'm floating through time and space with my most trusted allies: Chevy, POL-I, and Special Agent Bonesaw.

Just as the world starts to even out, I hear Chevy's voice. Completely monotone. "I think Lisa hooked up with him."

My body stiffens. What is it about weed that enables you to go from a state of unadulterated tranquility to twitchy-eyed paranoia in a matter of seconds? I play it cool, pretend I didn't hear him.

"Cam? Did you hear me?"

"WHAT?" I scream/say in the least cool way possible.

"I think Lisa and Teddy had sex."

"How?" I garble. "I don't mean how—obviously I know *how* sex works. Just, like, how could she have found time for that?"

Chevy's leering at his fingers, debating which unlucky nail

won't survive the evening. Left hand, ring finger. Fitting. "On one of her recruiting trips to Wisconsin."

"How do you know?"

"I just do."

"Did she . . . you know . . . get better?" *Stupid.* "At sex, I mean." *So stupid.*

"What?" He breaks eye contact with the TV and glares at me. "No, it is *not* because she got better at sex."

"Oh. Then how can you be sure?"

"I just am, alright?"

"Oh." *Try to make him feel better.* "But . . . isn't she allowed to? Technically? I thought that was the whole point of being in an open relationship." Chevy doesn't respond right away. "Chev?"

"I guess."

"So what's the problem? It's just like you said—now you can sow your oats or whatever while you're at school too. Everybody wins."

A lightbulb sparks deep in the recesses of my drug-addled mind. Like any guy in a relationship, Chevy talks a big game when it comes to his sexual prospects "if he was single." But in all the years I've known him, Chevy's never hooked up with anyone besides Lisa. She was his first kiss. First girlfriend. First to circle all the bases. Which begs the question: Why would a guy who's only ever had eyes for one person want to be in an open relationship?

He wouldn't.

"You don't want to do this." It's not a question.

Chevy let out a heavy sigh, hunches forward. "You know how I flew out to Stanford for a campus overnight visit, like, a month ago? The kids hosting me took me out to some of the bars. We met up with a bunch of girls they knew, including this one Brazilian girl. And you know how much I love Brazilian girls."

"Sure, yeah, right."

"At the end of the night, she invited me back to her dorm. When we got there, she ran to the bathroom. While I was waiting, I started looking around her room. She had these collages on her walls with, like, pictures of her hometown friends. And in almost every one of them, there was this guy. When she came back, I asked her about him and she told me flat out it was her boyfriend. Not her ex. *Boyfriend*, present tense.

"I was like, 'Won't he be mad if you hook up with me?' and she was like, 'You're ruining the mood.' That's when I realized I didn't really wanna get it in with some rando girl lying to her boyfriend an ocean away." Chevy takes a beat. "Also, her nipples were smaller than mine, and I wasn't sure how I felt about that."

My brain's operating with a lag time, so it takes me a second to process. "Just to be clear, you don't want to hook up with other people next year?"

"No."

"And despite this fact, you agreed to be in an open relationship?"

"Yup."

"That's the most backward-ass thing I've ever heard."

"Yup."

"Does Lisa know?" He shakes his head. "Well, there ya go. Just tell her you changed your mind. Boom, problem solved."

"It was her idea in the first place," Chevy says. "I can't risk losing her, man. I'd rather be miserable with her than sad and alone without her." He glances over me. "No offense."

Offense. Very much offense.

18

The next morning, a miracle: I sleep in.

My luck doesn't stop there. Sugary cereal, hours of uninterrupted TV time, and my best girl, POL-I, whirring by my side.
The summer I'd dreamed of. By the time Ally rolls in, I haven't
budged in almost twenty-four hours.

"You're just in time; they're about to introduce this season's
big villain," I tell her. "His MO is he forces his victims to walk the
plank into a vat of acid. Big pirate energy. Also, he may or may
not be Agent Bonesaw's long-lost biological father."

"Riveting." She flops down next to me. Her knee knocks my
good one. I cinch my blanket over my lap.

"Leave your sarcasm at the door, Tandy. This is an *NCIS* safe
space."

Ally's cheeks flush crimson. "Been a while since you called me
Tandy."

"Haven't I?"

She shakes her head, grinning. "Where's your fam?"

"Soccer tournament, I think?" I unlock my phone. Nothing
from Mom.

"Perfect." Ally snatches the remote out of my lap. I should really be better about protecting that thing. "No more TV. We have work to do."

I cross my arms in a huff. The full Maizy. "You never let me do anything fun!"

"Yeah, helping my ex-boyfriend find someone new to make out with. I'm an absolute monster."

"Pretty much!"

"You're such a baby." Ally rolls her eyes. Still grinning. "So, I've been doing some thinking. Regarding our approach. In light of yesterday's debacle—"

"I wouldn't call it a debacle."

"What would you call it?"

I think a moment. "Okay, yeah, *debacle* works."

"Like I said." Ally hops to her feet and starts on the move. "Look, Chevy and Lisa deserve all the props in the world for the work they did on the dossier. It's impressive. I respect them—I really do." She raises one hand, places the other over her heart. Scout's honor. "But it's limited to just those twenty candidates—all of them our classmates. So while we shouldn't abandon the dossier, I don't think there's anything wrong with expanding the pool of potential candidates."

I frown. "I'm not following."

Ally sets her feet. "High school's over in a week. It's time we expand your horizons—look outside the confines of STHS. I mean, clearly you've already had the best Shermer has to offer." She winks. I don't disagree. "But there's an entire world out there. Who's to say the person you're looking for even lives in Shermer?"

The very thought of meeting new people makes me want to walk into oncoming traffic. But I can tell the idea's already taken hold of Ally's imagination. Nothing wrong with humoring her.

"And how am I supposed to find these people?"

A glint in her eye. "How does anyone meet people today?"

"Church? Sock hops? Hospital waiting rooms? I dunno, Al. I haven't given it much thought—" My voice catches. *No.* She isn't saying what I think she's saying.

"Dating apps!"

Goddamnit.

"Never gonna happen." I hug a throw pillow to my chest. "Dating apps are for catfishing and lonely people in their twenties who don't know how to make friends."

"Not true! Plenty of people use them."

"In the suburbs?"

"Yeah! Divorcées, college students home for the summer—maybe even a teacher! Wasn't there a substitute you had a crush on?"

Ms. Baker. One time she asked me how much I benched. Greatest day of my life.

Ally rounds the coffee table, motioning for me to scooch back. I'm not sure what she means until she sits on the sliver of cushion between me and the edge of the couch.

"Here, the app is called AMO," she says, balancing her arm on my chest as she fiddles with her phone. "I already took the liberty of setting up your profile."

Sure enough, there I am. Er, there's my head, cropped and pasted from a different photo onto the body of a svelte gentleman covered in tattoos.

"Is this photoshopped?"

Ally cocks an eyebrow. "Gee, Cam, I'm not sure. Do you see a tattoo sleeve on your arm?"

I don't. "Why use a fake photo?"

"Because you have, like, no good pictures. Plus I thought the tattoos would give you more of an edge."

"And what happens when they meet me and they realize I don't have any tattoos?"

"Just say you had them removed."

Ally swipes to the next pic—another Photoshop. "Why am I holding a fish in this one?"

"I'm rebranding you as a fish boy. There's this whole subgenre of white guy on here that *loves* fishing."

"But fishing is stupid."

"Yeah, Cam, I know fishing is stupid! The point is to present an ideal version of yourself, even if you stretch the truth. Which is why it also says you have a great sense of humor."

"I do have a great sense of humor!"

"That's the spirit! If you believe it, maybe they will too."

Am I crazy, or is this flirting? *Right?* I don't hate it either. I could do this all day, and we might've, if my phone hadn't started ringing. It's Chevy. He slipped out last night after I dozed off. He's already mid-rant when the line connects.

"—don't know what to do, man, I'm freaking out!"

"Chevy! Slow down!" I shout over him. Ally shoots me a concerned look. I shrug. "Say that again."

Muffled static, then he's catching his breath, huffing directly into the receiver. "I'm in trouble, Cam." His voice is hoarse. Has he been crying?

"Get over here. Now."

CHEVY'S IN HIS kitchen when I come crutching in. He's sitting at the breakfast bar, feet up on his stool, knees pulled to his chest, his spindly arms coiled around his shins. Still wearing his Australia shit from yesterday.

"Hey, bud."

He barely acknowledges my arrival. In front of him, his laptop hums. Overheated. Surrounded by a summoning circle of junk food—chips, cookies, a party-size bag of Skittles.

"Parents out of town?" I ask. Mr. and Mrs. Wyatt are always traveling.

"Fundraiser," he murmurs. "One of Mom's foundations."

"What is it this week? Coding classes for Amish communities?"

"Bulldogs with cleft palates, I think."

"Ah yes, our nation's most pressing issue."

He grunts, hits his pen. Offers it to me. "I'm good."

Up close, he looks even worse. His eyes are bloodshot, saddled with heavy bags. He's chewed right down to the cuticle on both hands; there's even dried blood caked around his nail beds. A live breach—right thumb—oozes as we speak. Chevy notices me staring and licks the blood away.

Is this how I looked? *No way,* I tell myself. I hid the hurt well, maintained basic hygiene. But deep down, I know that's bullshit. I have the empty Oatmeal Creme Pie wrappers to prove it.

"Wanna tell me what's going on?" I ask.

Chevy coughs, then wipes his nose on his knee. Doesn't respond. But he doesn't have to. One glance at his laptop and I see it. Tab after tab after tab after—they just keep going. Chevy doesn't stop me when I reach around him and slide the laptop toward me. I click through the tabs, one by one.

Google search results for *Teddy Hall, Teddy Hall Shermer, Teddy Hall Wisconsin, Gemma and Ethan Hall*—is that . . . Did Chevy google Teddy's parents?! Sure enough, I click a page listing the family's political donations, their involvement in the local Rotary Club, even a newsletter for the Hall family reunion.

Jesus. Chevy's in deep. The internet is a dangerous place for the heartbroken—I know firsthand. Chevy's tumbled down the same obsessive rabbit hole every ex falls into. He just made the fatal mistake of skipping the breakup. Jealousy doesn't play fair and square; it blindsides you when you least expect it, unleashing sucker punches even after you've waved the white flag.

At least I'd built up a tolerance of sorts while I was with Ally—HE was always lurking in my rearview mirror. Chevy hasn't. Five years he's been with Lisa. Never a jealous word. But now? Jealousy is kicking his ass. The guy is in trouble.

"Why don't we leave this alone for a while." I start to close the laptop.

"No!" Chevy lurches for it, yanks it back. Breathing hard. Big "my precious" vibes. "I have to show you something."

He floats the cursor to one of the tabs I haven't checked. Teddy's Instagram. He opens a pic. Taken a couple months ago, judging by the snow on the ground. Teddy's bundled in a Canada Goose parka and a patterned knit cap with a puffball on top. His flow flips out the back. Behind him, the unmistakable red Wisconsin *W* graces the side of a stadium.

"What am I looking at?" I ask.

Chevy swipes one picture over. That's when I see it. Same Teddy, same parka, same stadium. Only this time, he has his arm draped around a female companion: Lisa Langer. Teddy's caption isn't helping matters. *From Wasps to Badgers. Can't wait to cheer each other on for another four years!*

"This was in February." Chevy sniffles. "In her tagged photos. I didn't even follow the guy until recently. Since his profile's private, I'd never noticed it before."

I look at the photo again. If there's one thing in the world I know, it's that Lisa loves Chevy. Every rational fiber of my being is telling me this is nothing more than Chevy's suspicions run amok.

That said . . . Lisa and Teddy do look awfully chummy. And they did have that elaborate handshake. He's going to Wisconsin; she's going to Wisconsin. Fuck. Is Chevy actually onto something here?

See, there I go again! *That's* how easy it is. Jealousy fits like a glove; we all wear the same size.

Right now, my job isn't to feed Chevy's conspiratorial mind. I need to talk him off the ledge. What to say, what to say . . .

"Dude, there's like forty thousand people at Wisconsin, yeah? That's so many people for Lisa to hook up with. Teddy Hall will be the least of your concerns once fall semester starts."

Nailed it.

"It's obvious you don't want an open relationship," I go on. "I don't wanna be the 'talk it out' guy. But . . . yeah. You and Lisa need to talk this out. Together."

Chevy's tummy lets out a rumble. He grabs a handful of Skittles and shovels them into his mouth. "I can't do it, man," he garbles between chews. "The minute she confirms it . . ." He wavers, his voice cracking. "It used to be we'd only had sex with each other. And now—"

"You don't really believe that," I insist. "And even if you did, the answer is still the same. Talk to Lisa. Otherwise you're gonna lose it."

"Do I look like I'm losing it??"

Yes. "Yes."

Chevy appears stunned by my assessment. If he considers my answer, it isn't for long. Then he's right back to his tabs. "I'm fine, Cam. Plus, I haven't even told you the best part yet." A few keystrokes . . . "There!" He moves aside so I can have a look.

Another photo from Teddy's feed. No Lisa this time, just Teddy and his dog from last Halloween. Teddy's dressed as Batman, the dog as Robin. It's cute. I don't say that aloud.

"So?" I give a little shrug. "Lots of people are obsessed with their dogs."

"Not the dog. Right here." Chevy moves the cursor to the geotagged location under Teddy's handle. Clicks. A pinned map comes on-screen. "I found where he lives."

"You geotag stalked him?" I'm impressed. Then horrified.

"It's his own fault, if you think about it," Chevy reasons. "What kind of dumbass doxes himself online? Some deranged psychopath could just show up at your door." I assume Chevy's doing a bit and laugh. He is not.

"Okay, so you found his address. What exactly are you planning on doing with this information? Mailing him a strongly worded letter?"

Without hesitation: "I'm going over there."

Again, I laugh. Again, he does not. "Why?"

"I'm not gonna do anything weird," Chevy whispers, the way a weirdo would. "Just to see if he's home. Maybe chat with him."

"You can't be serious."

Chevy's already shuffling to the mudroom. "Can you drive?" he asks, slipping on his moccasins.

It dawns on me then I could put an end to this madness. Right here, right now. Refuse to chauffeur him, rob him of his getaway driver. Then again, he'd probably just drive himself. I don't trust him behind the wheel, not in this state. And even if he did make it to Teddy's without ending up like Ally, Chevy's never been in a fight. Which is exactly what will happen if he does show up at Teddy's, coming in hot, tossing around wild accusations.

I take another look at the map. "Where even is this?" The street names are vaguely familiar, just not the neighborhood.

"Over by the highway."

Fuck.

"In West Shermer."

Double fuck.

Everything in Illinois that doesn't touch the Lake Michigan coast is basically Iowa as far as I'm concerned. That includes certain parts of Shermer—the other side of the (Metra) tracks. People jokingly refer to it as the "bad part of town," which of course is ridiculous since it's still Shermer. That's like saying you got accepted by a "bad" Ivy League school. But still, if it weren't for school or basketball games, I'd never leave the shore.

The fact that Ally's house is in West Shermer has absolutely nothing to do with my feelings.

I close my eyes and let out a heavy sigh. Pinch the pressure point between my eyes. "Remember last summer, when you convinced me to try mixing lean in my CamelBak before the Xandy Xanberg set at Lolla, and I told you that was your worst idea ever? Yeah, this is worse."

"Cam, I—"

"Remember the time we watched that movie *Twister*, and you convinced me we should become storm chasers?"

Go to YouTube, search "Teens Wet Pants as Tornado Approaches." Five hundred thousand people have seen the two of us sobbing under an overpass. (For the record, it was Mountain Dew.)

"I remember," Chevy says.

I open my eyes. Find his. *"This* is ten times dumber."

Chevy's eyes are damp, his shoulders slumped over his toes. I've never seen him like this. And yet, looking at him now is like looking in a mirror. Chevy's me a couple months ago, as my suspicions about Ally festered unchecked. I grew convinced she'd nuked our relationship in order to get what she really wanted: HIM.

I was too far gone. Just like Chevy is now.

"This is a terrible idea," I repeat, because it bears repeating.

Chevy nods. "Yup."

"We're gonna do it anyway, aren't we?"

"Yup."

I groan. "Alright, I'll get my keys."

19

I already have my keys. But since we're actually going through with this absurd mission, Papa needs his midday Delatrix a little early. Good thing Ally isn't here, I think to myself. Talk about making a bad situation worse.

Speak of the Devil and She shall appear. Just as I've buckled in, I notice Ally in the Geo's rearview mirror.

"Don't."

"I won't."

"I mean it."

"I know."

"Seriously, Allison."

"Okay."

We blink at each other's reflections. I break first. "What am I supposed to do here?" I turn and face her head-on. "It's not like Chevy's giving me much of a choice."

"Gee, that's a tough one." Ally furrows her brow and taps her chin. A look of faux contemplation. "Well, for starters, you could call his parents. Or one of his sisters. Or—and this might sound crazy—fucking Lisa. Seems like a good place to start."

I scowl, face forward. "You wouldn't understand."

"You're right. I don't understand why you're enabling your best friend while he's at his most vulnerable."

"He's going, with or without me."

"Not necessarily. But you just gave him the green light."

I fidget with the carabiner on my key chain. "Well, maybe it's not such a bad idea."

I don't hear the approaching footsteps. "What's not a bad idea?" Chevy asks.

"Nothing!" I yell, nearly jumping out of my skin.

Chevy gives me a weird look, then peers in the back seat. Directly at Ally. She gives him a wave. *Can he see her?* I find myself briefly wondering, only for logic to kick in. *No, Cam, only a small percentage of Delatrix users can see through time and space into the astral plane. Use your head.*

Regardless, Chevy's mind is elsewhere. As he climbs into the cab, I catch Ally's eye in the rearview. Stare daggers.

"Oh, I'm staying," she says defiantly. "Someone here needs to be the voice of reason."

Great.

Chevy already has the directions to Teddy's pulled up. He plugs the aux into his phone, and we're off. It's a quiet drive. Chevy isn't as talkative as earlier. Ally has the decency to pipe down. My mind wanders instead, to the last time the three of us were together like this. Must've been right before winter break, I think. We'd been studying for our AP Bio final. Same teacher, different periods. During a break, I drove us to the twenty-four-hour McDonald's drive-thru. We split a forty-piece McNuggets meal.

Damn. I miss that.

"The destination is on your right."

Siri—ever the buzzkill.

"Just pull into the driveway," Chevy says. "This won't take long."

I'm not sure I believe him, but I do as he says, sidling up behind a champagne-colored SUV. Teddy's car—I recognize it from the student lot at school. Bucky Badger, Wisconsin's mascot, taunts us from the rear windshield.

Chevy scowls. "Who actually puts those on their car? It's just tacky." Normally I would take this opportunity to remind Chevy of the Stanford yard sign staked in his front lawn. Or that the stamps on his graduation invites bore the Stanford insignia. Or that he was currently wearing Stanford red mesh shorts. But now feels like a bad time. Gotta pick your battles.

Teddy's house is set far back on their property. Big front yard. A hike to the front door. Over on the lawn, we've got a live one. One of those rotating sprinklers, the kind that goes *tcht-tcht-tcht*, then *tchttchttcht*. Chevy doesn't see it coming and startles when the stream splashes his door.

"Alright . . ." I put us in park. "We're here. Now what?"

My ears are thumping. No, wait, that's just Chevy's foot, drumming on the floor like a jackhammer. His moment of hesitation is all Ally needs to assert herself.

"Now's your chance," she says, swatting me on the back of

the head. "He hasn't done anything he'll regret yet. Tell him Lisa never has to know about any of this. Remind him how much she loves him. They can get through this. Okay? Cam? Say it to him *exactly* like that."

And so I do.

"Let's just go home, man—fuck! Quit acting like a baby, go call your girlfriend and tell her open relationships are for douchey coastal elites living on their parents' dime."

That's essentially what Ally said, right?

Chevy soaks in one last long look at the house. "Yeah. Okay." An audible sigh of relief from the back seat. It's premature—the next thing I know, Chevy's on the other side of the passenger door. "Keep it running," he says, stalking off.

Ally seizes me by the arm. "Cam, fucking do something!"

"I tried!"

"Try harder!"

I could. Try harder. Maybe I'd even succeed. But here's the thing: What if Chevy's right?

Slim as the odds may be, what if Lisa really is messing around with Teddy, her open-relationship idea merely a ploy so she can date him when they get to Madison? Isn't it better Chevy find out now, painful as it may be, rather than two . . . six . . . nine months from now?

"He deserves to know," I say coolly. "I'd want to."

"Not like this!" Desperation fills Ally's voice. "This will ruin their relationship. Trust me, if Lisa finds out, she will end things!"

"What would you have him do, then?" I spin around in my

seat. "Wait until after Lisa breaks his heart? Come to find out the guy he suspected all along—the one she *swore* she was 'just friends' with—is actually the one she was in love with the whole time? Huh?!"

Ally shrinks back to her seat, looking wounded. "Is that what this is about?" I turn away. "Cam, do you think that I'm in love with—"

I cut her off. "He's at the door."

Even at a distance, the tension in Chevy's shoulders is evident. I've never seen him stand so straight in his life. Is he flexing? Have I mentioned Chevy's never been in a fight before? I saw him throw a punch once, playing a VR boxing game. Let's just say I was . . . *unimpressed*.

In my periphery, I see Ally cover her eyes. "I can't watch."

I can and I do. Chevy's crouching now, peering through the sidelight windows, forehead right up against the glass. He stands back up and . . . nope, he's just standing there. I keep waiting for him to bang the knocker. Ring the doorbell. Do something.

Thirty seconds stretches on for days, but eventually Chevy turns and trots down the front steps. Cuts straight across the grass, sprinkler be damned. Doesn't flinch when the sprinkler leaves a dark slash across his yellow Aussie pinny. The mesh sticks to his stomach.

Back in the Geo: "I couldn't do it." He sags lower in his seat. Massages his eyelids. "I'll talk to Lisa when she gets back."

He looks defeated, exhausted. Like he could use a pick-me-up. Breakfast maybe? I'm in the middle of brainstorming nearby restaurants when I feel Ally's icy grip fasten to the crook of my elbow. I glance back. Her eyes are bugging out—more than usual.

She's looking past me, toward Teddy's house. Specifically, the woman in the plush violet robe, leering at us from the stoop.

"*Shit,*" I mutter.

"What?" Chevy tracks my gaze. "Shit!" He hits the deck, slides down to the floor mat. The same instinct gnaws at me, but I can't. Not with my cast locked at 180 degrees.

Then the woman turns over her shoulder, yells something into the house.

"Cam!" Chevy slaps me on my good leg. "What are you doing? GO!"

My palms are slick, my brain a step slow. I blindly paw at the gearshift—how many notches is reverse again? Fukkit, doesn't matter. I hit the gas. The Geo lurches out of a standstill—*Crunch!*—right into Teddy's SUV.

"Was that his fucking car?" Cradling his neck, Chevy clambers back into his seat. "Did you hit Teddy's car?"

"Working on it!"

I jam on the gearshift—the correct notch this time—and throw us into reverse. The engine revs; the wheels whirl. *Why aren't we moving?* Then I see it; my bumper's latched on to his. Something must be caught underneath. I only have one option: The full *Fast & Furious*.

I stomp the pedal flat to the mat and haul the wheel as far as it'll go. Metal rakes against metal. Teddy's car shudders, inching backward along with us, until suddenly—it gives. As we're thrown back, I catch a glimpse of Teddy's caved-in trunk door. The UW Badger decal is ripped in two.

Our victory doesn't last. In all the excitement I've forgotten to center the steering wheel. The Geo's hood swings out into the Halls' front yard, chewing through the wet lawn and spitting it into the air like a rifle laying down cover. In my ear, Chevy's screams are drowned out by Ally's. By the time we reach pavement, half of Teddy's yard is reduced to mud. Another scream now—I realize it's coming from Teddy's mom. RIP to her pristine yard.

There's no time to mourn. Back in the street, the Geo stalls momentarily, its tires wailing in their best falsetto. Once they find their footing, we're a rocket ship.

My bumper only makes it to the end of the block before taking a nosedive into the street. Chevy jumps out, scoops up the rusted steel frame—license plate and all—and chucks it in the nearest alley.

Then he climbs back in, and we book it the hell out of West Shermer.

20

By the time I arrive home, I'm beat. With a little help from POL-I, I'm out before my head hits the pillow. I sleep long but not deep, dreaming in brief, episodic vignettes, each one purged from memory before the next begins.

Later, when I come to, Ally's already here, engrossed in her phone, lounging on the other side of the sectional. Using POL-I as a footrest.

"Don't you knock?"

She doesn't respond, not right away. Instead she sits forward. What's in her hand? Then, it clicks: my Delatrix bottle. I watch as Ally unscrews the cap and slides two of the capsules into her palm. Hands them to me. I swallow them raw.

Once they're safely down the hatch, she speaks. "Morning, sleepyhead."

I squint at the grandfather clock. Almost 7:00 p.m. "Shit, have I been asleep all day?"

"Mhm." Ally tilts her chin at the coffee table. "Check your phone. You have a new *message.*"

There's something cagey about the way Ally says *message,* and when I unlock my phone, I see why. A text from an unknown number with a Chicago area code.

UNKNOWN

> Hey Cam, it's Jeannie Sprinkler, Lisa's friend from volleyball! She gave me your number . . . I think she really REALLY wants us to be friends next year lol. I'm totally cool with that—I don't know anyone else going to UC. Would you maybe want to meet up at some point?

I also have notifications from my various social media accounts. Seems Jeannie took the liberty of following me across the board.

"Who is it?"

I jolt—I'd actually forgotten Ally's presence. "Nothing! No one!" I stammer, clutching my phone to my chest.

Ally side-eyes me. "You're cheesing awfully hard at 'nothing.'"

"Right, sorry." I unclench. "It's just—it's still weird, you know? Talking to you about this kind of stuff."

Ally twists her lips to the side. "I get it. But seriously, Cammie, I'm here to help."

We hold eye contact then, Ally seemingly daring me to call her bluff. Unless, of course, she's not.

I cave, hand her my phone. "This girl Jeannie. Candidate #21 in the dossier."

"There is no Candidate #21," Ally says, scanning the message.

"Lisa made a late addition," I explain. "They play on the same club volleyball team. Oh, and Jeannie's going to UChicago too. That's why Lisa wants us to meet." And then for some reason I add: "Just as friends."

"Uh-huh." Cue eye roll. "I'm sure that's all Lisa wants for you guys." Ally settles into the couch, pondering. "A fellow future Maroon?" There go the eyebrows, the lower lip. "*Wow*, she must be quite the smarty-pants."

"Maybe, I dunno," I say with a shrug. "She's loaded, apparently. According to Lisa. So there's a nonzero chance her parents paid for a new dorm or something."

"Hm." Still holding my phone in one hand, Ally uses the other to fiddle with the drawstring on her joggers. I wonder what's going through her head right now.

Wait a second; is that—is Ally *jealous*?!

"Well?" Ally mutters. "Is she cute?"

WHAT DID I SAY?! Didn't I tell you Ally couldn't handle me hooking up with someone else?! I can't tell you how many times I've envisioned this moment the last few months, when Ally first lays eyes on her heir apparent. Never thought I'd get to see it in real time, the jealousy taking root in her brain, just like it did for me back in March, when Chevy informed me of Ally's newfound relationship status.

This is the proof I've been praying for. It's true, Ally cast me aside so she could be with someone else. But I wasn't just HIS placeholder. Cam Garrity is no one's also-ran. Not only that, I finally have my chance to start evening the score. Ally won the breakup . . . *so far.* Now's the time to make my comeback, finally give her a taste of her own medicine.

So why am I hesitating?

"Cam?" I snap to. Ally's watching me intently. "Do you think Jeannie's cute?"

"Uh . . ." I aim for benign. "She's fine, I guess."

Ally sits forward, elbows balancing on her knees. "I need to see a picture of her."

She still has my phone, by the way. Never a good idea to give an ex unfettered access to your unlocked phone. Too late now. Ally's already got Jeannie's socials pulled up. She taps open Jeannie's most recent pic, posted yesterday from the deck of some yacht in the Caribbean. Reader, when I tell you Ally's jaw dropped, I mean like the Tower of Terror.

"MOTHERFU—" Ally convulses before she's finished getting the word out. "*This* is who Lisa's setting you up with? *Her?*" Furiously scrolling now. "God, she must weigh like eighty pounds." Scrolling, scrolling. "Jesus Christ, how rich are these fucking people?" Scrolling, scrolling. "Oh, *come on.*"

Ally's reached the photos of Jeannie's recent trip to Turks and Caicos. Some of her more revealing bikini pics. I'll admit, I had a similar reaction.

"Stop smiling!" Ally scolds me, rapping me on my good knee.

"I'm not!"

I am. Look, I'm not a saint, okay? There's no harm in enjoying this just a little.

"That's it." Ally flings my phone at me like it's contaminated. I catch it before it bounces to the floor. "Executive decision. As chief consultant for the Cam Rebound Project, I forbid you from going out with this girl."

"You *forbid* it? And why's that?"

"Because. She's hotter than me."

I scoff. "No she isn't." I pull Jeannie's profile back up. "She only looks like this because of technology—you're the one who taught me that!" I swipe to the next pic. "Plus you're way prettier." Swipe. "I like your hair more, even when it's short like this." Swipe. "Your boobs are way bigger." Swipe. "And her feet aren't anything special—"

I glance up. A mile-wide smile stretches out across Ally's lips. It sinks in gradually; I've been had. Tricked. Bamboozled. *Fuck!*

Ally starts to sing, "Cam thinks I'm hotter than Jeannie! Cam thinks I'm hotter than Jeannie!" Her tone light, mocking.

"No—no I don't!"

"Yes you do! You already admitted it."

"I take it back!"

"Sorry, no take-backs."

I make a show of rolling my eyes, looking annoyed, but I have to press my tongue hard against the inside of my cheek to keep from grinning. "Fine. You caught me. I'm attracted to you. Would've thought you'd figured that one out during any of our many—" We lock eyes. "*Many* hookups."

Ally's cheeks light up. She shifts uncomfortably. "Anyway! What do you plan on texting this Jeannie? You know, the one who's not as hot as me."

I mull it over. "Maybe something like . . ." I clear my throat, get in character. *"How's it hanging, girl?"*

"How are you so bad at this?" Ally snaps her fingers. "Here, give it."

I don't protest. Ally gets right to it, reading aloud as she taps: "Hey Jeannie! Thanks for reaching out. So cool you're going to UC too! How excited are you for next year?"

My phone makes a whooshing noise; message sent. "The hell? I didn't say you could send it yet!" I try snatching my phone, but Ally smacks me on the wrist.

"Not done." She starts tapping again. "And yeah, I'd love to meet up. Want to grab food sometime next week? I literally have nothing else going on haha."

"Do we really need the last line?"

Ally winks. "I'm just trying to give her the full picture."

Whoosh.

"Al!"

"Relax! I know what I'm doing. In a few minutes, she'll respond. You guys will flirt back and forth for a little, and then—"

My phone chimes. Then again. And again.

JEANNIE

I'm so excited! My dad went there too and he makes it sound amazing!

My family leaves for Hong Kong on Thursday, but I can do earlier in the week.

Does Monday night work for you?

"Someone's thirsty," Ally snipes.

This time, I reply for myself. "Monday works great!"

Whoosh.

"Watch her suddenly be busy," Ally says, snorting.

"She wouldn't dare miss out on all *this*." I strike a pose, wiggle my hips, wind my tongue around my lips for added effect.

"No, she wouldn't." I wait for the insult, the joke at my expense. Ally offers none. I think she might actually be sincere.

"So," she goes.

"So," I echo.

"You have a date."

"I have a date."

"Congratulations."

"Thank you."

"Even though you did basically nothing to earn it and you just have good friends who do everything for you."

"A win's a win."

Ally laughs lightly, then pats herself on the thighs and rises to her feet. "Come on, then. We'd better get started."

I frown. "Started on what?"

"Getting ready." Ally's already on the move, beelining for the front hall.

"But the date's in two days."

"Exactly." She whirls around. "Cam, have you seen yourself lately? We haven't a moment to spare."

WHOEVER INVENTED STAIRS can suck on Optimus Prime's tailpipe. Humans as a species should've skipped stairs and jumped straight to elevators. Or ramps. Everybody likes ramps! Especially people named me.

My room is all the way up on the third floor. By the time I summit the final agonizing step I'm completely drenched in sweat. God knows what Ally's unearthed after ten unsupervised minutes in my room.

"I really thought that I'd imagined this." Her voice is coming from the closet. "When I'd think back, I'd go, 'No, Ally, that couldn't be real. You must have imagined it.' But here we are."

She throws open the closet doors. And there they are. Four years' worth of STHS Wasps basketball T-shirts. Some blue. Some gold. Most gray.

"My babies," I say, getting choked up. "How I've missed you."

Ally lifts one off the rod and balances the hanger on her pointer finger, holding it at arm's length like it's radioactive.

"What, are you afraid you'll forget the *only* extracurricular you do? You're eight feet tall! Look in the mirror and let deductive reasoning take the wheel."

She snorts, nearly falling over herself giggling when I snatch the hanger from her grasp.

"Is that why you made me come all the way up here?" I ask. "So you could slander my wardrobe?"

"Slander? Is that what I'm doing?"

"Yes, slander! I like my clothes fine, thanks!"

"And what about next year? Even someone as fashion challenged as you knows you can't wear your high school gear around
a college campus."

"Got it covered." I swing my crutch toward my desk. The
rubber nub lands on a half-opened care package strewn across
my swivel desk chair. Courtesy of UC Maroons basketball. They
hooked it up: car decals, dad hats, team-issued T-shirts—one
white, one maroon, and yes, one gray.

Ally groans. "I should've known." She looks to the closet. "Do
you own anything with buttons?"

"I might still have the white button-down I wore to my
confirmation."

"From five years ago? Cam, there's no way it fits you now."
She starts riffling through hangers. "What about the Henley I
bought you?"

"What's a Henley?"

"The shirt I got you for your birthday last year with the
buttons"—she turns, traipsing her fingers down her sternum—
"right here."

"Oh." *Oh.* "That one." *That one.* "I have no idea where it is." *I
know exactly where it is.*

Ally frowns. "You're being weird."

"No I'm not."

"That's exactly what someone being weird would say." She
squints at me. "Why do you keep glancing under your bed?"

"I'm not!" I totally am.

"Uh-huh." Ally pushes past me before I can think of an excuse. I watch her feel around beneath the box spring until her arm snags on something. An old Air Jordan shoebox with the logo colored in with Sharpie.

"This?" Ally asks, getting to her feet. "What's in here?"

"Shoes," I lie.

"Uh-huh." She shakes it. "Doesn't feel like shoes. Guess we'd better open it and find out."

"No, stop!" I lunge, but two legs are better than one, and Ally easily dances out of reach. "Okay, fine!" I throw up my hands. "It's my Ally Box!"

Ally makes a face. "Your what?"

"My . . . Ally . . . Box." I don't think I've actually said that phrase out loud before. Really wishing I'd come up with something better right now. "Leftover stuff from our relationship. Memorabilia, I guess you could call it."

Ally studies its exterior for a few seconds, then makes her way to my bed. She gently places the shoebox on my comforter. Flips open the lid. I haven't opened it in months, yet I can recite the contents from memory.

The ticket printouts for the Kid Xannabis concert Ally got me for Christmas last year. Technically our seats were in the rafters, but she'd photoshopped them to make it look like we had general admission on the floor. Postcards from her visit to Tokyo last summer—some trip for one of the clubs she's in. She was gone just two weeks, yet she managed to write me four times. Then there's the book she bought me after I confessed I hadn't read a book outside of class since sixth grade. Two days later, I opened my locker to find a well-worn copy of Jane Austen's *Pride and Prejudice*, complete with Ally's personal annotations. She'd scribbled notes in the margins of nearly every page. Later, she told me the main characters—Elizabeth and Mr. Darcy—reminded her of us in a lot of ways.

"How so?" I'd asked.

"Because . . ." Ally grinned. Then, without a trace of sarcasm, she said, "The whole book, Elizabeth and Darcy are at each other's throats. And yet, in the end, they wind up together. Because sometimes the person you can't stand to be around is the same one you can't bear to live without."

I read the whole thing in a single night. Then again the next. Plus a dozen more times since. Amazing, the crazy stuff love makes us do.

Finally, we have the Henley. Charcoal colored. Waffle knit. Balled up tight so it would fit in the box.

"You found it!" I feign surprise. "Been looking for that thing. Might be a little hot, though, with those sleeves. Let's just put it back. Now, weren't we looking for my confirmation shirt?"

Before I can interfere, Ally shakes the Henley loose. From the back—my vantage point—it looks normal. A few wrinkles crisscrossing the fabric like spiderwebs, but nothing more. It's the front I don't want her to see.

"It was an accident," I blurt out.

Ally turns to me, eyebrows on high alert. "*This* was an accident?" She flips it around so I can see and—*oh God*, it's worse than I remember. In my head, I'd only torn it a little, but now I see that's underselling the damage. The shirt's ripped clean from collar to hem. "It looks more like a cardigan," she adds.

I'm not entirely sure what a cardigan is, so I don't argue. "Alright, so it wasn't an accident. But it wasn't like I did it on purpose! Er, I mean I didn't mean to ruin it."

I can't get a read on Ally, which makes me nervous. And when I get nervous, I start to ramble. And when I ramble—well, you know by now.

"I'd just had the worst day . . . The night before, Chevy told me you'd started seeing someone else . . . I just lost it . . . My emotions got the better of me . . . One thing led to another . . . When I saw the shirt hanging in my closet, I just—"

I pantomime ripping it in half.

"So you decided to ruin my gift?"

"No!" I waver. "Well, yeah. But it's not like that. It was just hard having little reminders of you—of *us*—scattered everywhere. Like a constant barrage of 'Hey, in case you forgot, Ally doesn't want to be with—'" I cough to shut myself up. "It was just easier to stash it all. Out of sight, out of mind."

"Uh-huh," Ally says, turning her back to me. She starts gathering the memorabilia, repacking it into the Jordan shoebox.

"Come on, Al," I plead with her. "Don't be like that."

"Like what?" She glances back to me. "I totally get what you're saying. I dealt with the same thing with my—what'd you call it? Relationship memorabilia?"

I shouldn't ask. Nothing good ever comes from prying into your ex's new life, post-you. Everyone thinks they want answers. *What are they doing? Who are they doing it with? Are they thinking about me?* A couple weeks before Chevy informed me of Ally's new relationship status, I'd asked him straight up if she was seeing anyone. If the answer was yes, good riddance, I figured. Case closed. I'd be able to finally move on. Two months later, and the moving-on part is still a work in progress.

And yet. My brain is a dick and a masochist.

"What'd you do with it?"

Ally doesn't hesitate: "I got rid of it."

I flinch. "Oh." Ally drops to her knees and slides the shoebox back under my bed, so she doesn't see me run my forearm across my eyes. I pull it together by the time she's back on her feet.

"It's probably for the best," she says. "It might've been weird to show up to a date wearing a shirt your ex gave you. And since you can't wear one of your ratty T-shirts on a date with a girl like Jeannie, we'll have to come up with something else. What are you doing tomorrow?"

"Uh . . ."

"Trick question," Ally says. "Put on some deodorant and dust off your mom's credit card, because tomorrow—" She claps me on the shoulder, *hard*. It feels deliberate. "Tomorrow, you're getting a makeover."

21

No one in their right mind should wake up before noon on a Sunday. Hell, I bet even Jesus Christ Himself slept in until His mom shook Him awake. Day of rest and all that.

So imagine my frustration when, just after the sun's made its daily curtain call, I'm awoken by a commotion coming from the kitchen. Mom's voice comes through loud and clear, accompanied by another I can't immediately place. She's probably on the phone, talking over the TV. Wouldn't be the first time. The noise dies down a few minutes later, but by then I'm already up. Time for my morning dose.

Mom's over by the patio door when I venture into the kitchen. Her back is to me, her head bowed over a glowing iPhone screen. Er, wait—that's not Mom. Ally? Couldn't be—I haven't taken my Delatrix since last night. This person's too tall to be either of them anyway. I inch closer. By the time I recognize her, it's too late.

"Jesus!"

The figure jolts violently when she finally notices me. As she wheels around, her phone slips through her fingers and clatters to the floor.

"What was that?" Mom yells from upstairs.

"Nothing, Mom," I shout back. "Just saying hello to Steff." I lower my voice. "Hi, Steff."

"Hi, Cam."

Stefanie Ambrose, or Steff for short. My *ex*-ex-girlfriend. Now that she's in my crosshairs, I check off Steff's all-too-familiar characteristics one by one. Dark hair? Check. Bangs? Check. Teardrop-shaped beauty mark on her left cheek? Check.

"Sorry," Steff says then, flushing. "I know this is weird."

At that, I have to laugh. "What—*nooooo*," I deadpan. "What's weird about an ex-girlfriend appearing in your house unexpectedly? Happens all the time."

Steff offers an obligatory chuckle. "I haven't been feeling well lately. My throat's been really sore," she explains, crossing and uncrossing her arms. "Your mom's worried I have mono. Apparently it's going around."

"I heard that too," I say, beelining for the sink and my pills. "So you and QB1 are back together, then?"

Steff's eyes bulge. "How'd you know? We've been keeping it a secret."

I park it at the counter. "Just a hunch. How come you guys are sneaking around?"

Nodding, Steff fixes herself against the sliding door, finally deciding on arms crossed. "We're both tired of having to explain to people every time we get back together."

"I'll bet. What is this? The third time?"

"Fourth."

"What's different this time around?"

She considers this a moment. "I'm not sure it is," she says then, looking defeated. Defeated and ashamed.

"Is he being kinder at least?" I ask.

"He's always kind. He just changes his mind a lot."

"And you?" I arch a brow. "Has your mind changed?"

Steff shifts her eyes to the ground. "I made mine up a long time ago."

"I wouldn't know anything about that," I crack, which prompts a smile. Any awkwardness dissipates—like popping a balloon. Like I said, Steff and I are the exception that proves the rule. Exes rooting for each other.

"We haven't really talked in a minute," she says.

"Guess not," I say. "The last time must've been . . ."

"Yeah."

"Yeah."

". . ."

". . ."

"About the accident." Steff flounders. "I'm sorry I didn't check on you afterward. Knowing you, I just assumed you'd want to be left alone."

"Don't worry about it," I reassure her. "It was a crazy time." *Still is.*

"Yeah, I guess so." I watch as Steff struggles to swallow the lump in her throat. Probably the mono. "Did she text you at least? Before . . . you know."

"She totaled her car at the bottom of the ravines?" I laugh in spite of myself. It's all just so ridiculous. "No, Ally never texted me. Although I bet she would've if she'd found out about us. That, or she'd have cut the brake lines on the Geo."

"I told Robby," Steff says sheepishly. I give her a look. "QB1," she corrects, rolling her eyes.

"I know. He tried talking to me about it."

Steff tenses. "He promised me he wouldn't."

I shrug. "Told me he wanted me to know he didn't hold it against me."

"Oh God." Steff hits herself in the face, laughing. Then coughing. "What were we thinking? Was it just that we were . . . ?"

"Cold and lonely?"

We hold eye contact. "Yeah. Cold and lonely."

With Steff, there was always mutual attraction and affection. But our relationship always lacked that special *something*. The intangibles of falling in love. I found it with Ally. Steff found it with QB1. (God knows why.) It's what Ally always failed—or flat-out refused—to understand. Pinky promise or not, I had no intention of ever backsliding. Barring the most extreme circumstances, anyway.

"I haven't told anyone," I admit.

Steff cocks an eyebrow. "Not even Chevy and Lisa?"

I shake my head. "Probably for the best we keep it to ourselves from here on, yeah? Just because—"

Because what, Cam? Why do you feel so guilty?

"I get it," Steff jumps in, offering a life raft.

Overhead, the ceiling creaks. Mom's footsteps headed our

way. Self-preservation kicks in. "I'd love to stay and chat," I say, shifting to my feet, "but I woke up like five minutes ago and I have to pee."

Steff doesn't protest. "I'd give you a hug, except . . ." She points to her potentially mono-infested throat. Fair point. It's for the best, anyway. Wouldn't want anyone—or anything—lurking nearby to get the wrong idea.

I've been dreading this part. There's no good way to tell this story, so let's just plow through.

Back in January, over Martin Luther King Day weekend, Chevy decided to have a "small, unsupervised gathering" at his family's lake house—excuse me, their *other* lake house—over on the Michigan side of Lake Michigan. Twenty-ish people, give or take a few plus-ones.

Three weeks into my post-Ally era, I drank and sulked my way through the weekend. Late Saturday, I needed a break from the festivities. I bundled up and crept down the bluff. The beach was in a sorry state, erosion taking its toll on the shore despite the quarter-million-dollar revetment Chevy's parents had installed two summers ago.

I found a spot near the tall grass and settled on the cold, hard sand. Maybe twenty minutes later, I felt a presence. On that occasion, it wasn't an astral projection.

"Hey."

"Hey."

Steff unveiled her pen from the inside pocket of her parka. "Smoke break."

I motioned for her to join me. We traded hits, silently watching the gunmetal waves pound against the coast.

"So you and Ally broke up?" Steff phrased it like a question, but of course she already knew. "You doing okay?"

I inhaled deep. "Never better," I croaked, exhaling all at once.

"The waiting is the worst part," Steff said when she caught me sneaking a peek at my phone. "That is what you're doing, right? Waiting for Ally to text you?"

I shrank into my coat. "Is it that obvious?"

Steff shook her head. "I'm just way too familiar with the signs." She sounded pained as she laughed then. "Trust me, Cam. She will. When you least expect it too. Right when you feel like maybe—just maybe—you're ready to move on. Then bam! It's like they can sense it." Steff took a drag. "I'm not just saying this; it's a real thing. They call it the Ex Message. Get it—like text message without the Ts?" I give her a look. "It's a real thing, I swear! I found this whole article about it. Here, I'll send you the link."

It only took Steff a second; she had the link bookmarked.

"How are things with QB1?" I asked.

"I always forget you guys call him that."

"It's his official title."

Steff glanced up at the house. "We're . . . *okay*. Up and down."

"So, normal?"

Steff shot me a sad smile. "Yeah, I guess so."

We didn't say much after that. Instead, we took turns fighting back tears and frostbite. After a while, we rejoined the party. That was the end of that. Or so I thought.

Now, I should mention that—while we were dating—Steff and I did everything but. We'd hit a triple, if you're into baseball metaphors. And I'm glad it worked out that way, that my first time wound up being with Ally. That it felt like more than just checking off a box.

But in Ally's mind, Steff had a singular goal: complete her home run. I'd insist that wasn't the case, and that even if Steff wanted to have sex with me, I wasn't interested. Ally didn't buy it.

Things boiled over one day. Earlier, Ally'd seen us chatting at my locker, Steff's hand—*allegedly!*—on my arm. After school, Ally wasted no time addressing the matter.

"Why don't you guys just fuck and get it over with?"

"Al, for the last time, it's not like that with me and Steff."

"You sure looked pretty cozy earlier."

"What about you and [HIM], huh? I could say the same thing about you."

"That's totally different!"

"How?"

"Because I'm just friends with [HIM]! We've never even hooked up."

As I've said, these arguments happened all the time. This instance stands out, though, because of what Ally made me do once we reached my house.

"Pinky promise." Ally swiveled in her seat. "Pinky promise me you won't hook up with Steff."

"Seriously?"

"Yes, seriously." She extended hers. "Please? It'll make me feel better." I just wanted the conversation to end, so I relented, linking my pinky to hers.

"You have to kiss it," she informed me. "That makes it legally binding." So I did. I kissed my end and Ally kissed hers. "Just remember, Cammie: a pinky promise is a sacred oath. If you break it, I won't be able to protect you from the fallout."

I grabbed her wrist and yanked her in for a kiss. "I'm not worried."

And I wasn't; I had every intention of honoring the sanctity of our pinky promise—even after Ally dumped me. But then, in March, I found out about Ally and HIM. As fate would have it, a few days later I received the following text.

STEFF

Robby and I broke up

Then, to clarify:

QB1 lol

That weekend, Steff and I had sex while her buffalo-sized Bernese mountain dog snored in his kennel one room over. Afterward, as I got dressed, Steff's phone lit up.

She held it out so I could see. "See? What'd I tell you?"

Sure enough, QB1—er, *Robby*—had texted her. Two words: miss you.

"Are you gonna respond?" I asked.

"Not yet. He can sweat it out for a night."

I frowned. "But if you know this is what he does, why do you keep falling for it?"

And then Steff gave me a look that broke the last bits of my heart. "Wouldn't you?"

I can feel you judging me. Where do I get off, right? Resenting Ally for dating HIM, meanwhile I'm out here screwing my other ex. Breaking a pinky promise. But there's a big difference between relapsing once with an old ex and fully dating the "he's just a friend" guy two months after unceremoniously dumping your boyfriend of over a year. For all the shit Ally'd given me, she'd been the one who lied. Just because I didn't make her swear some childish oath didn't mean she was off the hook.

So yeah, I feel bad. But not guilty.

22

Okay, but seriously, what is it with my exes showing up randomly at my house? First Ally, now Steff. Who's next? Tallulah Chamberlin? Remember her? The girl I "dated" for forty-eight hours in middle school? Is she hiding in the mudroom?

Sorry, I'm just on edge. Seeing Steff really threw me off more than I expected. Obviously when we hooked up in March, I kinda, sorta (definitely) hoped Ally would find out.

But now—I don't know. If Ally knew about me and Steff, she would've said something by now. That she hasn't suggests she's still in the dark. Let's keep it that way. I'm having enough trouble getting a read on her as it is.

Take yesterday: Ally seemed legitimately upset about the Henley, only to turn right around and admit she'd gotten rid of all her Cam memorabilia. The hell is that? Okay, yes, I ruined the shirt. But I didn't throw it away! I kept it, just in case Ally and I ever, you know—

I am over Allison Tandy.

I'm not sure what to expect—which Ally I'm going to get—

when she rolls in just before noon. So I'm caught a little off guard when she starts acting . . .

"Cammie! Chop-chop, let's move!"

Normal? Like nothing happened. Weird.

"Where am I going?" I ask as I back the Geo out of the drive-way. "Macy's? Goodwill? Dick's Sporting Goods has button-ups—we could try there."

Ally looks at me like I just told her to jump off a bridge. "Please tell me that was a joke."

It wasn't.

"You cannot wear a Dick's Sporting Goods button-up on a date. Let's try Plaza Del Blanco; they should have everything we need."

To describe Plaza Del Blanco as a *strip mall* would technically be accurate. And yet, it might leave you with the wrong impression. Shermerites don't like to think of themselves as strip mall shoppers—they require a certain lavishness whilst purchasing their extra-value two-ply toilet paper. Thus, Plaza Del Blanco was born. It's supposed to resemble the Spanish Riviera . . . if the Spanish Riviera had a cryotherapy day spa.

We sail along, breezing through a string of green lights. The top is down. The music's loud. Ally's rapping along to "Mary Had a Tab of Xan" by Xan Savage. Squint and it almost looks like a scene lifted straight out of last summer.

I turn down the volume. "We should establish some ground rules for today."

"Ground rules?" Ally snorts. "Last time I checked, I was the one in charge here."

"You are. But there are simply some lines I refuse to cross."

"Uh-huh."

I clear my throat. "No blazers, no polos, no sweater vests, no golf wear, nothing pastel, no cargo shorts, none of those little zip-up vests, no boat shoes, no ironic T-shirts, and nothing with a little animal logo—the horse, the pink whale, the alligator, none of them."

"Does that seem like my style?" Ally asks, practically inviting me to ogle. So I do. Today she's in one of those striped onesies— like a jumpsuit that stops at her thigh. (I wanna say *pomper*? *Bomper*? Is that right?)

"Cam?" I snap out of my trance. "What did I just say?" She knows I don't know, and she knows damn well why I don't know it. No wonder she looks so pleased with herself.

"Finally," I say. "I will allow the purchase of one button-up."

Ally counters, "Five."

"*Five*? Absolutely not. I'll go as high as two."

"Four."

"Three."

"Deal."

I find a parking spot in front of Uncle Ruff's, one of three artisanal dog bakeries in the plaza.

"Okay . . ." I kill the engine. "Let's make this quick. In and out in a tight thirty."

Ally breaks into a low, menacing laugh, steadily growing louder and louder. Fucking Maleficent over here.

"Oh, Cammie. Sweet, sweet Cammie. We aren't simply here for a few shirts—oh no. Today is a full remodel. Starting with those two guys." She indicates between my eyebrows. "Are you prepared for what's about to happen?" she asks me as we approach the salon.

I roll my eyes. "So they're gonna yank out a couple of stray hairs. How bad could it be?"

Answer: Very, VERY bad.

Ally doesn't stop there. She puts me through the paces: haircut, professional shave, manicure. Finding clothes is the easiest part of the whole endeavor. We hit up Madedecent and Club Tropez, stores Ally frequents. She points stuff out, I try them on. Half an hour later, we're good to go.

Shoes are a different story.

"Don't bother browsing." Ally ushers me toward a pair of stark white Adidas. "Stan Smiths. Classic. Versatile. Won't make you look like one of those sneaker-head douchebags."

I pick up the display shoe. "Do they come in different colors?"

"Yes, but you have to get them in all white. It's the look."

"Ally, if I buy white shoes they're gonna get dirty immediately."

"Not if you take care of them. Or clean them once in a while."

"Right, like I'm gonna clean shoes," I scoff. "Shoes go on the ground, Al. That's where the dirt lives!"

Eventually we settle on a compromise: I buy the ones she likes.

When it's all said and done, the Geo's trunk is jam-packed with shopping bags and Mom's credit card feels substantially lighter. The call from my bank is a fitting end to the afternoon.

Hello, Mr. Garrity, we've noticed some suspicious activity on your card today . . .

Ally gets a kick out of that. "Even Chase knows you have no sense of style."

I laugh along. Today went a lot better than I expected.

Whatever weirdness I feared earlier never materialized. Good thing too; I'd much rather spend my time with Ally cosplaying our relationship. (Or some upside-down version of it.)

"Any word from Chevy?" Ally asks as I slam the trunk door.

"Nada," I say, opening my own and belting in. "Think maybe I should call him?"

"Give it a little more time," she says. "He'll pull himself together."

Ally's saying something else, but she's drowned out by the stereo when I start the ignition. I turn the knob down. "Sorry, say that again?"

Ally contorts in her seat so she's facing me. "I said, I've been thinking about your Ally Box. Now that we're back on speaking terms, there's no reason to keep it hidden."

My pulse quickens. "Good point."

"Great! Then it's settled." Ally smiles. "The Ally Box must be destroyed."

I do a double take—"Huh?"—braking just in time to avoid

backing into the minivan waiting for my spot. The driver, a white lady with a tattoo sleeve, flips me off when we pass her.

"It's a classic breakup move," Ally maintains. "You gather up all the shit from a past relationship—photos, gifts, that sort of thing—and you set it on fire! Then *poof!*" She claps, imitates smoke with her fingers. "Instant catharsis. Isn't that just the greatest idea ever?"

The greatest idea ever came in 1998 when Earth's greatest minds got together and inserted yogurt in a long, portable plastic sleeve. They called it Go-GURT and it won the Nobel Peace Prize. (Don't google that.)

This was no Go-GURT.

I fix my eyes on the road. "Is that what you did with my stuff? Set it on fire?"

Ally's quiet a moment. I tap the accelerator, breeze through a stale yellow. "No, that's not—I just threw it away." She doesn't sound quite so animated. "Look, if our goal here is to help you move on, I don't see how we can do that while you're harboring a box of bad memories under your bed."

"Who said they were *bad* memories?" My voice catches.

"No, of course not." Ally's tone softens. "But you know what I mean. It's baggage. If you're gonna give Jeannie—or any girl—a fair shot, then you need to get rid of it." A beat. "And what better way than to light an inferno so high they'll see it from the across the lake?"

"I don't think we're zoned for that."

I feel Ally's fingers tighten around my wrist then. "I think this could be really good for you, Cammie. Tell me you'll think about it?"

I glance down. Her nails are painted the same shade of blue as the veins buried deep under her tissue and flesh. And right then, I know no matter how much I bitch and moan, I'll end up doing whatever Ally says—even if I don't actually want to.

23

The next morning, Maizy joins me for breakfast. We're both in our jammies, eating Lucky Charms, watching *NCIS Boise* when Mom comes trouncing downstairs.

"Maizy's soccer coach is out of town this week," Mom says. "I told the other parents you would supervise their practice tomorrow."

"Can't . . ." My mouth's full. "Busy."

"Busy doing what?"

Damn. She got me there. Well played, Mother.

"Fine, I'll do it. But only if I'm allowed to trade players."

"No."

"Can I cut players if their performance doesn't meet my standard?"

"No."

"Can I give them all candy so they turn into nightmares for their parents when they get home?"

Maizy: "Yes!"

Mom: "No!"

"Why can't one of the other parents do it? I'm not the one

who got bored and decided the world needed more boring white people."

"Yay, no more boring white people!" Maizy cheers.

"See, Maizy gets it."

Mom isn't as amused. "Because I told them you would and I don't want people to think we're the kind of family that doesn't follow through on our promises. Are we a family that follows through on our promises?"

"Yes," Maizy and I recite together.

"Good. Get Chevy to help you. I was hoping he'd talk you into this for me, but I never heard back from him."

"Wait, what?" I wheel around, forgetting the bowl in my lap. Milk-logged marshmallows slosh onto the carpet. "Chevy hasn't responded to you?"

Mom shakes her head. It's one thing for Chevy to ignore me; it's another for him to ghost my mom. I should check on him. I mean, sure, he dragged me across town in a convoluted attempt to confront his girlfriend's (alleged) lover. But who among us, amirite? Once it's rooted in your brain, there's no telling what kind of chaos jealousy can incite. You know you're in trouble when your imagination starts working against you.

"Hey, Mom, one more thing." I leave the episode running for Maizy and hobble over. "You haven't heard anything new, have you? About Ally?"

Mom forms a sort of grimace. "There haven't been any additional involuntary outbursts, if that's what you're asking.

Otherwise her condition remains the same. Stable and indefinite. Why do you ask?"

Because Ally told me she'd wake up in time for graduation.

"No reason."

"Mm." Mom tries for a sympathetic look. "As soon as there's any new information, I'll let you know."

I text Chevy before we leave, then again after I drop Maizy off. When he isn't in school, I really start to worry.

"Have you tried facetiming him?" Ally asks me later in the afternoon. She's sprawled out on my bed, overseeing the final stages of date prep. Jeannie sent me a message earlier: Can't wait for tonight!

"Didn't think of that," I say, threading my arms through one of my new button-ups. "At what point do we call in a wellness check?"

Ally rolls off the bed and walks over to the window. "His car is gone," she points out. "Weird. He's supposed to receive this prestigious senior award at the debate team banquet tonight too. I thought for sure he'd pull himself together in time."

"Uh-huh." I'm barely listening. This goddamn button-up is already proving to be a liability. The cuffs are too tight; I feel like I'm losing circulation.

Ally sighs. "I feel bad for him."

"Why? I thought you said what he did on Saturday was inexcusable?"

"It was. But clearly Chevy isn't comfortable being in an open relationship. He's just too afraid of losing her to speak up. It's sad."

"Hm." *Fuck you, shirt! Why don't you have a zipper? Just be a coat!* I check my reflection in the mirror. "This still feels wrong."

Ally, without looking, "You missed one."

I look down. Sure enough, the shirttails are uneven. "Couldn't have told me a minute ago?" I mutter, restarting the whole process.

Ally peers over her shoulder and winks. My temper cools. Once I've corrected the mistake, she sidles over.

"Leave the top two open." She reaches up to undo them herself. Her breath is warm on my chest, her fingers cold. I shiver. "Give her a little preview of the goods underneath."

I flex. "You mean my massive pecs."

"Yes, you have a very nice chest. It's one of your best features."

Not a whiff of sarcasm. Suddenly, I feel invincible. *I've got this.*

Ally takes a small step backward—without moving her hands off my chest. They're welcome as long as they'd like. "Alright, game plan. What're you gonna do tonight?"

I count off on my fingers. "Smile, nod a bunch, resist dominating the conversation, ask her questions about herself . . ."

"And don't look bored at her answers, even if her answers are boring as shit."

"Be nice, Al."

"Sorry, sorry. Jeannie seems great. I bet she's an excellent conversationalist." Ally's sarcasm is back and better than ever. "Here, watch. Pretend I'm you." Ally closes her eyes, gets into character.

"Wow, it's so cool your parents let you drink with them when you vacation in Europe."

"Is that supposed to be me?"

"*Tell me more about your passion for influencing. At what age did you decide you wanted to be professionally hot?*"

"How are you this bad at impressions?"

"*I agree, capitalism is the only way poor people will learn.*"

Snorting at her own jokes, Ally vaults onto her tiptoes and smooths the wrinkles out of my collar.

"You're gonna kill it, Garrity."

"Thanks, Al."

She slides her hands down my neck to my shoulders. Gives them a squeeze. "I can't wait to hear all about it when we debrief tomorrow."

"You're not coming?" My stomach flips. "I thought we were gonna rendezvous in the bathroom like we usually do? So you could coach me up."

Ally's looking at her phone now, half listening. "That does sound fun. Unfortunately I have a prior engagement."

I figure she's doing a bit—what commitments could an astral projection possible have? So I laugh. Ally doesn't. "Wait, you're serious?"

"Yeah." She locks her phone, slips it in her back pocket. "It's just this thing. I'm sure I told you."

She most certainly did not. "You most certainly did not."

"Okay, well, I'm telling you now." Ally must sense my confusion. "Helping you find a new booty call isn't how I spend every waking minute of existence. What'd you think I was doing during the hours I'm not with you?"

Huh. I guess I hadn't put much thought into it. It's not like she has a ton of options; I am the only person who can see her. According to her, anyway. Unless she's lying. Now that I think about it, she could be going anywhere. With anyone. Even HIM—

No, that's crazy talk. She's not . . . I mean she wouldn't . . .

Huh.

"Relax, Cammie." Ally closes the gap between us. "Jeannie's gonna love you. You're well prepped, you look great, and most importantly, you're not a complete douchebag." A beat. "Most of the time."

I mimic her smile. But deep in my belly, the churning's begun. If Ally's discovered a way to permeate the astral plane and communicate with me, who's to say she hasn't done the same with HIM?

PARANOIA TAILS ME across town. Driving over: *She isn't with HIM . . . right?* Getting gas: *Why would she bail on me? Tonight of all nights?* Finding parking: *It's selfish is what it is. She knew I wouldn't be able to focus if I spent the whole date worrying about her and—*

"Sir?"

I snap back. A girl with curtain-style bangs gawks at me from behind the hostess stand.

"Sorry, I'm meeting someone." I check my phone. Jeannie's texted me; she's already here. I scan the room. The place is packed, one table on top of the next. It's gonna be a bitch crutching through this.

"Cam! Over here!"

I know that voice. I swing my gaze toward the source and there's . . . Lisa? What's she doing here?

And then I notice Jeannie is beside her. At a four-top. I recognize the back of Chevy's head seated across from them. Evidently my big first date with Jeannie just doubled.

"Hey, guys," I say, couching my surprise with faux excitement. "What're you doing here?"

"It's the funniest thing." Lisa takes her seat. "Chevy and I were just sitting down to a little date night of our own, when who should we run into but this beautiful creature." Lisa puts her arms around Jeannie. "When she told us she was here for a date with you, I was like, 'Um, here's an idea: What if we turned this into a double date?'"

I force a smile. "How about that." Lisa does the same. We lock eyes. I send her a clear message: *Are you seriously about to do this?*

She answers in kind: *This is happening. Don't blow it.*

Look, am I surprised The Happy Couple intruded on my date? Not entirely. (If you haven't noticed, they have serious boundary issues when it comes to my dating life.) What's weird is they're *together.* Like, physically. I thought for sure Lisa would be pissed at him—and by extension, me—when she found out about our little jaunt to Teddy's house over the weekend. Why hasn't she ripped him limb from limb yet? And how come Chevy's avoiding eye contact with me? Unless . . .

He didn't tell her. Goddamnit. I'm gonna kill him.

"Hi, I'm Jeannie!"

Shit. Almost forgot this is supposed to be a date. I introduce myself, then settle into the empty chair on Chevy's right.

"Chevy."

"Cam." He still won't meet my eyes.

"So . . ." Lisa's voice is light, unbothered. "Jeannie was just telling us about this incredible marketing opportunity she's been offered."

"It's nothing, really," Jeannie says with a practiced indifference that screams, *It's everything, really.* "This locally sourced chakra dispensary found my socials, and they're interested in partnering with me on a new collab."

"Amazing." I elbow Chevy. "Isn't that amazing, Chev?"

Mumbling: "Amazing, yeah."

"Yeah, I mean I've been working really hard to increase my engagement rate the past few months," Jeannie says. "My shaman says this is the universe's way of validating my work. Providing me what I deserve, you know? Like, I feel like I've really earned this."

"Cool," I say, just to say it. Lisa's nodding along, hanging on Jeannie's every word. Chevy's inspecting his plate for smudges. "So, I guess we're about to be classmates, huh? Go Maroons, amirite?" Jeannie looks confused. "Our mascot. The University of Chicago Maroons."

Recognition crosses Jeannie's expression. "Maroons, yeah. They wait-listed me at first, but my dad took care of it. He's an alum and we give them *so* much money."

Oh—*oh wow.* She just came right out and admitted it. No sheepishness whatsoever. I wait for the *just kidding.* Maybe a self-deprecating trust-fund-kid joke.

Jeannie goes a different route. "I was worried for a little bit I'd have to go to a state school." She turns to Lisa. "No offense, babe. I just don't think a state school would fit the brand aesthetic I'm cultivating."

"That's so funny. We make fun of Lisa all the time for going to a state school." I elbow Chevy again and he grunts. "Chevy's always saying how Wisconsin is just Arizona State with better PR."

Chevy snaps to attention. "I never said that!" To Lisa, sweetly: "Babe, I never said that."

But Lisa's cracking up. "It's fine. I'm gonna have more fun than all three of you put together anyway."

Soon the girls are swept up in their sidebar, leaving me to play a little game I just invented called *Glare at Chevy Until He Explains What the Fuck Is Going On.* It's easy—here, I'll explain the rules: All you have to do is glare at Chevy until he explains what the fuck is going on.

"We're gonna run to the bathroom before the rest of the food comes," Lisa announces. She and Jeannie rise to their feet. "Babe, will you order us more of those pot stickers when the waiter comes back?"

"Sure thing, babe." Chevy and I smile placidly as the girls pick their way through the maze of tables.

Once they're out of earshot, Chevy wheels around. "Look, I can explain—OW!" My foot isn't interested in explanations.

"*That* was for dragging me across town and ruining my Saturday!"

Kick. "OW!"

"*That* was for ignoring my texts all weekend!"

"Dude, I'm sorry—" *Kick.* "OW!"

"And *that's* for lying to Lisa! She sure seems relaxed for someone who just found out her boyfriend tried boxing a guy for posting a picture with her."

Grimacing, Chevy reaches under the table and massages his shin. "You agreed it was a suspicious-ass picture."

"That's not the point!" I take a sip of my Sprite just to munch on the ice cubes. "How much does she know?"

"Everything." Chevy sits up and starts fidgeting with his training-wheel chopsticks. "In a sense."

"The hell does that mean?"

Long, *loooooong* pause. "I told her it was your idea. Now, before you get mad—*OW!*"

I got him good that time—wound up and everything. Chevy keels over, forehead hitting his plate. He pounds his fist on the table in agony. "I deserve that," he wheezes. "But it's cool. All Lisa thinks is you *wanted* to go over to Ally's new boyfriend's house—not that you actually went. I wanted to see how she'd react, you know? Before I told her the truth."

"Let me guess—she wasn't big on the idea?" I deadpan.

Chevy cringes. "She said it was a good thing I was there to talk you out of it."

My eyes narrow. "I'm sorry. *You* talked *me* out of it?" I go for the kill shot, but Chevy's on the lookout. My toe whiffs, bangs against the underside of our table. The silverware trembles.

"Cam, chill! I took care of it!" Chevy pleads. People are starting to notice the ruckus coming from our side of the restaurant.

"I made her promise not to bring it up. Okay? So it's chill. No harm, no foul."

"Tell that to my goddamn bumper," I sneer.

"What happened to your bumper?" Lisa materializes at the head of the table.

Chevy. "Fuck!"

Me. "Jesus!"

The girls share a look and a laugh. "Why so jumpy, you two?"

"NOTHING!" Chevy shouts. "ABSOLUTELY NOTHING! ISN'T THAT RIGHT, CAM?"

I nod. Jeannie looks convinced. Lisa, less so.

"Cam?" Lisa arches an eyebrow. "Everything okay?"

Is everything okay? If you're me, you have to laugh at a question like that.

So I do. I laugh until tears are streaming down my face, in spite of their confused expressions—spurred on by them, in fact. I stop for a drink before I choke. As I chug, Lisa leans over and says in Jeannie's ear, "Cam's on a lot of drugs right now, with the surgery and everything. This new painkiller called Delatrix—have you heard of it?"

"Oh yeah." Jeannie turns to me. "My stepmom takes Delatrix too. I can't remember if it's for her hot flashes or for her crow's disease."

"You mean Crohn's disease?" I ask.

"No, crow's disease. She fell from the crow's nest on my father's sailboat last year in Martha's Vineyard. Fractured her collarbone."

"Right." I belch into my elbow. Not exactly proper date etiquette, but who even cares at this point? I'm calling it.

"Well, Jeannie, I'll be honest. I thought tonight would go a lot differently. I don't really get the whole influencer thing, but it's cool you're into it. Maybe we can be friends next year. My hobbies include drinking—"

"Me too," Jeannie cuts in.

"Perfect." I throw up my arms—*ta-da!* "Look at that, fast friends after all. I look forward to doing all sorts of dumb shit in the next four years. But I've gotta be honest; right now, my heart just isn't in this."

It's in the ICU at Shermer General.

I go to stand then, which of course takes me a minute, robbing me of the dramatic exit I would've preferred. "Chevy will take care of everyone's meal, won't you, buddy?" I take off before he can object. Can't imagine how Lisa plans to spin that to Jeannie. Whatever. I have my own relationship to look after. The Happy Couple can sort theirs out on their own.

24

Tuesday is the last full day for seniors. So long, eight-hour school days, you will not be missed. The hallways are buzzing. You can practically taste the excitement in the air.

I don't share in my classmates' jubilation. In fact, after last night, I'm feeling pretty anxious. I'd kinda hoped to see Ally back at my house when I got home last night. No luck, even after my bedtime dosage.

It occurs to me (now that I'm dwelling on it) that outside of Senior Olympics, I haven't seen Ally during school hours. That was normal, pre-accident. Our schedules and STHS's labyrinthine hallways made it so that we never crossed paths. Made my life a helluva lot easier after Ally dumped me. I could go about my day without having to worry about any chance encounters. But now—I don't know. What else could she be doing? The better question—who is she doing it with?

Chevy shows up late second period, not that our teacher, Ms. Estevez, gives a shit anymore. Chevy's yearbook lands on the table we share with a smack. A fat Sharpie dangles from the spine.

"Dude, it's so weird," Chevy whispers. "Instead of HAGS,

people have been writing HAGL—like, 'have a great life.' It's the end of the world, man."

I pretend not to hear him, focusing instead on the movie. This week it's *Sense and Sensibility*. Young Emma Thompson could get it. Alan Rickman too.

Chevy gives it five minutes before trying his luck again. "Look, Cam, I just wanted to—"

"Not here." I shut him down. "Make it up to me after school. Mom wants us to supervise Maizy's soccer practice."

"Done," he agrees without missing a beat. "Are we allowed to trade players?"

"Already asked—Mom says no."

A few hours later and we're back at Ringwald Park, only this time, instead of a few hundred wasted almost-grads, the fields are populated by a dozen fourth-grade girls chasing around a neon soccer ball. On the sidelines, Chevy and I relax in lawn chairs, sipping Capri Suns and munching on the orange slices someone's mom brought for the team.

"I think Maizy's scored like twenty goals since we got here," Chevy says.

"She's a legit prodigy," I say. "Mom says big-time travel teams are already sniffing around."

"Such a better athlete than you."

"Oh, no question."

Chevy still has plenty to answer for, but I will say it's nice to see him acting like himself again. For all his talk, Chevy's a "girlfriend guy" to his core. Life is better with The Happy Couple intact.

"So . . ." I gnaw the remaining pulp out of my rind. "You ready to beg for my forgiveness?"

Chevy lets out a long sigh. "It all happened so fast."

I roll my eyes. "Uh-huh."

"I'm serious! Lisa got back from Madison late Sunday and spent the night at my house. She didn't tell me she wanted to crash your date until the next morning. Sorry, by the way." I wave it off. Chevy continues, "I knew I had to tell her." A beat. *"Something."*

"Something like, 'Cam tried to fight Ally's new boyfriend'?"

"Right." Chevy's hands won't sit still; they keep finding their way to his pressure points. "I dunno, man. She was giving me this weird look, and I had this weird cramping feeling up and down my sides. I thought I was having a stroke. Swear to God, I could smell toast." He sighs. "So I put it on you."

"And what did Lisa say?"

Chevy waffles, then caves. "She said it sounded like something you would do."

I laugh in spite of myself. "Right, because Cam's lost his mind."

"Dude, it's not like that."

"What's it like, then?"

Before he can answer, the sound of a wailing ten-year-old erupts across the park. Down on the ground is this girl Katie— the only one wearing Rec-Specs.

I cup my hands around my mouth. "Y'okay, Katie?"

"We should probably go over there and check on her," Chevy says to me.

"Definitely."

Neither of us budges.

"She's probably fine."

"Yeah, I wouldn't worry."

"Walk it off, Katie," I shout.

"Rub some dirt on it," Chevy joins in.

Katie manages a shaky thumbs-up. Before long, she's back on her feet.

I turn to Chevy. "You know you can't go on like this."

Chevy slurps what's left of his juice. "Yeah, I know. I really am sorry. Blaming you was a shitty move."

"I'm not just talking about what happened this weekend," I say. "Chev, you don't want to be in an open relationship. Look at what it's doing to you, man. We haven't even graduated yet, and you're already freaking out about every guy she puts her arm around."

Chevy snaps to attention. "Who'd she have her arm around?!" I cock an eyebrow. "Oh." He deflates. "Maybe you're right."

We end practice a little early, let the girls chase each other around on the playground until their parents come to pick them up. Maizy and I make it all the way home before I realize I forgot to collect the cones.

Ringwald Park is deep in the throes of golden hour when I return. A young couple pushes their chubby-cheeked baby on the swings, snapping pictures. Under the floodlights, two vocal women trade shots on the tennis court. On the soccer pitch, I spot someone lying in the freshly trampled grass.

Ally clocks me without getting up. "Well, if it isn't the man of the hour," she quips. Her hair is arranged in a fiery halo. "How was the big date? You and Jeannie getting married?"

"It was fine," I say absentmindedly. To Ally's left are the soccer cones, stacked neatly. To her right is a shoebox. Let me rephrase: not just any shoebox. My Ally Box.

How the hell did she move that here herself?

Ally reads my mind. "You know, it's the strangest thing." She gets to her feet. "The closer I get to waking up, the stronger I'm getting. A few days ago, I had to be in the same room as you. Now I can pick things up, even when we're miles apart. For example . . ." She scoops the stack of cones up, flings them at me. "You're welcome, by the way."

Ally traces my line of sight. "Oh right, I went ahead and snagged your Ally Box. I hope you don't mind." She flutters her lashes. "Now, I know you were on the fence before, but I really think this will be good for us—for *you*," she corrects. "Put the past behind you. Burn the boats. So to speak."

She's not letting this go. This is happening whether I like it or not.

"Okay, fine." I relent. "We can use the firepit in my backyard later. Or, I don't know. Maybe a coffee can. If Mom asks what I'm doing, I'll just tell her I'm burning Dad's old baseball cards."

Ally has this twinkle in her eye. "I have a better idea."

Q<small>UICK</small> G<small>ARRITY</small> <small>FAMILY</small> history lesson: We have a boat nicknamed *Leisure Rules*.

It really isn't anything to write home about, just a little motorized thing with more cup holders than life jackets. It was my dad's. Er, it still is, I guess. Mom only hung on to it after they separated because she wanted to maintain her membership status at the Shermer Shores Yacht Club, where it's moored. (In her defense, their seasonal galas are quite tasteful.)

Personally, I've never found any use for it. The call of the sea, yada-yada. I think it's because I saw *Jaws* too young. Freshwater or not, you can never be too careful.

Ally is well aware of my nautical *deficiencies*. And yet, she's decided tonight is the night to put them to the test.

"You know I haven't driven this thing in like eight years, right?" I tell her once we're aboard. At least Mom hasn't changed the code for the padlock; it's still 1-2-3.

"How hard can it be?" Ally flops down in the copilot's chair. "I'm sure it's just like driving a car." I give her a look. "Cameron, I swear to God if you make a car accident joke right now, I will push you overboard and leave you for dead."

I manage to clear the harbor without running into another vessel, puttering well below the wake limit past ships that far outweigh (and outvalue) ours. The club's jurisdiction extends only so far—an invisible line of demarcation strung between a pair of converging stone revetments. Beyond the breach, it's open season. I goose the throttle, and we're off, charting a course parallel to the coast.

Not a minute later, Ally makes a slashing motion across her throat. Kill the engine.

I look back the way we came. "You sure we shouldn't go farther?" I can still make out the club, perched on a hill overlooking the harbor.

"Nah, here's good."

"Alright, well, there should be an anchor around here somewhere—"

"Cam, relax," Ally stresses. "We'll be fine. This shouldn't take long."

I don't share her ease of mind. Out here on the water, I can't escape the feeling I'm doing something wrong, like when I was thirteen and tried beer for the first time. But then Ally's hand closes around mine. My uneasiness disbands instantly.

She looks at me. I look at her. Together, we turn and set our sights on the rapidly obscuring horizon. God's making cotton candy; the sky's splashed in brilliant pinks and reds. How easy it would be to play pretend, indulge in the fantasy of a normal summer night with my normal non-comatose girlfriend—no *ex*. Such a lovely thought.

And then I see the lighter.

"What do you think?" Ally cranks the wheel on her Bic, teasing the flame. She nudges the Ally Box with her toe. "Should we go one at a time? Or all at once?"

"Wait a second!" I blurt. "Let's just think about this for a second." Suddenly I'm a hostage negotiator, desperately trying to prevent Ally from shooting someone in the head. For every excuse I come up with, she's ready with an answer.

"Those clouds look pretty ominous. Maybe we should head in."

"Already checked the weather; those clouds are moving west."

Fuck.

"Should we really litter like this? We only have one planet, you know."

"We can plant a tree tomorrow to offset it."

Double fuck.

"Are we sure this is safe? For all we know, astral projections are extremely flammable."

This time Ally gives me a pointed look. "What's going on? Why are you trying to bail?"

"I'm not!" I am.

"Uh-huh." She isn't buying it. If I can't get her to release the hostages, then maybe I can stall her.

"I just don't feel like this is very fair, you know," I say. "You get to watch me dispose of all my memorabilia from our relationship. Meanwhile, you just, what—got rid of it? Hell, I don't even know what you kept."

Ally stares straight ahead. "Would that make you feel better? If I told you what I held on to?"

"Honestly, yeah," I say, and I find I'm being sincere. (Shocker, I know.) But I've spent months thinking Ally could give a shit.

"Alright, deal." She kills the flame. I breathe a sigh of relief.

"Let's see . . ." Ally plunks back down in her chair. Starts to swivel back and forth as she reminisces. "First, the obvious: notes, letters, anything with your handwriting."

I wince. Keep it together, Cam. You asked for this.

"The box from the cupcake ATM, when you took me after my speech team lost at State."

"Oh, I remember that," I say, a little too excitedly. Ally was crushed after the loss. She's not Lisa competitive (who is?), but when it came to academics, she always rose to the occasion. On a whim (and a school night!) I snuck her out of her house and drove us to the city. Our destination? Sprinkles Cupcakes, this pink-clad bakery right off the Magnificent Mile. Home to Chicago's only twenty-four-hour cupcake ATM. Ally'd mentioned it in passing once before, and I'd made a mental note to take her. I watched her order—then consume—the worst flavor imaginable. Banana Marshmallow. Still, I let her kiss me afterward.

I can't believe she kept that.

Ally continues: "There was the mood ring you bought me at Suburban Infitters . . . the punch coupon book you made me use every time I hit you . . . squares and scratch-offs you bought me on my eighteenth birthday . . . Oh! And the hockey sweater you let me borrow."

"You threw out my Red Wings jersey?!" I pipe up. "I wanted that back!"

Ally shrugs. "Too late."

I'm not a hockey guy (again, too white). But this one time, after Lisa dragged me and Chevy to go thrifting in Chicago with her, I found this sweet-ass Detroit Red Wings jersey (some guy named Howe) for, like, twelve bucks. That thing was so god-damn cozy. On one of the chillier nights last summer, I lent it to Ally while we went to look at stars over on Chevy's beach. She kept promising to give it back, then conveniently "forgetting." Now it's probably in a landfill somewhere.

That one hurts, I have to admit. The nostalgia high is wear-ing off. Just as I'm about to give in, Ally perks up. "Oh! And the receipt from our fourth date."

I frown. "Our fourth date?" I rack my brain. What was so spe-cial about our fourth date?

"I wouldn't expect you to remember," Ally says. "We went to Froman's for pizza?"

It's coming back to me. "Is that the time I asked them to put Skittles on my half of the pizza? Because I stand by that request."

Ally snorts. "We are not having the Skittles-on-pizza debate again." The wind's picked up, tossing her hair. She brushes it aside, fits the loose strands behind her ear. "No, this was the time we had that terrible waitress. She barely spent any time at our table, came off super condescending and annoyed when she did, and then she messed up our order.

"When the check came, I thought about saying something, but you paid before I had the chance. Curiosity got the better of me, so when you ran to the bathroom, I snuck a peek at how much you tipped."

Ally's beaming now, a beacon silhouetted against the en-croaching darkness.

"The bill was $32.54. I remember it exactly. The worst waitress in history, and you still tipped more than fifty percent."

I wait for her to elaborate. "Is that it? You kept a receipt because of some tip?"

Ally tosses her head back and groans. "Jesus Christ, rich people are so frustrating. You can tell a lot about a person by the way they treat service workers. And you always tipped well. But that wasn't why I kept it. What stuck out to me was the amount—$17.46. Exactly enough to round the total to fifty bucks." Her smile returns. "And I thought that was so weird! But . . . also super cute? Does that make sense? Like, why would I find something that barely qualifies as a personality quirk to be *so* endearing unless my crush on you was very, *very* real, you know?"

I don't.

"So you went out with me because . . . what? I'm anal when it comes to tipping?"

"No, Cam. I went out with you because you're cute and charming when you want to be, and I liked talking to you as much as I liked kissing you, and you made me laugh. More importantly, you weren't surprised I was funny."

"You are funny."

"Yeah, I know I'm fucking funny. But I can't tell you how many boys say shit like"—she distorts her voice to a low rumble—*"You're funny . . . for a girl."* Ally scowls, shakes it off. "You were everything I was looking for then. And more." A beat. "In a lot of ways, you still are." I realize that there are tears in her eyes.

"Hey, come here," I say, spreading my arms open. Ally goes

slack, falling face-first into my chest. She nuzzles the top of her head below my collarbone. I recognize the smell of her shampoo. We stay like this for a while—Ally's body braced against mine. The last of the sunlight is gone when suddenly Ally stiffens.

"I'm fine," she mutters, smearing the sleeve of her flannel across her face.

"You don't have to be," I say, placing my hand against the small of her back. This time, she's allergic to my touch.

"No, no. I'm fine," she insists, climbing to her feet. "Let's just get this over with." She heads for the bow, my Ally Box tucked against her hip. Lighter at the ready.

Shit. She's about to shoot one of the hostages.

"Ally, wait!" She looks back at me. "Don't do it."

"Why do you even care?" The tears are rolling. "I thought this was what you wanted."

"*Me?* This was your idea! Why would I want this?"

"Because clearly you hate me."

I feel my expression twist. "I never said that!"

"Yeah, well, you didn't have to. From the moment you first saw me in your bathroom last week, you've gone out of your way to remind me you want nothing to do with me. And I get that you're still pissed about how—" Pause for breath work. "*Everything* happened that night. I know I could've handled the whole situation better. But my body is rotting in a hospital room as we speak. You're the only connection to the real world I've had in two months. How much more punishment do I deserve?"

On instinct, I open my mouth to respond. Nothing comes out. What is there to say?

"You're right." That gets her attention. "I've been acting selfish. Petty. And I know I haven't exactly made this easy on you—"

Ally scoffs. "Understatement of the year."

"I deserve that. But, Al—I don't hate you. It's a physical impossibility. And yeah, I still have some"—I put it mildly—"*unresolved* feelings about the way things went down. But hate you? Never that." This time, I take her hands, cup them together between mine. Offer up a smile. "You're my favorite person in the world. Full stop."

Ally sniffles. "Ahead of Lisa?"

"*Way* ahead of Lisa."

"Chevy?"

"He couldn't catch you if he tried."

"Maizy?"

"Alright, don't push it."

Ally lets out a wet snort and breaks into a smile. Her gaze keeps flickering—my eyes . . . my lips . . . my eyes . . . my eyes . . . my lips . . .

And then—out of nowhere—Ally's expression hardens.

"If you don't hate me, Cam, then why did you break up with me?"

25

Here are the facts.

The morning of January 1, I received the following text from Ally: We need to talk.

It snowed all day.

I arrived at Ally's house around seven.

Mrs. Tandy was visiting Ally's aunt in Indiana for the night, so we had the place to ourselves.

Ally was baking cookies.

I felt sick to my stomach, so I declined when she offered samples.

I couldn't handle the suspense, so I broke the seal, asked her outright: "What is it you wanted to talk about?"

Ally rambled for what felt like hours, waxing poetic about how she didn't think long distance could work, how she was worried we'd grow to resent each other, and how she still wanted to be friends.

I could tell she was dancing around the issue.

I just wanted her to be honest.

So I asked: "We're breaking up, then?" A question. Simple. Direct. Pleading.

She couldn't even look me in the eyes.

She barely flinched when I got up to leave.

I blacked out then; it's a minor miracle I made it home in one piece without meeting a fate like the one Ally would face just a few months later. Next thing I knew, I was sitting in my driveway, headlights kissing the garage door, a single recurring thought—a mantra, if you will—circling in my head like water down a drain.

I am over Allison Tandy.

26

Hiccup. I have the hiccups. *Hiccup.* In case you couldn't tell. *Hiccup-hiccup.* A nasty case too. This happens to me sometimes, when I laugh too hard, for too long. When a joke tweaks my funny bone in just the right way. Blame Ally and her deadpan delivery.

"What the hell is so funny?" Ally demands, brows furrowed, nostrils flaring. Still committing to the bit.

"Sorry, sorry . . ." I hold up a finger—*one sec!*—overcome by another round of giggles. "It's just (*hiccup*) for a second there (*hiccup*) I thought you said *I* broke up with *you.*"

Ally steels herself. "That is what I said."

The giggles wane. Not as funny the second time around.

"Al, come on (*hiccup*). Quit messing around."

"Do I look like I'm messing around?"

She doesn't.

"You're confused," I say then. "Is this related to your accident? Mom told me you suffered a brain injury (*hiccup*). Maybe it scrambled your memory."

"Oh, fuck off," Ally snaps. "My brain's fine, asshole. I remember that night perfectly. *You* were the one who ended it."

"LIAR!" *Keep a level head, Cam. She's just trying to get under your skin.* I hurry the pin back in the grenade before I detonate completely. Voices carry, and without an anchor, we've drifted within shouting distance of the shore. But what the hell?! Is Ally seriously trying to rewrite our history right now? Erase it altogether? And for what—just to screw with me?

"See this?" Ally gestures wildly between us. "*This* is gaslighting. Congratulations, Cammie; it turns out you're just like every other shitty guy in the world."

Gaslighting. We covered it in freshman health class—after the unit on abstinence being the only safe sex, before the STD slideshow. It's when you intentionally manipulate someone, essentially warping their reality, in an effort to make them feel crazy. Remind you of anyone?

"Bullshit," I counter. "If anyone here is gaslighting (*hiccup*), it's you!"

Ally scoffs. "Just what a gaslighter *would* say."

I'm feeling light-headed. How many times in the last week have I been forced to question my reality because of Ally? She may have robbed me of my sanity, but she doesn't get to undermine the one thing I know to be true.

Allison Tandy broke my heart. End of story.

In one move, I burst to my feet, the stabbing sensation in my knee be damned. Ally flinches but doesn't back down. We square up, nose to nose, two boxers locked in at a pre-fight press conference.

"Alright, Al," I snarl. "Let's piece this together step by step. True or false: *You* were the one who texted *me* saying *we* needed to talk."

Ally waffles. "Okay, true, but—"

"NO! No more (*hiccup*) buts! It's my turn now." My voice fans out across the water. Oh well. I'm past worrying about discretion. "True or false: You were the one who didn't want to stay together next year."

Ally's gaze falls to the deck. "True."

"Honesty—would you look at that?" I feign delight. "True or false: *You* didn't want to be with *me* anymore because *HE* was the one you actually wanted all along."

Ally's head pops up suddenly. "Cam, that's not—" She stumbles over her tongue, almost looking flustered. "Is *that* what you think happened?"

I screw my eyes shut. Crying will only make the hiccups worse, but I don't have much choice. The tears are already en route.

"Please don't make me say it," I mumble.

"Say what?" Ally asks. "Cam, I honestly don't know what you're talking about."

I turn away before she can see the waterworks. "You had a choice (*hiccup*). Me or HIM. And you chose HIM. Just like I always knew you would."

I wasn't paranoid *needlessly*, without cause. One minute, Ally and I were head over heels in love with each other. The next, she bailed. Just like that. Left me for dead. Classic hit-and-run. Now she's back to finish the job.

I am over Allison Tandy.

Who cares if I believe it or not. Right now, I need it to be true.

"Fine," I say. "Have it your way." Before she can react, I snatch the shoebox from her clutches.

"What are you doing?" Ally asks, panic rising in her voice.

"What does it look like?" I say, fishing my lighter out of my pocket. We've switched roles; now I'm the one taking hostages. "You were onto something earlier. Why bother doing this one at a time? It's all gonna end up in the same place anyway."

I flick the wheel. The flame stirs.

"Cam, stop!" Ally surges after me, arm outstretched. "I'm sorry, okay? This was a bad idea. I was just upset about the Henley and I wanted to get even. It was stupid! Can we please just go back?" The waves have come alive; Ally has to shout over them. "I lied before. All the stuff from our relationship, *my* Cam memorabilia. I still have it—all of it! I never threw anything away."

"I don't believe you!" There she goes, changing her story again. "You were right before." I hardly recognize the hard edges of my own voice. "We can't hold on to something that doesn't exist anymore (*hiccup*). Better to cut the cord now, get it over with. And you know why?"

I am over Allison Tandy.

I am over Allison Tandy.

I am over Allison Tandy.

JUST FUCKING SAY IT!

"Because I am over—"

Suddenly, the boat lurches, bucking like an enraged bull. Under me, the deck shifts, then vanishes. In an instant, my feet are out from under me, then over my head. I'm falling, I realize. I brace for the impending crunch—my back slamming into the deck. Only, it doesn't come. Why isn't it (*hiccup*) happening?!

I catch a fleeting glimpse of *Leisure Rules*, pitched on its side, before I strike the water and am swallowed by the blackened surf.

I am over Allison . . . It's over, Ally . . . Overboard . . .

"Hey? You alright?"

Good question, disembodied voice in my head. To be honest, I'm not doing so—

Ow! Who the fuck keeps prodding me? I crack open my eyes, blink out lake water. A shadow towers overhead.

Ally?

No—just some kid. Middle schooler, if I had to guess. I spot the culprit, the slab of driftwood he's holding, aimed once more for my rib cage.

"Poke me again and . . ." I can't even finish my threat without coughing up a liter. "Where am I?" I manage to croak out.

"Central Street Beach," the kid tells me, at which point I become aware of the sand supporting my head, clinging to my arms, down my shorts. *Everywhere.* "My friends and I were over there." He points to the other side of the beach. My head lolls to the side. I make out two girls and one boy perched in the guard chair. A regular double date. I can't imagine how I must look to them, washing ashore in the dead of night.

"We thought you were a dead animal," the kid says. "Until we saw these." He moves out of my line of sight. I hear him sloshing around in the shallows. He returns, holding my crutches. "What happened to your leg?"

Little man won't lay off. My pruning fingers make it impossible to snap. Instead, I wordlessly extend a hand—the universal signal for *help me up*. The kid's tall, gangly. With a little effort he manages to haul me to my feet. My shirt feels like it weighs fifty pounds. I strip it off, wind it tight, then wring it out. Pop it back on. That's when I remember—

"The boat?" I wheel around, swing my gaze from one jetty to the other. We'd beached it, I'd assumed. On a sandbar maybe. Or just plain run it aground. But as I squint at the opaque horizon, *Leisure Rules* is nowhere to be seen.

"The boat." I grab the kid by the shoulders. "Did you see a boat?"

He shakes his head. "Nah, man. No boat. Just you."

But . . . I was there . . . I piloted it out the harbor . . . the Ally Box . . . we were arguing . . . and then—

Why did you break up with me?

"You know you're bleeding, right?"

I look down. Splatters dot the right side of my T-shirt. I lift it up. No cut, wound, abrasion, anything. *Could it be Ally's?* I wonder for a fleeting second. But then I spot it: the wide, seeping gash sliced across the pad of my middle finger. Must've nicked it during my fall. Because I did fall off the boat! That happened! *Right?*

My head thrums. Ally's got me all turned around. Just like she wanted.

"You dating one of those girls?" I ask the kid, nodding toward the guard chair.

"What? No!" Defensive. Obvious. Very middle school.

"You like one of them?"

This question he considers, eventually nodding sheepishly. Confessions are always easier with a stranger.

"Consider this your first warning." I hold my lacerated finger up to the moonlight so he can get a better look. "A girl did this to me."

To say nothing of the damage she's inflicted on my heart.

27

I have a new mantra. (The old one clearly wasn't working.) Well, maybe not a mantra so much as a sound bite my brain insists on rewinding every ten seconds or so. Say goodbye to *I am over what's-her-name* and hello to *Why did you break up with me?*

See, this is what Ally does. She wants me fixating on what she said. All part of her twisted little game. Maintain the upper hand. Spin me around. Save me in her back pocket for later. Just in case.

Why did you break up with me?

I sank my family's boat last night! At least I think I did? She did mention feeling stronger, but what does that even mean? The fact that I'm not entirely sure is cause alone to be worried about my declining mental health. And yet, it's the furthest thing from my mind.

Why did you break up with me?

I mean, what she's implying is provably false. Ally broke my heart. Period. End of story. Canon locked. Everything since has just been the epilogue. So why do this? Just to get a rise out of me? Make me feel even crazier than I already do?

Why did you break up with me?

I didn't! You broke up with me! (Great, now I'm even arguing with her in my head.)

Why did you break up with me?

You think I wanted this? The depression, the second-guessing myself? Feeling like shit? God no! I wanted you.

Why did you break up with me?

This loop—constant, vicious, and unceasing—I just want it to stop. A voluntary lobotomy sounds preferable to being locked in my head right now.

Why did you break up with me?

Why can't I make it stop?

Why did you break up with me?

Please.

Why did you break up with me?

Why did you break up with me?

WHY DID YOU BREAK UP—

Morning offers some minor respite. Mom's already awake when I hobble into the kitchen. She's second-screening it, scrolling her Facebook feed, sipping a green smoothie hands-free through a plastic straw. Not a fan of the turtles.

Without even glancing at me: "What happened to your finger?"

Oh, right. The mystery cut. Eyes in the back of her head, my mother.

"Dunno."

"Put some Neosporin on it before it gets infected. There are Band-Aids in the junk drawer."

The Band-Aids are Disney themed. I pick one at random

(Buzz Lightyear, it's your lucky day), then squeeze out a dollop of Neosporin and curl him around my finger.

"Before you ask, I haven't heard anything about Ally," Mom says.

Just the mention of her name—*Why did you break up with me?*—prompts a relapse.

"Okay."

"You asked me if I thought she would wake up in time for graduation. So this is me telling you it seems less than likely."

Right. Graduation's in three days. Ally's self-imposed deadline, the day she's (allegedly) set to wake up. Funny, she's been mentioning it less and less. Too busy turning my world upside down.

Why did you break up with me?

I stuff the Band-Aids back in the drawer, hip-check it closed. "Thanks for the heads-up."

"Mhm." Mom brings her mug to her lips. In her glasses, I make out the reflection of the PTA website for Maizy's school. "I'll take Maizy this morning," she continues. "So you can enjoy your last day of school."

Shit. I'd forgotten that too. "Thanks," I say.

"There's just one thing." Mom frees a stapled packet from underneath her laptop, slides it across the island. "This was in the seat pocket in my car. Basic recovery exercises, for your knee. Rich—I mean *Dr. Vernon* . . ." she clarifies, "gave it to you last week. You were supposed to start these the day after your procedure."

I blink.

"Right, well, you won't be able to start physical therapy until you do, so you need to do these twice a day. Can you commit to doing your exercises twice a day?"

I tell her I will. Best to tread lightly with her right now, especially with the nonzero chance her ticket to Shermer Shores membership currently sits at the bottom of Lake Michigan.

About an hour later, after Mom's left with Maizy, I make good on my promise. I clear space on the family room floor so I can spread out. The exercises look easy enough. Mostly stretching with some light core work. Nothing I haven't done before. With my good knee bent, I lay my injured leg flat out in front of me and wrap a towel around the arch of my foot. I grab the towel by the ends and slowly draw my heel in toward my butt, gradually bending my knee in the process. I count the reps aloud as I go.

"One . . ."

CHRIST'S THIRD COUSIN SEBASTIAN THAT HURTS!

"Two . . ."

BODIES ARE A FLESH PRISON! EXISTENCE IS PAIN!

"Three . . ."

I USED TO BE ABLE TO DUNK! WHAT HATH BECOME OF ME?

"Four . . ."

SURE, IT WAS A NINE-AND-A-HALF-FOOT RIM. BUT THAT'S PRETTY GOOD FOR A WHITE GUY!

"Five . . ."

OKAY, FINE, IT WAS NINE FEET! HAPPY?!

When I reach ten, I flop onto my back, breathing hard. One set, and I'm sweating like it's the fourth quarter. I notice one of

Mom's throw pillows within reach. As I use it to mop under my arms, the doorbell rings.

Chevy? I wonder. Why doesn't he just come around back? Unless he's purposely luring me to the front door. I bet he and Lisa have some sort of celebration planned for the last day of school. I should've known they'd pull some shit like this. They're testing my patience too, ringing the bell a second time.

"Coming!" I holler, hopping toward the door, sans crutches. "Guys, can we not do this—"

HIM.

It's HIM.

HE's here. On my porch. Ringing my doorbell. Dating my ex-girlfriend. HE's . . . HE's . . . HE's . . .

HIM.

Blane Duckworth. Not the boogeyman. Not the monster in the closet my imagination made him out to be. Just . . . *some guy.*

"Are you Cameron Garrity?"

Look, I know I only met Blane like five seconds ago, and I may be biased here, but I can already tell he is the worst person who has ever existed, or will ever exist. I hate everything about him. I hate that he's taller than I'd hoped—a true six feet, like he's listed in the Rush Tech lacrosse team roster I found online. (Of course he plays lacrosse. I hate that too.) I hate his sandy blond hair, the way it's shaved on the sides, long on top. Looks crunchy, like uncooked pasta. Probably gets up super early just to fix it that way. I hate his pale blue button-up—there's that fucking whale again. His top two buttons are undone. Just like Ally instructed me to do.

I hate his—actually, his eyes are kind of mesmerizing. They're this deep, rich hazel color I've never seen before. You could get lost in those bad boys . . .

No! Pull yourself together, Cam!

"I'm Blane. Blane Duckworth." He offers a hand. I pretend not to notice. "I was Ally's—well, actually, I guess I'm still Ally's boyfriend."

I wince. My gut curdles. Still stings, hearing someone else claim that title. Blane's gaze travels to my damp T-shirt. "Sorry, did I catch you working out?"

"Lifting," I lie. *This motherfucker.* I bet he's here just to rub his two functioning knees in my face.

"Nice," Blane says. Is it just me, or is he acting nervous? Jittery, even. He keeps shifting his weight from the balls to the heels of his feet. Checking over his shoulder like someone's after him. "It's brutal out here," he says. "Is it cool if I come inside for a few minutes?"

"That depends." I give him a once-over. "Are you here to fight me?"

Blane laughs to himself. "No, I'm not here to fight you. I just wanted to talk."

No. That's what I should say. *No, Blane, you can't come in. Because I desperately need you to remain a figment of my imagination. I can't cope with your existence or the fact that Ally chose you over me. So please. Just go. Please.*

I don't say any of that. In fact, I don't say a thing—I simply turn and start inside, leaving the door ajar. I hear it close behind me, Blane's New Balances squeaking on the floor.

The Delatrix bottle catches my eye when I enter the kitchen. Right where I left it after I took my morning dose. An hour ago, at most. Plenty of time for Ally to make her presence known. That's why Blane's here—I'm sure of it. What other possible reason could there be?

I round the island, fix myself against the sink. Blane idles kitty-corner, hands buried deep in the pockets of his chinos. He scans the kitchen, then homes in on the glossy lookbook that arrived in the mail yesterday.

"You're going to UChicago?" I nod. "That's awesome. I did a campus visit there too actually. I bet you're playing basketball, right?"

"Why? Because sports are the only way I could've gotten in?"

"What? No!" Blane's eyes bulge. "Ally just told me you were really good. And I have some friends on our team—I go to Rush Tech." *Oh, I know.* "They said they tried everything and still couldn't stop you."

"Hm." I always did play well against Rush Tech. A little added motivation. "Yeah, I'm playing next year. After I recover."

"Oh, nice. I bet you'll be in the starting lineup pretty quick after that, huh?"

"Hm." If these compliments are Blane's attempt at sucking up to me, then I hate to break it to him, but it's not gonna work.

Okay, so maybe it's working a little.

"What about you?" I ask.

"Notre Dame," he says halfheartedly. "Just like my parents. It's where they met. Not my first choice, but it made them happy."

"Hm." That would suck, feeling obligated to go somewhere because your parents expected it. My mom went to some obscure liberal arts school downstate. I'd rather snort chili powder every day for four years than go to—

Wait! Am I actually starting to feel bad for this guy? Okay, this has officially gone far enough.

"Alright then . . ." I settle the small of my back against the edge of the sink and cross my arms. "Where is she?"

Blane knits his brows. "Sorry?"

"Don't play dumb with me, man. You've had your fun, but the joke's over. Just tell me where she is."

"What are you talking about?"

"Right, like you don't know." Cue eye roll. "How'd she do it? Are you taking Delatrix too, or has she found some new means of being seen?"

Blane still looks lost. And then, a wave of realization crashes over his face. "Wait, are you—you're talking about—" He lowers his register. *"Ally?"*

"Yeah."

"Did you not—hasn't anyone told you?" Blane looks horrified. "Ally's in the hospital."

If he's bluffing, then Blane deserves an Oscar for this performance. Or at least a Daytime Emmy. He's serious, isn't he? *Shit.* This one's on me, guys, my bad. Time to overcompensate.

"Psh, *whaaaat?* That's not—I wasn't referring to Ally . . . for obvious reasons . . . like the fact that she's in a coma . . ."

Nailed it. Wait a second—if Ally's not behind this, then why the fuck is Blane here? I put the question to him.

"Right. About that." Blane squirms where he stands. "Sorry, I know this is weird. Normally guys in our position never have to meet. It's just . . ." Blane grabs hold of the counter. Steadies himself. "I just miss her so much."

It comes out a whimper. Blane quickly turns away. Even in profile, I recognize the pain etched in his beleaguered expression. I've seen it in the mirror for months. And suddenly, despite my best efforts, I feel this bizarre sort of kinship with the guy. Sure, he'd pined after Ally the entire time we were together. Yes, he pounced the moment we split. True, when he spoke, it sounded like his uvula was slathered in peanut butter. But he clearly cared about Ally. Hell, if I'd been the one in his situation, I probably would've done the same thing.

"I'm good," he says, aggressively clearing his throat the way guys do when they don't want to cry in front of each other. "You know, I hated you for a long time," he says then, laughing a little. "Like, I couldn't even say your name without feeling sick."

I know the feeling.

Blane continues: "Like, full disclosure, man: I've been in love with Ally since before I hit puberty. When we were like ten, I actually tried telling her how I felt. She shut me down so fast I never worked up the courage to try it again. And then along comes this guy I've never met, and suddenly you're all she can talk about. It was 'Cam this,' 'Cam that.' And in my head, you know, I pictured you like this cartoonish bad guy in old high school movies. Throwing kids in lockers and shit." Laughing, Blane shakes his head. "But now that I've met you, you don't seem so bad."

"Give it time," I crack, and again he laughs. I feel a smile coming on. Seriously, what the fuck is happening to me right now?

"It's funny," he goes. "I don't even resent you anymore. You fell for her, same as I did. You know better than anyone how easy it was."

I steel myself. "Yeah." *Don't you dare start crying.* Jesus Christ, Cam, pull it together. Change the subject or something.

"It must suck for you too," I say. "You only got to date her for what—two weeks? Before her accident."

Blane knits his brows. "Two weeks? What do you mean?"

"You and Ally. You guys had been together a couple weeks before . . . you know."

Understanding lurches across Blane's expression. "Oh, you mean when we started dating *officially*. Yeah, it had only been a couple weeks."

I frown. "What did you think I meant?"

Blane hesitates. "Just, like, when we started hooking up."

"Oh." *Is he saying . . . ?* "Wait—hold on." I shouldn't ask. It isn't fair—to Blane or myself. Nothing good will come from this. And yet.

"When did you guys start hooking up?"

"What?" The blood drains from Blane's face. He heard me. I repeat myself anyway.

"You and Ally—when did you guys first hook up? What day?"

"I, uh, don't really feel comfortable sharing that information with—"

"Blane."

"So much has happened since then, it's hard to remember the exact date we—"

"Blane. You just admitted to being in love with Ally since you were kids. You expect me to believe you can't remember what day you first hooked up?"

I can sense the fight in him evaporate. He knows I'm right.

"January tenth."

I do the math. Suddenly my limbs go limp, my good knee buckles. Blane leaps into action, but I catch my balance at the last second.

"I'm fine!" I snap. Blane jumps back, hands raised, mouth agape, words stalling on the tip of his tongue.

"Look, bro, I dunno when you guys broke up, but Ally swore there wasn't any overlap. Otherwise I wouldn't have done it."

I hold the heels of my wrists over my eyes and scrub. "New Year's Day," I manage to bite out.

"Oh." Blane perks up. "You guys were done. So we're good. Right?"

I'm not listening. January tenth. Where was I that day? I think we had a game that day—my first post-breakup. I couldn't hit a shot. Wound up getting benched in the fourth quarter. I remember looking up in the stands. Spotting Chevy and Lisa in the front row of the student section, like always. But no Ally. Because she was with Blane.

Ten days. It took her ten days to move on from me. I turn to Blane, eyes wide, pleading. But this, he can't understand. How could he? Ally didn't annihilate his heart unprovoked. Our relationship meant that little to her. *I* meant that little to her.

"You need to leave," I say to Blane.

Blane starts to argue. "Bro, I know it's a small window, but—"

"Blane." He falls silent. "Get the fuck out of my house."

Blane can sense it, the dormant rage stirring inside me, slowly making its way to the surface. He makes the smart career choice. Without another word, Blane turns and walks out the way he came in. As soon as the door slams shut, a sob escapes my throat. Just the one; this isn't the time for crying. That's not what I'm feeling. A more appropriate response is in order.

I reach for the closest thing to me—the Delatrix bottle. Heft it in my hand. Unscrew the cap. Then hurl it blindly, as hard as I can. It connects with the refrigerator, a splash of red-and-white pills fanning out upon impact.

I could end this now. Grab a broom. Sweep away the capsules, the rest of my supply. Empty the dust pan in the dumpster outside. Unburden myself of Allison Tandy, at least in her current form.

But that would be too easy. I've already tried waiting around for Ally to explain herself. Not this time. Time to go on the offensive. Ally won't get away with this again. Which is why, in spite of my knee's objection, I find myself on the floor, gathering up the Delatrix pills, stuffing them one by one back into the bottle.

28

School's already started by the time Blane leaves. Seniors only have an hour anyway, so I decide to opt out entirely. POL-I and I have better things to do. I wheel her outside and plug her into the outlet behind the grill no one's touched since Dad left. A dab of sunscreen here, a tab of Delatrix there. On go the sunglasses and *voila!* Summer break, y'all.

I've cooled off a bit since earlier. Guys, I'm jazzed. Yeah, I said it. Fucking *jazzed*. And do you know why? Because for the first time since Ally's initial late-night ambush, I have the upper hand. So Blane's not such a bad guy after all. Hell, maybe Ally was right; maybe we would've been friends if we hadn't fallen for the same girl. But he slipped up—said more than he should have.

My lids start to grow heavy. Just as I start to nod off, everything goes dark. The temperature drops and I break out in goose bumps. I open my eyes, lower my shades. Not a cloud in the sky. Just Ally, towering overhead, looking down at me.

"Hi."

"Hi."

"Can I?" I shrug. She half sits on the edge of the adjacent chaise. "Last day of school."

"Yeah."

"Pretty crazy."

"It is."

Small talk isn't gonna cut it; we both know it. Ally breaks the seal. "I was hoping we could talk about the other night."

"Of course." I inch my sunglasses down the bridge of my nose. Originally, I'd planned to slow-play the Blane reveal, holding out until the perfect moment before unleashing it on her, just like she did the other night.

But now that she's here, well . . .

Why did you break up with me?

Yeah. No. This can't wait. Time to even the score.

"I had a visitor this morning." I leave her in suspense while I power POL-I down. "You mind explaining why Blane Duckworth paid me a visit?"

Ally's face collapses. "He didn't." It's delicious.

"He most certainly did."

"Cam, I—" Ally swallows her words. She pops up then and starts pacing the length of the deck, all the while massaging her temples with her thumbs. "I can't even begin to tell you how sorry I am, Cam," she says, which is something people do when they begin telling you how sorry they are. "I just— Why the *fuck* would he do that?"

"I have a theory."

Ally picks up what I'm putting down. "You think *I* had something to do with this?" She comes to an abrupt halt. "That's the last thing I want!" Shouting now. "I don't even know how he found your address."

"Probably Instagram geotag."

"What?"

"Never mind."

Neither of us speaks for a few moments. In the distance, a thumping sound. Speakers. Someone's blasting Kid Xannabis. The sounds of summer.

"You're mad," Ally says, ending the stalemate.

"It's fine," I say. "Totally fine. Couldn't be more fine. One hundred percent fine."

"You keep saying *fine*."

"Because it is."

I wait a beat.

Then another.

And then . . .

"So there I was! Minding my own business . . ."

Ally groans. "I knew it."

"Enjoying my breakfast! Catching up on my stories . . ."

"I get it, Cam."

"When who comes knocking at my door, but Mr. LinkedIn personified, flaunting his steam-pressed chinos and his stable two-parent household. Just what I needed today: a visit from my ex-girlfriend's new boyfriend."

"*Boyfriend?*" Ally spits the word like it's tainted. "Blane wasn't my boyfriend."

"He literally introduced himself as your boyfriend!" Suddenly I'm trembling with anger. *Of all the bald-faced lies* . . . The surge in adrenaline propels me to my feet. "Are you seriously about to lie about this too? It's not exactly breaking news, Al. Chevy told me you and Blane were exclusive *before* your accident."

"That's not—" Again, Ally's at a loss. She regroups. "Okay, yes, technically Blane and I were exclusive. But it wasn't like that. And he definitely wasn't my boyfriend. Not by a long shot."

"How is that any different?"

"It just is! I never thought of Blane in that way—regardless of how he interpreted it." I'm not buying it. Ally can tell. "Look, I know you think I lied to you about Blane, and I've been madly in love with him for years, and dating you was just a placeholder until I could be with him or whatever."

"I'd go with *warm-up* instead of *placeholder*," I sneer. "But yeah. That's basically it."

"Fine, warm-up, then," Ally shouts over me. "It doesn't matter, because it isn't true! Did I figure Blane had a crush on me? Yeah, Cam, I did. You were right. Another guy who was only friends with me because he liked looking down my shirt. I *so* appreciate the reminder."

I start to argue, but Ally rounds on me, snapping her fingers, shutting me up. She gets right in my face, practically standing on my toes.

"Put yourself in my shoes," she says. "Try walking into school after a devastating breakup and finding out the entire student body—including some people you've never even spoken to—

they've all already taken your ex's side. *Team Cam*," she mocks. "Those dumb fucking shirts. And oh, by the way, the two people who made them? Your *friends* Chevy and Lisa? Not anymore! They won't even look at you!

"Maybe I got tired of feeling like complete shit—did you ever think of that, Cam? Maybe I got tired of driving past the water tower on my way to school and seeing TEAM CAM painted across it. Maybe I went looking for a confidence boost in the one place I was guaranteed to find one. And yeah, I figured you'd find out eventually." She clenches her jaw. "Maybe I liked the thought of that too."

We stare each other down for a moment. The silence seems to stretch.

"Believe what you want," Ally scoffs, ratcheting down the hostility in her tone. "But I'm not in love with Blane Duckworth. He was a rebound—that's it. And I had nothing to do with him coming over here earlier. You're the only person I've had any contact with since . . ." She flits her hand in the air. "*This* happened."

The laundry list of unanswered questions isn't going away, but for a moment they don't seem quite so pressing. Something's happening inside me, spreading quickly, infecting my nervous system at lightning speed.

Relief.

Ally wanted to make me jealous. She cared enough to want to make me jealous. And knowing that makes me . . . *happy*? How fucked up is that?! But look, after months thinking she could give two shits about me, waiting anxiously for a text that would never come, I finally have proof she wasn't itching to jump right into the next thing.

Ally's staring at me intently, watching me process in real time. She absentmindedly scratches the back of her head, messing her hair. I'm still not used to it being short like this. Back when we were together, her hair would always interfere while we hooked up, snaking in between our swollen lips until we'd come up giggling for air. Ally would pull it back, quickly stashing the troublemaking strands behind her ears. Then we'd get back to it. Ally wouldn't have that problem with her hair at its current length. Not with Blane. I wonder if she cut it before they started hooking up.

And then I remember.

Ten days. It takes longer for milk to spoil. For a mosquito to complete its life cycle. For Kate Hudson to lose Matthew McConaughey.

Bitterness curdles in my belly, crowding my intestines. Blinding white rage paints my vision until I can't see Ally or the patio or the rest of my backyard. The faint rumble of my own voice cuts through the fray.

"I had sex with Steff."

Color returns to my vision in time to see it drain from Ally's face. "Say that again." It isn't a request. Something's happening with her eyes. They're expanding, swelling to unholy dimensions. Seriously, her face is like thirty percent eye. Is it just me, or are they turning red?

"Uh, well . . . me and Steff," I squeak. "We, uh . . . you know."

"You told me you were over her." Her voice is a glacial monotone.

"I was—I mean, I am!"

"We pinky promised."

"I know. But it only happened once. It's not like we're dating or anything." I can't help myself. "Not like you and Blane."

Ally stills. "Blane and I haven't had sex."

I scoff. "*Right*, okay."

Her breath quickens. "I'm telling the truth." Tears percolate in the rims around her eyes. "I told him I wanted to wait." She clenches her lids together, as tight as she can, but before long the tears are streaming down her cheeks. "I wasn't ready to do it with someone else. Someone who wasn't you."

Then, Ally begins to weep. Silently, her entire body shuddering under the weight of each muted sob. She's being serious, I realize, and again I feel a surge of relief. *What is wrong with me?!* In an effort to comfort her, I reach for her exposed shoulder.

Big mistake.

"Don't fucking touch me!" Ally explodes, rocketing out of reach. I snap my hand back, raise my arms overhead in a defensive posture.

"Can I just say, in my defense, I don't think it's very fair of you to hold this against me, considering you just admitted going out with Blane because you knew it would make me jealous."

"That's completely different," Ally sneers.

"How?"

"Because you didn't get your heart broken *and* lose your entire friend group overnight." She's battling another wave. This time, she manages to hold them at bay. "And because you were the one who dumped me in the first place."

"What!" I try—and fail—a second time to jump to my feet. "Allison, stop with these bullshit mind games. *You* broke up with *me*."

"I AM NOT DOING THIS WITH YOU AGAIN!"

I throw up my hands. "Alright, alright." As I gradually rise to my feet, I say, "Look, obviously we've both done things intended to hurt each other. You had Blane, I had Steff. We're even now, yes?"

Ally drops the menacing scowl, and as I lower my arms, I think maybe—*just maybe!*—she agrees. There are more important things to discuss. And then I hear it.

Cackling.

Low and menacing, growing louder by the second. The kind of hair-raising bark you'd expect from a deranged serial killer, or the Joker moments before he cooks a hospital. Before I can react, she grabs me by the collar, hauls me down to her eye level. "I'm sorry, Cammie." *Why's she smiling at me like that?* "But you broke our pinky promise. Now you must face the consequences. So, no, we are NOT even." She tightens her grip. "But we will be."

"What the hell does that"—*poof*—"mean?"

The pixels composing her complexion erode from view until I can see right through the space and time she occupied only moments earlier, as though she's been cropped from the frame, her ominous threat and the unshakable recollection of her demonic grin the only proof that she'd ever been here at all.

29

When I finally check my phone, I have eleven missed calls. Ten from Chevy, the other from Lisa. Like, fifty texts from them too. I skip to the most recent one.

CHEVY:

> You have 5 minutes to call me back before we come and drag you over here

Sent four minutes ago.

Chevy answers on the first ring. "CAAAAM!" He's shouting to hear himself over the drunken symphony in the background. "Where are *yooou*?" Slurring. He's trashed. Just what I need right now. "Dude, get here *NOW*!"

I hear him addressing his congregation. "Should Cam . . . should he get his ass over here?" His flock whoops and hollers. To me: "The people have spoken."

"I'm not sure I'm up for it tonight. Something happened earlier—you know the guy Ally started dating after me? He showed up at my door and—"

Chevy groans, drowning me out. "Is this about Ally again?

Dude, I cannot talk about this shit right now. Quit being such a fucking buzzkill. This is our night! High school's over! You're really gonna sit in your house sulking over some girl who didn't even want to be with you? That's what you're about right now?"

Background commotion on Chevy's end; someone asking about the bathroom. I sit in silence as Chevy shouts back directions.

"Fukkit," he says finally. "Either get your ass over here or find a new best friend."

The line goes dead.

THE FEDS MUST be taking the night off; I can hear drum machines coming from Chevy's the minute I step outside my house.

Inside Chevy's house, it's bedlam. More people than I can count. Upstairs, downstairs, spilling out into the backyard, all the way down to the beach. Like we're in a real Hollywood high school movie. Before I've even made it to the kitchen, I'm stopped by no fewer than three people, each one declaring with boozy sincerity how much they'll miss me next year. Give it a week; half these kids will be knocking down my mom's door with "mono-like symptoms." Among the crowd, I notice a few people wearing their SAVE ALLY ringer shirts. That's all they are now, a memento from senior year—Hey, remember when that girl from high school crashed her car and fell into a coma? Another T-shirt at the bottom of their dressers for when they don't feel like doing laundry.

I do a lap around the first floor. No sign of Chevy. I try my luck out back. Outside, the air is thick with skunk weed. I even see someone holding a real live cigarette like it's 1950 or something. Suddenly, someone shrieks my name.

"Cam!"

I about-face and spot Lisa, carving her way through the throng. "Where have you been all day?" she asks, lassoing me into a hug. "We've been trying to reach you." Her nose is bright pink. Someone's been out in the sun all day. Drinking too, from the looks of it, the way her hands linger on my traps.

"I had a thing." I peer over her head, scanning the premises. "Where's Chevy?"

"He's inside. No, wait!" Lisa teeters. "The beach, I think. Yeah, he and some people went to see if they could start a bonfire. I told him it wouldn't work but he didn't wanna listen." Lisa makes a face: *It is what it is.* "Hey, guess what?" She slides her hands to my chest. "Jeannie told me she likes you."

"No she didn't."

"Okay, so maybe she didn't use those *exact* words. But she had fun at dinner!"

"No she didn't."

"Okay, so maybe she thought you were a little weird. But I filled her in and she totally gets it. She dated this college guy, Gunner, off and on for a couple of years, so she knows all about how breakups can make a person crazy."

"That sounds problematic."

Lisa waves it off. "It's *fine*, he's only given her chlamydia like twice." She glances around suspiciously, then motions for me to come closer. "Just so you know, I didn't tell Jeannie about what happened this weekend." I give her a look. "Chevy filled me in."

"Did he now?"

Lisa nods excessively. "You wanted to drag him to that guy's house. The one Ally was dating—what was his name again? Blake? Blaze? I can't—I'm too drunk to remember. But don't you worry." She jams her knuckle on my sternum. "Your secret's safe with me." Lisa pantomimes locking her lips, throwing away the imaginary key. "For what it's worth, I totally get where you're coming from. If you'd gone through with it, I would've supported it."

"Really?"

"Oh yeah!" Lisa doubles down. "I mean, you always knew that guy was after Ally. Then she starts hooking up with him right after you guys break up? No, sir. Doesn't sit right with me."

While she talks, Lisa reaches around my neck and tucks in my tag on my T-shirt. If an uninformed third party walked by and saw us right now, it might look as though Lisa and I were moments from kissing. Especially if that third party was Chevy. Give him a taste of real jealousy, not that watered-down version he's concocted for himself.

Or I could do him one better.

"Wow, Lis, thanks for being so cool about it. I know someone who's going to be very relieved to hear you feel that way."

Lisa's still cheesing. "What do you mean?" Not for long.

"We didn't go to Blane Duckworth's house."

"Yeah. Because Chevy talked you out of it."

285

I shake my head. "It was never about Blane, Lis. It was Teddy Hall's house."

Lisa laughs a little, looking confused. "Teddy's house? Why would you be jealous of Teddy?"

I arch an eyebrow. It takes her a second. Then another. (Alcohol, man.) And then . . .

"You mean . . ." I nod. "Chevy was the . . ." Still nodding. "You went to Teddy's?" I could do this all night, but Lisa's off her game. I give her an assist.

"Look, Chevy just wanted to talk to Teddy. You know, man to man. See if there was any funny business going on between you two. But don't worry, Chevy came to his senses. Once he got to Teddy's front porch."

Lisa's jaw hinges open. "But Chevy said—"

I cut her off. "Chevy blamed me because he didn't want you to get pissed at him. Plus, let's be honest, who wouldn't believe a story like that about me?" Time for the grand finale. "Doesn't it sound like something I would do?"

I force a laugh. Lisa doesn't reciprocate. She casts her gaze across the dune in the direction of the burgeoning flame taking shape, the cluster of bodies stumbling around it. Lisa looks like she might scream. Or cry. Both?

"Look, if it makes you feel any better—"

"Shut the fuck up, Cam." The playfulness is gone; Lisa sobered up real quick. She recoils from me, scowls at the water another minute, then disappears inside the house. Something tells me she won't be spending the night.

I follow her example, head for the exits. If eight years of friend-ship hinges on a single party, then maybe Chevy and I weren't such good friends in the first place. Besides, look around. He won't have any trouble finding a new best friend, if that's what he wants.

Even as I'm leaving, new groups continue rolling in. Not just seniors either, from the looks of it. No wonder things are spiral-ing out of control. I'm halfway home when I hear—

"Cam?"

Bridget Kaplan peels off from her pack, stepping out into the street. She bounces right up to me and yanks me into a hug. Didn't realize we were that close, but I'm not exactly complaining.

"Did you just come from inside?" Bridget asks, her breath vodka-soaked. Behind her, the kids she came with are idling, not-so-subtly eavesdropping. Girls in front, guys in back. Taking the lead, whoever has an in.

Oh. I'm their contact, I realize. Bridget just wants an easy way inside for her and her friends.

"The side door's open, guys," I say. "No one's checking." Whooping and thanks follow as they make their way by.

Except for Bridget.

"You're not staying?"

"Nah, I've caused enough damage tonight."

"Ha! Been there." Bridget extends her bottom lip. "Too bad. We could've continued our conversation from last week."

Yeah, I think. It is too bad. And then, before I can talk myself out of it, I'm like, "Hey, can I ask you a question?" Bridget nods.

"At Jake Cooper's party last week, would it have been weird if I'd asked you out?"

Without skipping a beat. "Not at all."

"Huh. Good to know." I laugh to myself. *At* myself. "And now? Would it be weird if I asked you out now?"

"Are you?"

A beat. "Yes?"

"Yes."

"Yes, you want to go out?"

"Yes, it would be weird."

"Oh."

"But that doesn't mean I'd say no."

"Oh!"

Bridget chases after the rest of her friends a couple minutes later—after she's texted her number from my phone and added a new event to my calendar.

Tomorrow @6:30. Dinner w/Bridget

SOWING CHAOS IS exhausting work. I head straight to bed when I get home. Just as my consciousness wanes, I remember—POL-I! But when I flip her switch, nothing happens. I flip it again. Did she come unplugged? I dig my phone out of my pocket and switch on the flashlight, shining it at the wall socket. POL-I's cord is still embedded; I track it from the socket, along the cord, until the beam reaches her. As she comes into focus, my heart sinks.

"POL-I, NOOOOOOO!"

Hello, 911? I'd like to report a murder!

"You're gonna be okay, old girl. Just hang on." My words conceal the reality of the damage; POL-I's in bad shape. Her display screen's been caved in, with multiple points of impact. Frantically I start pressing buttons—one at a time, then all at once.

But it's no use. She's gone.

That's when I see the Post-it note tacked to one of the suction tubes.

Hastily scribbled in all caps: YOU'RE NEXT.

30

"Maizy."

My sister's asleep.

"Maizy!"

Mom won't wake her up for another hour or so.

"MaizyMaizyMaizy!"

Unfortunately for her, I need her up and at 'em.

"Uhhhhhh," Maizy whines, ducking her head under her comforter. "Cameron, I'm sleeping."

"Sleep? Sleep! Maiz, do you think the women of the US national team sleep this late? No! They're up before the sun so they can practice with their super-cool brothers. Now, let's see some hustle."

"Uhhhhhh."

Look, I'm not proud of this. Under ordinary circumstances, I'm the last guy advocating for extra practice. Four years on varsity, and not once did I show up for voluntary workouts. But these aren't ordinary circumstances. POL-I's murder made that clear.

As I tossed and turned and winced my way through another

sleepless night (only made worse by POL-I's absence), it occurred to me that in spite of all the time we'd spent together, the full extent of Ally's supernatural powers remained a mystery to me. Now that she's on the warpath, there's no telling what she might be capable of.

I've seen enough horror movies to know that any evil spirit worth their weight begins a successful haunting with the little kid. Which is exactly why I wake Maizy up as early as I do—for her own protection. And not at all because I'm convinced every bump on the roof or creak in the floorboards is Ally coming to finish me once and for all.

Completely unrelated, you wouldn't happen to have any holy water on you, would you? Silver bullets? No?

I can only use Maizy as a human shield for so long before I'm forced to drop her off at school. Then it's just me. Alone. In this enormous hundred-year-old house. Nothing creepy about that. If I can just keep it together a few more hours, everything will be—*WHAT WAS THAT?!*

Just my phone, thank Christ. An incoming call from Chevy. He probably wants help cleaning after last night's festivities. Not gonna happen. I let it go to voicemail. No sooner has my phone fallen silent than I hear the patio door fly open and slam shut.

"Cam!" Chevy. In real life this time. Screaming bloody fucking murder. *"CAM!"*

"One sec," I shout back. Guess he doesn't need help cleaning.

In the kitchen, I find Chevy furiously pacing laps around the island like the floor is lava and if he stands still for too long, he'll burn alive. He looks off. For one, he's glowering. Almost looks ready for a fight. Is that what he's come for?

"If you're here to break up with me as your best friend, you could've just done it over text," I quip, hoping to cut the tension.

Chevy stops on a dime and glares at me. "You told her!" His bottom lip quivers. "You fucking told Lisa!" His eyes are soaked. "Why?"

Oh. Right. That.

Amid all the uncertainty with Ally, I'd almost forgotten my little confession to Lisa. Guess she confronted him about it.

I try playing dumb. "Is this about the Jeannie date? Because Lisa and I already cleared the air. Everything's cool."

Chevy slams the counter with his fist. "You know exactly what I'm talking about! You told Lisa what we did! You told her we went to Teddy's."

Time to roll out the prepackaged excuses.

"It was an accident. The whole thing just slipped out."

"Something like that doesn't just slip out!"

Next.

"I was drunk."

"I thought you weren't drinking while you're taking Delatrix?"

Next.

"She figured it out on her own."

"Bullshit she did!"

Next.

"My clone did it."

Then, a fatal mistake: I giggle.

"You think this is *funny?*" Chevy's expression mangles in agony. "Lisa just fucking dumped me, and you're over here making jokes?"

Wait, did he just say—?

My chest tightens. "Wait, what?"

"She broke—" Chevy falters. He looks green, like he might yuke any second.

"That—that's impossible," I stammer. Because it *has* to be. Because I *need* it to be. Chevy and Lisa are *The* Happy Couple. So Chevy did some dumb shit—big deal. That's not worth pulling the plug on a five-year relationship. Right? If Chevy and Lisa can't navigate this stuff, then what hope is there for any of us?

I go on the defensive. "It's not like you can blame me for that. Lisa was the one who brought it up! She kept going on and on about how she didn't fault me for wanting to confront Ally's boyfriend, how she understood the impulse. I figured she wouldn't care if I told her what really happened. Seriously, Chev, I thought she'd laugh."

I didn't. But it never occurred to me she might leave him over this. Lisa's the one who escalated the situation, not me. Come to think of it, Chevy's the one who set this whole thing off.

"And I hate to be *that guy*"—I don air quotes—"but in my defense, you were the one who lied in the first place and told her it was me. If you'd just been honest . . ." I offer a shrug as an answer to my own rhetorical.

Chevy's facade cracks; a single sob springs from the back of his throat, causing his whole body to shudder. "I was going to tell her—I swear! After graduation, when everything calmed down. I just needed to buy a little time."

He's pleading his case; for me or for himself, I can't tell.

"But now I won't even get the chance. All because *you* went and fucked everything up!"

I scoff. "Alright, simmer down over there. Should I have spilled the beans to Lisa? No, probably not. Was it a dick move? Perhaps. Do I regret it? With all my heart."

"Stop asking yourself easy rhetorical questions!"

"Fine. You want an honest answer? *I* told you not to go snooping through her socials. *I* told you not to agree to an open relationship if you didn't want one. *I* told you driving to Teddy's was a mistake. *You* freaked out over nothing. *You* made me the fall guy. *You* were the one who couldn't sack-up and talk to your fucking girlfriend about what you want next year!"

Chevy isn't listening. "And here I thought you were looking out for me. That's part of the deal when you're someone's best friend. You look out for them."

He gestures wildly to an invisible audience. "Look around, man! Lisa and I are the only ones left on Team Cam. You have been a complete buzzkill all fucking year. Do you have any idea how obnoxious it is, listening to you constantly whine about Ally? Even after the accident! She almost died and you're still out here complaining about your stupid breakup. Everyone got sick of it! But Lisa and I kept trying. Even when you acted like an ungrateful toddler, we kept trying. And *this* is how you repay me?"

Bile rises in my throat. "I had no idea I was such a charity case."

"Jesus Christ, *that's* your takeaway?!" Chevy throws his head back. "I can't with your shit right now."

"Maybe you were onto something last night," I say, folding my arms, willing my eyes to stay dry. "Maybe our friendship ends with high school and we leave it at that."

Chevy seems taken aback. For a moment I think—I hope—he'll call my bluff. I can admit I fucked up telling Lisa what I did. He can retract what he said about Ally. Together, we can move forward.

But then his brows knit, his nostrils flare, his jaw sets.

"Yeah, maybe we should."

Neither of us speaks for a while. Eventually, Chevy turns his back to me. "Fuck this. I'm done."

"Fine."

"Fine."

Ladies and gentlemen, for the first time in history: a mutual breakup.

SIRI, TAKE THE wheel. Tonight is date night.

I'm driving north, headed to the address Bridget texted me a little while ago. When did dating become the only thing going well in my life? Weird. Earlier, I considered canceling; now hardly seems like the right time to put myself out there. But then, wasn't this the point all along? Chevy, Lisa, Ally—*they* were the ones who pushed me into this. Find a rebound. One could argue bailing on Bridget would only make my situation worse.

Yeah, let's go with that.

I shoot Bridget a message when I pull up to her house. An old colonial, impeccably landscaped. It takes a few minutes before she emerges. Clinging to Bridget's shoulders is a shawl of some kind, blanket-like, swishing by her calves with each step. Once Bridget clears the property line, she sheds it. I nearly choke on my gum.

Her top is exceedingly low-cut. The straps don't collide until her navel, in what has to be the deepest V-neck ever made. She can't be walking in slow motion, can she? Probably just a mirage. Blame the heat. Or the male brain. Or the pills. One of them. All of them.

"Hey, Cam!" Bridget gives a little wave as she steps off the curb. I wave back, reaching across the passenger seat to shove her door open. Neither of us is sure how we're supposed to greet each other once she climbs into the cab. We settle for an awkward hug over the clutch, made worse when I impulsively decide to kiss the top of her head, the way a good-natured grandparent might.

We're off to a banner start.

I hadn't given our date itinerary much thought. So when Bridget asks, "Where to?" my instincts take over. Next thing I know, we're at Walker Bros. Pancake House. I'm sure Ally won't mind sharing our spot with someone else.

Bridget and I follow the hostess to a table by the window. We're joined by a middle-aged couple in the corner booth trying to salvage their marital spark at the bottom of a maple syrup bottle. Judging from his resting stink face and her empty shark-eyed stare, it's not going well. God, I hope I never turn forty.

"So I know girls don't like it when guys order for them"—*terrible way to start a sentence*—"because of, you know, sexism." *How are you making this worse?* "But I highly recommend the chocolate chip pancakes. Best thing here. If you order anything else, I'm legally obligated to contact the proper authorities." *Great, now you're threatening her. Why don't you go home and leave this poor girl be?*

I scrub my face. "Sorry, that was weird, wasn't it?"

"No, no! It's okay!" Remarkably, Bridget's laughing. "Normally, yeah, I wouldn't be thrilled about a guy ordering for me. But obviously these chocolate chip pancakes are very important to you. I can appreciate being passionate about something."

I tried ordering for Ally once when we first started dating. I'd seen it on one of those "dating guru" YouTube channels. *"Ordering for her shows confidence and subtly asserts your dominance over the situation,"* the haircut in the ten-thousand-dollar suit promised. *"Trust me, she'll be impressed."*

Ally had not been impressed.

"Order for me again and you're walking home," she threatened. Complicating matters, I'd actually been the one who drove us to the restaurant. But I didn't push my luck.

Bridget's still scanning her menu.

"Unfortunately, I'll have to pass on the chocolate chip pancakes. I actually just found out I'm allergic to chocolate. And gluten. And chocolate-flavored gluten."

"Seriously?"

Bridget's eyes flit to meet mine. A joke, I realize, and now I'm laughing. We're both laughing. *Look at us laughing!*

God, I wish Ally was here so I could rub it in her face. Of course, the one time a date goes well and she's not here.

Our waitress, Ginny, is an older woman with permed chestnut hair. She calls us *dearies*. We put in our orders: egg whites and grapefruit for Bridget ("sugar on the side"), the aforementioned chocolate chippies for me. As she collects our menus, Ginny chirps an encouraging "You kids have fun now."

Right. Fun. This is supposed to be fun. And nothing's more fun than a list of predetermined conversation starters! Discreetly, I place my phone on the table and tap open the Notes app. Earlier, while I was getting ready, I googled "things to talk about on first date." I'd jotted a few things down, then sprinkled in some topics of my own. The key, though, would be bringing things up organically.

"How's SAT prep going?" I sound like a nosy parent.

"Where do you see yourself in five years?" Like a job interviewer.

"Favorite color, don't explain why." Like a camp counselor.

"Are you okay, Cam?" Bridget cocks her head to one side and squints at me. "You seem nervous."

"*Me?* Nervous? What gave you that impression?" My eye twitches. "Is it really that obvious?"

"Little bit. You also have what looks like a list of conversation starters open in front of you. Looks like it's called . . ." Bridget leans across the table, her head turned so she can read from my screen. She smells nice. "How to Have a Camtastic Conversation," Bridget recites. She sits back down. The booth lets out a whoosh. "You were that worried about talking to me?"

"No!" *Just tell her.* "I mean, kinda." *She'll find it endearing.* "Completely terrified." *I take it back—you shouldn't have said anything!* "It's just—I haven't done this in a while."

"Gone on a first date?"

I nod. "My first date with my ex was in my kitchen. During a checkup." I cringe. "Thanks for that, Mom."

"Believe it or not, I've actually been to your house for an impromptu exam," Bridget admits, offering that generous laugh again. She doesn't mention Ally by name. I'm grateful. "My ex took me to a party for our first date. He asked me to be his beer pong partner, then yelled at me when we lost."

"What a romantic," I crack.

"Tell me about it. Should've been my first clue he was the worst."

Who did Bridget date before this? I rack my brain but come up empty. In any case, I return the favor and don't ask.

"So what you're saying is, as long as I make it through dinner without yelling, I'll be in great shape."

Her smile invites mine. "Exactly."

Things settle after that, and by the time Ginny returns with our plates, I don't even need my list of conversation starters anymore. I learn Bridget was born in London and her family moved to the States when she was two. She auditioned for the role of

Penny in the theater department's production of *Hairspray* this spring, but settled for the chorus. She's killed at least two iPhones because she insists on texting in the shower. She loves all of her siblings equally, but baby Mikey (the youngest) is her favorite. She prefers Twizzlers to Red Vines, the Cubs to the Sox. We're so busy chatting that I barely make a dent in my pancakes.

Okay, I eat most of them.

Okay, I eat *all* of them! Happy?

I get the feeling things are going well, but it isn't until after dinner, once I've paid the check and Bridget and I are back in the Geo, that I realize just *how* well.

"Where to next?" Bridget asks once we're buckled in.

"Oh." A burst of terror surges through me. A second location? No one prepared me for this! "We could grab dessert or something? Have you ever been to Sprinkles?"

Bridget shakes her head, but I get the sense she isn't sold on the idea.

"How about the beach? The movies? Mini-golf? I have some EpiPens in my glove box; we could take those and see what happens."

"Maybe another time," Bridget says, locking and unlocking her phone absentmindedly. Great, now she sounds noncommittal. Maybe I had this all wrong. Maybe she's having a terrible time and can't wait for this to be over.

"If you're tired, I can just take you home," I offer, conceding defeat.

"I'm not tired," Bridget says quickly. "I feel great, actually."

Okay, now I'm really confused. On the one hand, she doesn't want to go home. On the other, she's shot down every suggestion I've made. What else could we possibly—

Oh. *Ohhhhhhh.*

"Did you, uh . . . you know?" My heartbeat picks up the pace. "Wanna go back, uh . . . back to my house?"

Bridget teases a closed-lip smile. Nods gently. She's as nervous as I am, I remind myself, because it's easy to forget when your armpits could double as a Slip 'N Slide.

31

Mom's watching TV in the family room when we pull into the driveway; the screen waltzes across the curtains. I'm banking on her being asleep, an empty bottle of Chardonnay still clutched against her chest. Just to be safe, we sneak in through the back and tiptoe straight down to the basement. Bridget's all for the covert operation—turns out, most people don't want to run into their doctor when they're about to get it in.

We let out a collective exhale once we're safely downstairs. "Oh my God," Bridget gasps. "That was intense."

"Yeah, seriously," I pant, stealing another peek up the stairwell to ensure we weren't followed.

"My heart's beating so fast," Bridget says, holding her hand flat over her chest like she's saying the pledge. "Here, feel." She takes my hand and guides it to her "heart."

"That is fast," I say. "Mine's racing too."

I mirror her move, lift her free hand to my heart. And now we're just two people with our hands casually pressed against each other's chests. It's a game of chicken—each of us waiting for the other to make the first move—one we're both losing the longer my clammy hand rests awkwardly on her upper boob.

So I close my eyes, slowly twist my neck to the side, and lean forward.

Lips are a lot like fingerprints—maybe even more unique in some ways. No two ever feel the same when mushed against your own. It's an entirely unique experience, despite requiring a partner. The catch is, you can't know what yours feel like to the other person.

And if the person on the other end of the kiss can't know the feeling of their own lips on yours, how could they even begin to understand theirs are the only lips you ever want to mush on again? Or how the prospect of dating long distance isn't an obstacle but an inconvenience so long as those lips are waiting on the other side? Or how your fear of other guys like Blane stemmed not just from jealousy, but frustration at your own inability to articulate just how fucking happy she made you? Because she did. She does. Even after everything.

Bridget's lips are nice, though.

Next thing I know, we're horizontal, and Bridget's tongue is sparring with my tonsils. Below deck, she tussles with the drawstring on my shorts. The knot is tricky and demands her full attention. She briefly rips her mouth from mine. When they return, my shorts are on the floor. Right next to her shirt.

It's been a minute since I've seen a girl naked in person, and I find myself transfixed. Bridget has on a flesh-colored bra. Clasps in the front. At first glance, I'd wager her left is bigger than her right. (Ally was the opposite.) They are equally captivating. There's an adorable mole next to her belly button—an outie, by the way. Don't see many of those.

"Wow," I say. "You are . . ." *Say something sexy. Or romantic. Something sexy and romantic.* "So hot." *Nailed it.*

As we braid our bodies together, Bridget's careful to avoid my cast, even going so far as to ask repeatedly, "Is this okay?" and "Am I hurting you?" Still, there are a couple instances where an errant limb knocks into it, causing me to grimace. Occupational hazard. The fact that Bridget's being so careful, so outwardly kind, is a change of pace for me. Strangely intoxicating. Deserves to be rewarded.

Gradually, my right hand begins its descent, tracing down Bridget's chest . . . her stomach . . . her pelvis. Bridget tenses when it reaches its destination. Her eyes flutter closed and she lets out a hushed moan—*"Yes"*—as her body relaxes into my grip.

Then, and only then, does it sink in that yes, this is happening, yes, I am going to have sex with someone other than Ally. Other than Steff. Other than an ex. An entirely new person who finds me attractive enough to allow me to fumble around inside of her. Nothing can derail this now, not even—

"Look at you, just diving right in on the first date."

I stiffen. She wouldn't.

"Remember the first time you did that with me?"

Not like this. Not right now.

"You just stuck one in and let it sit there; I had to show you a YouTube tutorial."

I lift my gaze. Ally's seated just beyond Bridget's unsuspecting head, looking all sorts of pleased with herself.

The interruption hasn't gone unnoticed. "Cam? Is everything okay?" Bridget asks.

Ally snorts. "Yeah, Cam. Is everything okay?"

"Everything's fine," I say to Bridget without breaking eye contact with Ally. "Just needed a second to catch my breath."

My fingers come back online. Bridget seems to buy my explanation. She offers an encouraging smile before her eyes roll back in her head.

WHAT ARE YOU DOING? I mouth carefully, painstakingly exaggerating each syllable so she'll get the message.

It works; Ally reads my lips. "Oh, don't mind me. I'm just here to enjoy the show," she claims, smile ranging from ear to ear. I'm fully aware she's just trying to get under my skin. So why is it still so goddamn effective?

Still mouthing: *THIS ISN'T FUNNY.*

"I don't know, Cammie. From this side of the couch, it's pretty funny."

GO AWAY!

"Ugh, you never let me have any fun," Ally huffs. "Fine. I can tell when I'm not wanted. Even though you clearly could use some assistance."

My eyes dart to Bridget. Still oblivious, preoccupied by sensation. When I look back, Ally's vanished. Good riddance.

Where does she get off trying to ruin this for me? She

explicitly said she wanted me to hook up with someone else. She got her wish.

But even after Ally's gone, I can't seem to recoup the rhythm Bridget and I established before. I'm too pissed, too paranoid about another appearance. I remain on high alert until Bridget makes it clear she's primed and ready to go.

"Do you have a condom?" she asks after hauling me in for another kiss.

"Lemme check," I say, feigning ignorance. Just this morning, I'd slipped a condom in my wallet. Quadruple-checked before I left. But when I track down my shorts, flip open my wallet, all I find are credit cards and my deli punch card.

"Looking for something?" Ally waves at me from behind the wet bar, condom snared between her first and middle fingers.

ARE YOU FUCKING KIDDING ME?

"Language, Cammie."

My blood's boiling. Ally's gone too far this time. She broke up with me. She didn't want me. I'm not about to let her ruin this for me too.

"I have to run to the bathroom!" I announce suddenly, glaring Ally down.

"Everything alright?" Bridget looks at me with concern. "Was it something you ate? The same thing happens to my little brother when he eats too much sugar. Here, I might have Pepto in my purse."

Ally snorts. Nails on a chalkboard.

"Nope, nothing like that," I say, already teetering toward the bathroom. "I'll just be a minute. Make yourself at home. The Wi-Fi password is 16—like the number—Handles. Uppercase H in *Handles*."

When Bridget turns, I level a glare at Ally. It's met with an eye roll.

"Yeah, yeah, I'm coming."

BREATHE. BREATHE.

The bathroom door slams closed behind me.

Breathe. Breathe.

I lock us in. Start the fan. Run the sink. White noise. Try to compose myself.

BreatheBreatheBreatheBrea—

It doesn't take.

"WHAT THE FUCK IS WRONG WITH YOU?"

Ally situates her waist on the grooved radiator cover and leans the back of her head against the dated floral wallpaper Mom always complains about but never replaces. She snickers to herself. Barely perceptible by design. The big stupid grin on her big stupid face gives her away.

"Okay, I know you're mad. But can you really blame me? This is, like, the most high-school-ass hookup I've ever seen. Watching that made me physically ill." She mimes dry heaving. Added effect.

"Why are you here?" I demand. "This is next-level petty— even for you!"

Ally looks at me warily. "Same reason I've been here all along.

To help you. Speaking of, you might want to ease up on the teeth."
She bares hers. "I got used to it while we were dating, but most
girls don't want to feel like a chew toy while they're making out."

I didn't use teeth that much . . . did I?

She's just trying to burrow her way under my skin—I know
that! I just hate that it's working.

"Nobody asked for your advice, alright? I know what I'm
doing."

Ally snorts. "Oh really? Here's a game. Let's see if you can
guess how many times I finished while we were having sex."

A knot coils in my stomach. "I don't like this game."

"Come on, it'll be fun."

"It definitely won't be."

"Just gimme your best estimate." It's a trap. Of course it's a
trap! She wouldn't be asking me right now if the number was
high. She wouldn't be asking me right now if she wasn't sure curiosity would get the better of me.

"I don't know. Like . . . half the time?"

"HA! You're joking, right?"

"No, I'm not joking!"

"Okay, well, I promise you, it was *a lot* less than half!"

My heart sinks. "I don't believe you." I sound thoroughly
unconvincing, but what other choice do I have? When our relationship imploded, I took solace in the fact that she enjoyed hooking up with me. Those intimate moments were real, even if the
rest was a lie. But if she never finished, then . . .

Don't go there, Cam. "Is this about Steff?" I ask, pivoting as fast as possible. "Because I already apologized."

Ally's mouth gapes open. "Of course not. Why would I be upset about you sleeping with Steff? It's not like I didn't expect you to go running to her as soon as you had the chance."

"Goddamnit!" I'm approaching full volume. A sharp pain sears between my ribs. My left eyelid keeps twitching. "I'm gonna kill you."

"Might be a little late for that. And I'd suggest you keep your voice down. We wouldn't want your little friend out there to think you're talking to yourself. Or worse. What's usually happening when someone rushes to the bathroom?" I don't need her smirk to figure out what she's getting at, but she provides it nonetheless. "It's in your best interest to hurry back out there."

"Okay . . ." I close my eyes and force a calming breath. Form prayer hands above my nose, driving my palms flat against one another, bending my wrists until they've reached their limit. "Here's what we're gonna do." I let my hands fall to my sides. "I'm gonna go back out there and have sex with Bridget Kaplan. And you are gonna pretend you aren't the world's most possessive ex-girlfriend for like twenty minutes—"

"More like three." Her lips are more scowl than smirk now.

"Stay in here, go somewhere else. Doesn't matter to me. Maybe you can go haunt someone who actually gives a shit about you. If there's anyone left."

Her expression wilts entirely. "Fine. Go have your fun with

diet *me.* I'm done interfering." She takes a beat, and for a second, I think I've won. "Oh, but, Cam? One last thing."

"What!" I snap. "What else could you possibly want?"

Ally gestures at my right hand. "Didn't you have a Band-Aid on your finger earlier?"

"What does that have to do with—"

Oh no.

I already know, even before I look down. The pale, shriveled, once-protected, now-exposed finger I'd torched. Band-Aid-less. Exposed for all the world to see. I'd been fidgeting with it at Walker Bros., yanking at the stitching whenever the conversation slid into a lull. *Maybe it came off in the car?* Maybe. Wishful thinking, more likely. No, I'm pretty sure it was there when we snuck in the house. That leaves only one logical explanation, one place it could've come off in the last fifteen minutes. I glance at Ally, hoping—no, *praying*—she won't confirm my suspicions. Wishful thinking, once again.

"No . . ."

"Oh yes." Ally snickers, unable and unwilling to contain her delight.

"You don't think . . . ?"

"Afraid so."

"Fuck." I can't breathe. "Oh fuck." I'm breathing too much. "*Fuckfuckfuck.*" Can both be true at the same time? Ally's only making it worse, standing there like this is some joke. I can't look at her. The light will do. Another light-titty.

"What do I do?" I manage between desperate gulps of air. "What if she finds it?"

"Forget Bridget; what's Woody gonna say when he finds out you lost Buzz?" She cracks up. I shoot her a glare. "Fine, fine. Want my actual advice? You have to go get it. That would be the gentlemanly thing to do, anyway." More laughing. She's enjoying this too much. "Time to send in the search and rescue team."

"But what if it's gone?" I ask sincerely. "Oh shit, what if it got, like, swallowed up or something?"

Ally snorts. "Where's it gonna go? There's not a whole lot of room in there. Your Band-Aid isn't floating around like . . . damn, what's that movie you made me watch where George Clooney floats off into space?"

"Gravity."

"*Gravity*! Thank you, that's it."

"What?" It takes me a second. "No, I'm not talking about the movie! I'm saying, won't it fall out on its own?"

"Uh, I realize you're not an expert in vaginas, Cam, but you should know by now that's not how they work."

There isn't room to pace, so I settle for pivoting in a small semicircle. "Goddamnit, Allison! This is all your fault!"

"Me? What did I do?"

"If you hadn't shown up, none of this would've happened!"

"Don't put this on me. I wasn't the one who forgot to check his fingers before he stuck them inside someone else."

"How was I supposed to know she had a Dustbuster vagina?"

Out goes her bottom lip. "Aw, poor baby. Everything always happens to you! It must be hard having absolutely no control over what you say or do!" She steps toward me, then again, so she's standing on my toes. "I should run. Gotta go find someone who, how'd you put it again? 'Actually gives a shit about me'?"

Suddenly her hands clamp around my cheeks, yank me down to her level. She catches me off guard—I'm too in shock to fight her off. I shiver instead—her hands are freezing.

Her lips aren't.

They're warm. And soft, always so soft. She's kissing me tenderly, and in an instant, I forget to be worried about—what was I worried about again? That's a problem for later because Ally is kissing me. I'm kissing Ally. The hair on my neck stands at attention. Overhead, the heavens have opened, just like they used to. Every kiss with Ally, a religious experience.

My ascendance ends abruptly, unceremoniously, when Ally shoves my face away from hers. My head bangs into the door, filling my vision with stars. They dance around Ally's head as she wipes her flushed mouth with the back of her wrist.

She isn't smirking anymore. "Good luck out there" is all she says. It's the last thing she says before receding back into my imagination.

A<small>RE YOU THERE</small>, *God? It's me, Cameron . . . I know we haven't talked in a minute . . . that's on me . . . but I feel like I've been dealt a pretty shitty hand recently . . . I'd really appreciate it if you could come through right now . . . Lord, please help me get my Band-Aid out of this girl's vagina.*

I splash some cold water on my face and hit send on my prayer before returning to the scene.

"Hey, sorry about that," I say a little too cheerily for someone who just wrapped a ten-minute bathroom break. "I was just—"

I come to a sudden halt when I see Bridget. Fully clothed. Gathering her belongings. Panic sets in. She must've already found the Band-Aid.

"You're leaving?"

"Oh!" Bridget startles and wheels around to face me. "I didn't hear you come out. How are you feeling?"

"Me?" *Who else would she be talking to?* "Oh, I'm fine. Totally fine!" *Except for the fact that I misplaced my Band-Aid inside of you.* "Just a little stomach trouble. You know how it goes." Everyone knows what *stomach trouble* is code for. I try again. "It's just, I'm on all of these painkillers for my knee, and they're screwing with my system."

Bridget mutters a response, but she's busy looking at her phone. I try reading her expression, without success. Then again, what expression does one emote when they discover a used Band-Aid in their vagina?

"Sorry, I'm distracted. My mom just called—apparently one of my brothers got thrown out of his Little League game, so I have to pick my sister up from her friend's. I hate to do this, but can we do a rain check?"

"Yeah, of course." For a second I forget the debris stranded inside her. "Wait, no! Shouldn't we at least finish what we started?"

I motion to the couch suggestively, but Bridget's too busy tracking down her belongings to notice.

"Next time," she says absently, once she's stuffed everything into her bag. "My ride's outside. Sorry tonight didn't go according to plan."

You have no idea.

Bridget loops the bag over her shoulder and scurries over. "Text me when your knee is feeling better." A quick peck on the cheek. "And your stomach."

I watch helplessly as Bridget retreats, shoes in one hand, bag in the other, waving one last time before she darts up the stairs and out of sight.

What the fuck just happened? Shell-shocked, I wander over to the couch. It took Ally all of, what, twenty minutes to derail things with Bridget? On top of derailing my senior year. My life. And I let her.

I did. No more denying it. Why have I gifted her this power over me when all she does is take advantage? Whenever it suits her. Only this time, she took it too far. The straw that chopped the camel in half.

This has to end. Right here, right now. If only there was some way to cut her off for good.

32

Hours Since Delatrix: 0

Dr. Vernon made it very clear: twenty-four hours without Delatrix, and I could ditch the stuff. Piece of cake. What's the worst that could happen?

Hours Since Delatrix: 2

Before bed, I take two ibuprofen. This would be way easier if POL-I were still alive (RIP). I settle for Ziploc bags stuffed with ice cubes.

Hours Since Delatrix: 4.5

I wake up underwater; the plastic bags have been leaking. Once again, Mom's throw pillows come in handy. So absorbent.

Hours Since Delatrix: 8

"Your grandparents are arriving soon," Mom reminds me in the morning. "I expect everyone else will be here by dinnertime."

Shit. Of all the days to wean myself off Delatrix, I picked the one when my entire extended family descends on my house. I try getting up—BIG mistake. Won't be doing that again.

Hours Since Delatrix: 11

Maizy: "Cameron! Wanna go outside and play—"
Me: "No."

Hours Since Delatrix: 13.5

Like Mary in the manger, or the Godfather on the day of his daughter's wedding, I receive various family members from my perch in the living room as they arrive. They each pepper me with the same questions: summer plans, rehab, college. I should just print out my answers, hand them out as they arrive.

Hours Since Delatrix: 15

The lights are flickering. At first, I assumed it was the bulb going out. But after a few minutes I start to wonder if it's—

Nope. Not gonna go there. It's weird, sure, but weird things happen all the time. Doesn't mean there's a paranormal explanation.

Hours Since Delatrix: 17

Can you overdose on ibuprofen?

Hours Since Delatrix: 21

Around dinner, Mom asks me for a minute alone. "Your father's plane is delayed, so he won't make it tonight. He'll meet us at the ceremony tomorrow." I tell her it's fine, no big deal. She seems lost in her own train of thought, though. In a trance.

"Mom?"

She snaps to. Looks at me. Frowns. "Where's your ice machine?"

Hours Since Delatrix: 23.99

Count it down, like New Year's Eve. Three . . . two . . . one . . .

Hours Since Delatrix: 24

So long, Allison Tandy.

33

It isn't quite six when I get up the next morning. Graduation isn't for another few hours. Plenty of time for a quick round trip to Shermer General. The Delatrix bottle bulges in my shorts pocket. Sure, without it, my knee feels like a lamb shank tenderizing on one of those vertical rotisseries. A small price to pay for my sanity.

Outside the house, the air smells funny. Like the third-floor bathroom in the east wing at STHS, where kids would go to—

"Mom?"

I almost didn't recognize her without her athleisure on. With a cigarette in her hand.

"Shit," Mom mutters, quickly stubbing the butt on the deck. It's a stunning sight to behold. I can't tell you how many times I've heard the "cigarettes will kill you" lecture. And yet, here she is, whipping a pack out of the fuzzy pocket of her robe. Sparking up another.

"Why are you up so early?" Mom asks me. She spots my keys. "Where are you going?"

"Since when do you smoke cigarettes?"

Neither of us feels like explaining. So we don't.

"Graduation's at eleven," she says. "You'll be back well before then?" I nod. Mom takes a drag, signaling the end of the conversation, were I simply to leave now. And I almost do. But then—

"Mom, can I ask you something?"

"I haven't heard anything new regarding Ally's condition."

"Not that." I rock back on my heels, contemplating. "Maizy is eight years younger than me."

Mom nods.

"But we have the same parents."

Mom frowns.

"Even though you and Dad hadn't lived under the same roof in—what? Seven years?"

"Is there a question in there somewhere?" Mom's starting to sound testy. It's a fair question. What exactly am I getting at here? My thoughts swirl and bleed into one another, until finally . . .

"Why did you take Dad back?" I hardly recognize my own voice. "You knew what he was like. He'd already bailed on us once before. And you just . . . let him back into our lives."

The question seems to baffle her. "If you have an issue with your father, take it up with him after the ceremony."

"I don't give a shit about Dad." It just comes out, and it strikes me how natural it feels leaving my mouth. I've never admitted that before—not even to myself. But . . . yeah. I don't. I've been talking your ear off this whole time and only mentioned the guy like, what, four times? Is that weird? Actually, you know what—I don't even care if it's weird. No, what I want to know is why my mother, famous for taking no shit, couldn't move past her shitty ex after seven years.

"There are plenty of decent guys out there," I say. "Why him? Why'd you let him back in?"

Mom looks taken aback. "Cam, your father—"

"Is a piece of shit," I finish for her. I'm not talking to my mother anymore. Dr. Garrity never would've taken my dad back. I once saw her make a pediatric surgeon cry because he drank her Diet Coke. No, I'm talking to Cindy, who got back together with her ex—even had another kid with him—then watched as he pulled the curtain over her eyes a second time.

I don't take much after my mom; it's not immediately clear what I inherited from her. But what if it's this? What if heartbreak runs in the family—genetic—and seven years from now I'm still waiting for Ally to text me?

Staring out into the garden, Mom takes a long drag on her cigarette, then whistles a thin line of smoke. Like a pro. "I was younger," she starts to say. "I wanted another kid. The one I already had missed his father." She gives me a look. I feel a pang of guilt. "But the real reason? Your father left me with a laundry list of unanswered questions the first time he left. Why did he do it? Was there something I'd done wrong? That sort of thing." Mom shrugs. "Did I worry history would repeat itself? Of course. But seven years on, and those questions continued to eat at me. I knew I needed answers."

Unanswered questions—*Why did you break up with me?*—I might have one or two.

"And? Did you get them?"

Mom nods. "I did."

"So it was worth it?"

"Your sister was."

"But after you got your answers, you were over him? Right?"

And then, one of the rarest sights in nature: Mom starts laughing. She's in stitches as she reaches in her pocket and pulls out the pack. "Do you know when I bought these?"

I shake my head.

"The last time your father was in Shermer. Twenty years after our wedding and the mere thought of being in the same room as him has me acting like my mother."

Grandma Dorothy: known smoker, died before I was born.

"Getting over someone isn't a straight line. Your father leaving didn't change the way I felt about him—not really. Not to the person I was before I became your mom. But that little relapse did provide the clarity I needed to make the best choice for my family."

In my pocket, I feel my fingers curl around the Delatrix bottle. Clarity, not closure. I could do that. Of course, it'll require me to break my Delatrix fast. So be it. One more trip.

I tell Mom I'll be back soon and turn to go. "Was that Bridget Kaplan I saw rushing out of here last night?" she asks before I can escape.

Shit. So much for Bridget's clean getaway.

"Was it?" I act surprised. "Hm. Maybe, I'm not sure."

"She seemed to be in a hurry. How come she was in such a hurry, Cameron?"

"Why do you always assume I did something wrong?" The eyebrow elevates. I simmer down. Mom takes another drag.

"Did you know Bridget had a twin? Well, at first. She absorbed the second fetus in her mother's womb."

"Mom!"

THE FREE PARKING lot is full when I get to Shermer General. I bite the bullet and fork over the ten bucks for the garage. Business must be good; spots are hard to come by on the lower levels, even at this hour. I corkscrew from one level to the next until I run out of ceiling. The top level is completely deserted—finding a spot is no trouble.

From up here, the lake looks gloomy and placid. So does the city, gleaming off in the distance.

I'll just sit here a minute, I tell myself. *Calm my nerves.* My stomach's a mess; the butterflies have evolved into fire-breathing dragons. Always eat something with your meds; I should know better. The Delatrix bottle leers at me from the cup holder. Looking a little lighter than it did when I left my house.

Commotion now across the tarmac. A horde of seagulls cawing bloody murder as they pick apart the remains of someone's Happy Meal. One of them looks right at me. Squawks.

"Don't you have somewhere better to be?"

"Jesus!"

Two weeks, Ally's been doing this, appearing out of thin air, and yet I frighten just as violently now as I did that first night. She approaches the driver's side and pokes her head in the window.

"Hi, Cam." I give her a blank look. "Are you still upset about the other night? Because you can't really be mad at me about the Band-Aid thing. Like, *yes*, it was super petty of me to ambush you like that. But how could I have predicted you'd lose it inside of her?"

That's it. I undo my seat belt abruptly. Ally leaps out of the way as I punch open the door. Slam it closed.

"Cam, come on!" she calls after me as I start for the elevators. "It's not that big a deal. You barely even liked her anyway."

I wheel around. "That's not for you to decide!"

There's a burst of noise—flapping—from across the tarmac. The gulls take flight, soaring overhead. Survival instincts; there's a storm coming.

"Is this about your ice machine?" Ally spurs me on. "Because I'm more than happy to reimburse you. The Save Ally Fund will cover it. Just as soon as I wake up."

It's not even subtle; she's practically begging me to detonate. Mission accomplished.

"Nothing!" I don't bother keeping my voice down. "All I wanted this summer was *nothing*!" No one's gonna hear us up here—not over the wind. "Then you show up spouting off about how sad I look, and how bad you feel, and how you want to help me move on. Blah-blah-blah. Except when I actually do find someone I'm semi-interested in, you can't help yourself. And do you know why, Allison? Because you can't stand the thought of someone making me happy who isn't you!"

As I'm ranting, Ally keeps perfectly still, hands folded by her zipper. I hate that even now, as I'm ripping into her, I can't help imagining her lips on mine. She's right. I barely liked Bridget, at least by comparison. But that's the point. That's exactly what Ally wants. For me to dream of her and her alone.

I finish by asking the obvious. "What is wrong with you?"

"What's wrong with *me*?" Her face clouds over. "Gee, I don't know. Maybe it's the fact that I'm out here arguing with you while the rest of me is inside, deteriorating as we speak!"

I scoff. "You don't get to play the coma card right now."

"Yeah, actually I do." Ally's quick to close the distance between us. "Seeing as I'm still in a fucking coma!"

"About that." My eyes narrow. "I asked my mom. She said she hasn't heard anything about your condition in over a week. Graduation's in five hours, Al." I check my wrist for an invisible watch. "Cutting it a little close, don't you think?"

Ally sets her mouth in a grim line.

"Unless—" I feign a gasp. "You lied about that too! Because if you could *actually* control a coma from the inside, then you would've woken up by now."

From the jump, I'd assumed as much. Ally's claim was far-fetched, to say the least. Of course, I wanted to believe her. Maybe she was trying to talk herself into believing. But it was always too good to be true.

"Look at Sherlock Holmes over here." Ally's voice is hollow, devoid of its usual firepower. "Fine. You win. I don't know when—or *if*—I'm gonna wake up. Happy now?"

No. But then, I haven't been happy in a long time.

This high up, there's an added charge to the atmosphere. The wind responds in kind, doling out haymakers one after another. Ally and I are forced to stoop down, shielding our eyes until the gusts die down.

"What happened, Cam?" Ally's done away with her sarcastic facade. I assume she's referring to the other night.

"You got what you wanted. Bridget bailed right after you."

Ally screws her eyes closed and shakes her head slowly. "With *us*, Cam. What happened with us? Things were *so* good. I was *so* happy. And then . . ." She lifts her shoulders. Sets them down.

"Blane Duckworth happened."

"*No.*" Ally's firm. Adamant. "I told you, I never wanted to be with Blane."

"Yeah, well, you clearly didn't want to be with me either," I say, my voice cracking. "Otherwise you wouldn't have ended things the way you did."

For a minute, Ally just stares at me funny. Probing with those big blue eyes. Then, in an instant, her expression changes. "You really believe that, don't you?"

I am over Allison Tandy.

"It's the truth." My heart rate cranks up. I've said it a hundred times now: Ally dumped me. Full stop. So why does it suddenly feel like I'm missing something?

Suddenly, the ground starts to shake. An earthquake? In Shermer?

No—just the El. A southbound train whooshing past. Folks destined for better days than mine. "You asked me to come over!" I shout over the tracks. "You said we needed to talk!"

"About next year," Ally yells back. She waits a beat until the train's out of sight. "How much of Jake's New Year's party do you actually remember?"

New Year's Eve . . . Shots of Malört . . . Throwing up in Jake's theater room . . . Dancing with Ally . . . *Fukkit, let's do long distance next year . . .*

"Bits and pieces," I say.

"Do you remember what you said to me?"

I nod slightly. "I told you I loved you. I wanted to be with you." Ally shoots me a look. *And . . . ?* "And I was willing to try long distance."

A stinging sensation radiates inside my nostrils, signaling tears. I hang my head, stare at the concrete. I couldn't have picked a worse way to tell her. If I could take it all back, do it over, I would. No questions asked. But a do-over wouldn't change the way I felt. Or what I wanted. And what I wanted was Ally.

"Everything happened so fast," Ally's saying now. "I panicked, okay? I panicked and I texted you without thinking it all the way through. I just—I wanted to be honest with you."

"Honest about what?"

Ally's bottom lip shivers. "Long-distance relationships never work, Cam. They're messy and emotionally draining and they always end badly."

My heart's doing barrel rolls in my chest. "You don't know that."

"Just look what it's doing to Chevy and Lisa. They haven't even left for school yet and it's already chipping away at their relationship. And *that's* The Happy Couple—that's what you call them, right? Now imagine *us*," Ally says. "How jealous we both get. You know I'm right."

She is.

"I was afraid the same thing would happen to us," she continues. "We'd just end up resenting each other after a while. And I wasn't willing to risk that. Not if it meant losing my best friend."

"If you were so concerned about losing me, then why—" The questions stalls in my throat. What's she saying exactly? My head's killing me. I'm losing the thread. *Pull it together, Cam. Ask her what you really want to know.*

"But why tell me then?" I ask finally. "Why not wait until—"

"Until when?" Ally interrupts. "When was I supposed to tell you? When's the right time to break the heart of the person you love?"

There's a desperate quality to Ally's tone. Like she's really asking me. But I don't have the answer.

"I thought maybe, if I warned you—if I told you how I felt about next year—then it wouldn't come as a shock later. We could mentally prepare ourselves, you know? Make the most out of the time we still had left. Together. Maybe we could even skip the awkward breakup phase and go straight to being friends. Obviously that didn't happen."

Ally shakes her head, then looks up. Locks on. "I couldn't bear the thought of losing you altogether. But that's exactly what happened. Trust me, if I could go back and redo everything about that night, I would. If I'd known you'd walk out on me, I would've kept my mouth shut."

That night. The perpetual night in question.

I am over Allison Tandy.

Suddenly, a stabbing sensation pierces the spot between my eyes. I let out a howl and drop to my good knee. The pain is excruciating, leagues worse than any migraine I've had before. An aneurysm? Could be. Or something worse.

The guardrails have been lifted. My subconscious is succumbing. Memories rush to the surface, gulping for air, attention. Kept at bay for months. Now it's all coming back. The way the snow stuck to my jeans as I sat in her kitchen. Ally's chunky fisherman sweater, with a hole under the arm. The way the Tandys' house smelled like real pine, not the fake tree we'd used since neither Mom or I felt like making the effort.

The grief on Ally's face.

I am over Allison Tandy.

I sense Ally inching toward me. I lurch upright and stumble back, away from her, still cradling my head in my hands.

I'm over Ally.

I'm not looking where I'm stepping. My heel catches on a parking block and I stumble . . . teeter . . . closer to the edge. A five-story fall. Nothing compared to the danger lurking every time I close my eyes.

The call is coming from inside my head. The memory's at my doorstep.

It's over, Ally.

34

Here are the facts. *(Including Ally's.)*

The morning of January 1, I received the following text from Ally: We need to talk. *(I didn't mean for it to sound so ominous.)*

It snowed all day. *(Most melted by sunset.)*

I arrived at Ally's house around seven. *(I received a text—Here—timestamped at 7:42.)*

Mrs. Tandy was visiting Ally's aunt in Indiana for the night, so we had the place to ourselves. *(Michigan, but that's not important.)*

Ally was baking cookies. *(Brownies.)*

I felt sick to my stomach, so I declined when she offered samples. *(He ate at least ten.)*

I couldn't handle the suspense, so I broke the seal, asked her outright: "What is it you wanted to talk about?" *(The tension was getting to me. Finally I was like, "So, I should probably explain my message earlier.")*

Ally rambled for what felt like hours, waxing poetic

about how she didn't think long distance could work, how she was worried we'd grow to resent each other, and how she still wanted to be friends. *(I rambled for what felt like hours. But I wanted to be thorough—check every box. Lay out exactly how I felt; the push-pull of wanting to be with him and wanting independence.)*

I could tell she was dancing around the issue. *(I could tell he didn't believe me.)*

I just wanted her to be honest. *(I was just trying to be completely honest.)*

So I asked: "We're breaking up, then?" A question. Simple. Direct. Pleading. *(So he said, "We're breaking up, then." A statement. Flat. Unemotional. Unambiguous.)*

She couldn't even look me in the eyes. *(I was in shock—it was the only way to keep from bawling.)*

She barely flinched when I got up to leave. *(I never thought you'd leave me.)*

I blacked out then—

(I didn't.)

(I remember more about those ninety seconds than I do my own accident. You don't forget the moment your best friend abandons you. The moment your heart fractures in two.)

(It's all still fresh in my mind. The sigh he let out as he went to stand. The plastic drawstring tips on his hoodie, ravaged by his anxious chewing. The last thing he said to me—"It's over,

Ally"—before striding out of the room. He couldn't leave fast enough—he didn't even bother lacing up his boots. The pummeling silence reverberating inside the house after he'd shut the door. Gone. The way the wind whistled outside as I sat rooted in place, waiting for him to double back, to fight for us, even if I'd spoiled the ending. After an hour, I gave up. He must hate me, I thought to myself. I hated me then too.)

(I assumed he just needed to cool off. He'd text me—I knew he would. Then we could sit down and properly talk. About next year, yes, but more importantly about all the things we still had left to do before our time in Shermer came to an end.)

(And so I waited for him, and I kept waiting—even after I started hooking up with Blane. I waited until one overcast day on my way home from school, I took my eyes off the road just long enough to see why my phone had lit up, when—)

35

It's over, Ally.

She's right. It was me. I was the one who pulled the plug. I broke up with Ally.

I broke up with Allison Tandy.

My world feels like it's spinning off its axis. How is this even possible? How could I let this happen? *I* was the jilted ex. The dumpee. The sympathetic one. The heartbroken one. I've grown used to it, adopted the persona. Grown into the role. But this . . . this upends all of that. Places the blame squarely on my shoulders.

I broke up with Allison Tandy.

"But . . . but . . . you didn't want me," I stammer. Another gust of wind screams past. Ally's hair is sentient. It moves like fire as she shakes her head.

"I did," she says. "I do." The expression in her eyes is intent, pleading with me to believe her. To understand. "You abandoned me, Cam. You were my best friend in the whole world and you just—*walked out.* Like I meant nothing to you." She's crying, I realize. I think I might be too. "We had so much time left. So many things we were supposed to do. What, like eight months before either of us had to leave? That's so much time, Cam."

Eight months. I could've had another eight months with Ally.

"I'm not a corny person," Ally says. "And we were never *that* couple. Making out in the hallway or posting gross captions about how *in love* we were. But I wanted to be corny with you. Do all the stuff. Prom photos and matching Senior Olympics outfits. Paint *CAM* across my stomach with Chevy and Lisa for your Senior Night. You made me feel less self-conscious for looking forward to those things. And you—"

Ally spins away from me suddenly. Like she can't stand the sight of me.

"And *you* couldn't wait to be rid of me."

I feel sick. Woozy. Guilt has me by the throat. My brain's racing to keep up. I'd lie down if we weren't surrounded by pavement on all sides. What I really need are my pills. Or a time machine. Then I could go back. To that night? No, further. Jake Cooper's New Year's Eve party.

If I hadn't been so drunk that night, I never would've admitted that I wanted to date long distance. If I hadn't admitted that I wanted to date long distance, Ally wouldn't have asked to talk the next night. If *that night* doesn't happen, then we don't break up. If we don't break up, Ally never dates Blane. I never hook up with Steff. If we never break up, then maybe I don't tear my ACL. Maybe Ally doesn't drive home through the ravines. And if Ally doesn't drive through the ravines, then maybe Ally never crashes her—

No . . . *NO!* That's unacceptable. I can't survive in a reality where any of that is true. Where it's all my fault. Not just the breakup— Ally's current condition too. A world where it's all my fault.

This needs to end. Once and for all.

Self-preservation kicks in. Sure, I might've been miserable before all this, in my old reality, before Ally showed up. But at least I knew where to lay the blame.

My body lurches forward, almost of its own accord. The few remaining Delatrix capsules rattle as I march. My supply seemed unlimited that first day home. Now I'm down to the stragglers.

"Cam?" Ally's right on my tail, keeping pace. "Cam? What are you doing? Where are we going?"

The other side of the parking lot. The ledge directly above the El tracks. I don't even realize I've forgotten my crutches leaning against the Geo until I'm almost across.

As I sidle up to the wall, the wind lands another blow, thrashing my cheek, snapping like a rubber band.

"Cam, seriously!" Ally's protests sound increasingly desperate. "Please, this isn't funny!"

"I agree." Another train should be headed our way. They run every few minutes. I dangle my neck out over the side of the garage. Look one way, then the other. Sure enough, headlights on the horizon—northbound this time. Still a ways off. Long enough for one final answer.

"Was there a chance?" I ask, turning to face her head-on.

Ally seems confused. "A chance for what?"

"Say I didn't walk out that night. Say that we stayed together and did all the corny senior year stuff you talked about. Say I waited until the end of the summer to tell you I wanted to try long distance. Say we fell deeper in love—" I'm interrupted by a clanging sound. Railroad crossing bells, one street over. "Was there any chance you would've changed your mind?"

Ally opens her mouth as though to answer, only to snap it shut. "That isn't a fair question," she eventually asserts.

She's right. It isn't. But I have to know. And the locomotive ever approaches.

"Answer the question, Al. Was there any possibility of you changing your mind? Where we could've stayed together?"

"Cam, I—"

"ALLISON!"

"NO!"

The train is upon us, trumpeting its horn. But I don't hear it. Not over the audible, thunderous crack coming from my rib cage as my heart finally splinters in two.

I have to act now. Any longer and Ally will talk me out of it. I'll talk myself out of it.

I turn my back on Ally. Mind the chasm head-on. Tighten my grip around the Delatrix bottle. Unscrew the cap.

I'm not over Allison Tandy. But I need to be.

I'm half expecting the pills to plummet straight down, instantly reduced to powder upon impact. Instead, the capsules take flight, corralled by the wind's seeping undertow. Ripped from sight.

My first thought: *It's over.*

My second: *What have I done?*

I wheel around, but it's too late. Ally's gone. Like she was never even here.

36

Graduation unfolds without incident. We do all the things. File in to "Pomp and Circumstance." Walk (or crutch) the stage. Throw our caps in the air.

Ally doesn't show. Still, her presence is felt, our superintendent assures us before inviting the crowd to partake in—what else?—a moment of silence.

THE POST-GRADUATION FANFARE lasts all day. I don't have a moment to myself until later, once everyone's gone to bed. Alone with my thoughts at last. What a nightmare. Being inside feels claustrophobic, so I mosey outside to the patio. Park it on one of the chaises. Bask in the celestial rubble. Not much to look at, save the dieting moon. Usually the light pollution from Chicago curbs any chance of stargazing. Still, I give it a shot. I'm homing in on what is either a plane or a very slow, very red shooting star when I sense someone enter my periphery.

"Hey."

"Hey."

Chevy plops down and offers me his pen. Twist my arm. "I tried texting you," he says.

"Phone's dead." My dot blinks. Definitely a plane.

We're quiet for a while then; an orchestra of cicadas fills the void. I get the feeling we both know what needs to be said, and we're both just waiting for the other one to say it.

"Look, Chev—"

"Cam, I—"

"You were gonna say something?"

"No, you can go ahead."

"You sure?"

"Yeah, you're good."

"Okay, well, I just wanted to apologize . . ."

"Me too . . ."

"I didn't mean any of that stuff . . ."

"Me neither . . ."

"It was really wack . . ."

"I'm sorry I changed the Netflix password . . ."

"I feel terrible about the Lisa thing . . ."

"We good?"

We both grunt an affirmative. Would you look at that? Friendship restored, good as new. Chevy takes another hit. "Lisa and I are talking again." He subs his cuticle for the mouthpiece. "Looks like I may have jumped the gun."

"How so?"

He hesitates. "Technically we never broke up."

"*Technically?*"

"It turns out there's a difference between breaking up and 'needing time apart.'" He shrugs. "Who knew?" He's smiling now, in spite of himself. "It's possible I'm not as well versed in confrontation as I thought."

"Or jealousy," I add.

"Or jealousy." He nods. "It's been a fucked-up couple of weeks." A beat. "Months, really."

I laugh in spite of myself. "You have no idea."

"I guess not." Chevy exhales, sliding his hands behind his head. "I really miss her, man."

I can't help laughing. "You only thought it was over for, like, twenty-four hours. It's not like you guys haven't spoken in weeks."

"Not Lisa," Chevy quickly clarifies. "I'm talking about Ally."

The cicadas take their intermission.

"Oh" is all I say.

"She should've been there today." I hear Chevy sniffling, but I don't trust myself enough to look. "Can I admit something to you?" I give him the go-ahead. "Every night—like, *every* night— since Ally's accident, I've had the exact same recurring dream. It's graduation—today—and I'm sitting there in the audience next to you and Lisa watching Dean Stein read off names of kids I don't recognize. Until they get to Ally's name. And suddenly . . ." Chevy pauses. "There she is. Walking the stage. Accepting her diploma. Just like everyone else. And I'm the only one in the audience freaking out about it—no one else reacts."

"I've had that dream."

"It's fucking brutal." Another sniffle. "I always try talking to her. In the dream, I mean. Like, I'll bum-rush the stage or something. But I never make it. I wake up just before I can reach her." Chevy flicks a gnat grazing on his thigh. "I stopped talking to her, you know? Lisa too."

"Yeah, she told me."

"Lisa did?"

No, Ally did.

"I can't remember." Chevy's not the only one being feasted upon. I claw at a penny-size bite on my shin, but it only makes the itching worse. "I never asked you guys to do that."

"I know you didn't," Chevy says. He takes a hit, holds it. Exhales. "You were in bad shape, man. Straight up, just a zombie. The lights went out and it scared the shit out of me." He sets his pen down on the armrest. "So Lisa and I talked about it—how we could help. And I made the call." He hunches over, rubbing his forehead with one hand. "All of it. Not talking to her. Team Cam. The merch. My idea. Talked Lisa into it and everything. Even though Ally was my friend. I thought it was right call. Now I'm not so sure."

There's no fending off his tears any longer. Chevy tries anyway, burying his face in the crook of his elbow. I don't know what to do, what to say. But then, by now I know better. There is nothing to do, nothing to say. So I just put my hand on Chevy's shoulder, give him a little squeeze with each sob. Hold firm until his ducts run dry.

"Have you been to see her yet?" he asks, wiping his face on his shirt. "At the hospital, I mean."

I shake my head.

"Good. I wouldn't. Don't put the image in your head if you don't have to." Chevy shivers. "I know Cindy and all of Ally's doctors say that she'll wake up eventually. But if you saw her—what's left of her . . ." He trails off. The fear in his voice turns my blood cold. "I don't know, man. Sooner or later, *eventually* runs out."

37

Time moves a lot faster when your head's on straight.

One minute it's May, we're graduating, semi-furnished adults granted a summer free from responsibility. The next, the dog days have arrived and the final countdown is on.

After graduation, my summer becomes the one thing I've long coveted: predictable. Physical therapy, *NCIS Boise*, hanging out at Chevy's.

Lather. Rinse. Repeat.

My leg remains a work in progress. By June, I'm off the crutches. The Robo-cast lingers a bit longer, but soon I'm walking raw. Feels about as structurally sound as a high-rise built with Styrofoam, but hey, it's a start.

Bridget and I text a bit, but it doesn't really go anywhere. No word on whether or not my Band-Aid ever surfaced. On the other hand, Chevy and Lisa mention it every chance they get. They even come up with a name for the incident: Band-Aidgate.

Lisa is the first to go. Volleyball is a fall sport, so they're expected on campus a month before everyone else for training camp. The Happy Couple is forging ahead with long distance—

minus the open-relationship policy. Lisa agreed on the condition of complete transparency. Honestly, they both seem kinda nervous about it, which of course makes me nervous for them. But what else can they do? Chevy puts on a brave face the morning of Lisa's departure. He saves the breakdown for later that night, right around his sixth beer.

A few weeks later, it's his turn. I tag along as he makes the rounds, says his goodbyes. Everybody and their mom wants to see him off. Later, when it's just us, Chevy's a bit more direct.

"Promise me you won't kill yourself." He's kidding. I think. "I know that suicide is, like, the only fun thing to do at UC, but seriously. Please don't."

"Fifty-fifty." I'm also joking (I think).

"Fine, but if you do, I'd better get a shout-out in your suicide note." His smile subsides, giving way to a more serious expression. "I'm on the first flight the minute she wakes up."

People clear out pretty quickly after that. Soon I'm the only one left. Well, besides Ally. No updates there either.

Mom is more than happy to fill the gap in my social life with chores and errands. Today I'm at the supermarket, weaving through the aisles, running down her list. Mindless work. Fine by me. Thinking never led anywhere good.

When I turn down the frozen foods aisle, my arms break out in goose bumps, and not because of the dip in temperature.

Mrs. Tandy. In the flesh. Scanning the nutrition facts on a sleeve of frozen plant-based burgers.

I used to joke that Mrs. Tandy could be Ally's older sister—a foolproof way to score points with your girlfriend's mom (Chevy taught me that). With Mrs. Tandy, though, it was hardly just a one-liner. Even under the unforgiving supermarket lights, the similarities are uncanny. Mrs. Tandy's wearing a plain blue T-shirt and bleached skinny jeans. A sprinkle of white garnishes her reddish-brown hair. That's new. No doubt the result of late nights spent at Ally's bedside.

"Mrs. Tandy," I breathe, and then, because I still don't totally trust my cognitive function, I ask, "Mrs. Tandy?"

She glances up. Looks confused. Like she's trying to place me. Or figure out where I've been.

But then . . . "Is that really you, Cameron Garrity?" Before I can react, she sets her cart alongside mine and pulls me into a hug. I don't deserve one, but I reciprocate anyway. "I was wondering when I'd see you," she says, stepping back, but not away.

My eyes sink to the floor. The shame cuts worse than Dr. Vernon's scalpel ever could. "Sorry," I hear myself mutter. "I've been meaning to get over there to see—"

I stop short. Why even lie at this point?

"No." I lift my eyes to meet hers. Same as Ally's. "It's just—I didn't want it to be real."

"Oh, sweetheart." Mrs. Tandy's bottom lip wobbles. "I only meant I'd hoped to see you. So we could have a chance to talk. It's been a while. I know things between you and Ally didn't end on the best of terms, but you were such important parts of each other's lives."

Mrs. Tandy always gave off the vibe of someone who, when you asked them a generic *How are you*, instead of the stock answer— *Good*—would say something like *Tired*. Who, in another life, was every bit the life of the party her daughter was. *Is*.

Until her husband died. Until she became a single mom. Until life happened. She always turned it on when it mattered, though. When it came to Ally. I'd see the two of them interacting, laughing, being affectionate and think, *So that's what a healthy parental relationship looks like.*

Mrs. Tandy's lips are moving, I realize; she's been talking this whole time. "Sorry, what?"

"I asked how you're feeling." She nods at the ground. "Your leg, hon."

"Oh, right." Forgot about that for a second. "It's fine. Getting better. So that's good. How are—" I cut myself short. I know damn well how she's doing. Instead, I go, "Any updates? I'd heard she—*Ally*," I add, as if that needed clarifying. "She showed some positive signs earlier this summer. But I'm not sure what the latest is."

Mrs. Tandy frowns. "How did you . . ." A smile breaks through. "Your mom?" I nod. "You know, some of the other Sunday school moms used to joke that Cindy Garrity knew they were pregnant before they did. Only, I'm not sure they were joking."

She snorts. Like I said—*uncanny*. "I'm sorry, I know I must look like an absolute loon right now." Mrs. Tandy blinks a tear onto her thumb. Rubs it into the rest of her fingers. She studies me for a few moments, probing my expression. I don't mind.

"You love her."

My mouth instinctively drops open, ready to protest, only to snap shut. She's right. Of course she's right.

"That's alright; you don't have to say it. But moms know these things." Mrs. Tandy's beaming at me. I wish she'd stop. My cheeks are on fire. "Ally thought the world of you, you know?"

I huff. "I don't know about that."

"Nonsense." She dismisses me with a wave. "Can I tell you? Last fall, she and I went dress shopping before homecoming. Took us all day. God knows she can be picky. She must've tried on something like fifty dresses, spread out over like four different stores. And even though she looked spectacular in every one, she refused to settle for anything that didn't meet her expectations. But eventually we found *the one*. And, well, you remember, Cam. It was well worth the wait."

She's right. With Ally, it was always worth the wait.

"And as we went to pay, I made some offhand remark about the next dress we'd buy would be for your senior prom in the spring. The one after that would most likely be her wedding dress. And I asked, just for fun, if she thought you might be the one she was buying that dress for. That it would be you she was marrying. And do you know what she told me?"

I shake my head, unable to feign composure any longer.

"She got this little grin on her face and she said, 'I don't know, Mom, but I can't think of anything better.'"

That.

That breaks me.

Mrs. Tandy isn't far behind.

We stand there in the dairy aisle sobbing, holding each other in equal measure, because it's the only thing to do.

38

I wait until the day before I'm set to leave before I go to see her.

The main lobby at Shermer General Hospital is this massive, cavernous atrium fitted with a glass ceiling, expensive-looking marble, and a waterfall five stories high.

And there's this piano. But not just any piano. A self-playing piano. Same one they've had since my mom worked here. Even as a kid, it freaked me out. Seems like a pretty weird call for a place where people vanish every hour.

It's quieter in the ICU. Less foot traffic. As I pass one of the nurses' stations, one of the staff offers me a brief smile before redirecting her focus to whatever's lighting up her phone. I wonder if she's the same nurse who answered my late-night phone call all those months ago.

Room 19B. Ally's home since March. I can't bring myself to enter right away. I double . . . triple . . . quadruple check that I have the number right.

I knock. Then feel silly. My heart splinters anew.

I hear it before I see it. Right when I open the door, before

I've even crossed the threshold. Ally's ventilator. The thing keeping her alive. Thumping and pumping air into her chest. Kinda sounds like POL-I (RIP), I think. Only much, much louder.

I can't bring myself to look at her—at least, not right away. Instead, my gaze travels everywhere *but*. Her TV's off; no *Family Feud*. Lining the windowsills are various flower arrangements. The larger bouquets have been relegated to the floor. Some still have price tags attached: $24.99 at Whole Foods is all it takes to assuage your guilt. A number of empty vases are confined to the corner, their original tenants long since passed. The fakes are the only ones left standing.

Beside her bed is a little nightstand packed with photographs. Most are of Ally with her extended family. I recognize one from Ally's house; it sat on the mantel over their fireplace. Ally's just a toddler, her mouth bright red thanks to the Popsicle she's holding. She sits atop her dad's shoulders. He seems strong in his Cubs hat and tropical short-sleeve button-up. Vibrant. A man with everything. Not someone who would succumb to cancer in just a few short years. He stares directly into the camera with Ally's eyes. Mrs. Tandy stares at him—at them. Her family.

It's too much. I tear my eyes away and—

Ally. In the flesh.

A while back, Mom gave me the rundown on Ally's condition. Cracked ribs, broken collarbone. They've sewn up her left wrist, placed it in a splint. Couple broken fingers, for good measure. Throw in a nasty case of whiplash, and a knee injury to match mine. Part of her head is shaved, due to a procedure to remove the fragments of windshield glass trapped between her skull and her scalp. Her hair's starting to regrow, to paper over, but it isn't thick enough yet to mask the purple scar lurking underneath.

That old cliché suddenly pops into my head—*It's like a car crash; you can't look away.* Guilt clots behind my forehead. It's easy to watch the crash when you don't have to see the aftermath.

I find a chair in the corner of the room and scoot it to her bedside. To lighten the mood, I try an icebreaker. "Well, you look like shit."

Instinctively, I defend my stomach. But Ally isn't punching back today. The machine answers for her. *Thump. Pump.* My own scar burns just from looking at hers, but my pain seems trivial by comparison.

Her right hand made it out relatively unscathed. I take it in mine. Still fits perfectly.

"How're we feeling today, Al?"

Thump. Pump.

"Don't give me that look. You know I hate that look."

Thump. Pump.

I don't realize I'm crying until tears begin splashing onto her wrist, pooling around the IV drip. I always knew this would suck, seeing her like this. Up close. I thought I could take it.

I was wrong. It feels like someone's scooping out my heart with a melon baller, clump by clump. I screw my eyes shut, press my forehead to the mattress. I'd give anything just to hear her voice right now.

"Oh, so now you want to talk to me?"

My eyes bolt open. Ally's don't. I glance at the door, ensure the coast is clear, then whisper a simple "Al?"

Thump. Pump.

She sounded so clear in my head. I could've sworn—

Not this time. It's just me. My chance to say what I should have.

"I've been thinking about you a lot." A beat. "Understatement of the year." I let out a snort she'd be proud of. "I think you were right, by the way. Which you know how much I hate admitting. But yeah. There was no good way to tell me about next year. Whether you told me in January or the day before you left, I was always gonna act like a huge baby about it."

Thump. Pump.

"Eight months is a really long time. And right now, I'd take eight months with you over a lifetime with anyone else in a heartbeat."

I rehearsed some of this in my head this morning. Things I wished I could say to her. Performed it for my mirror.

"I'm sorry, Al. For all of it. Walking out on you that night. Not texting you sooner. Hooking up with Steff. Letting Chevy and Lisa make those shirts." I could go on, rattling off my fuckups. I bet Ally'd like that, actually. I'll leave her an itemized list.

"What does it say about us that we both hooked up with certain people because we knew it would make the other person jealous?" I laugh. "We're either the worst match in history or perfect for each other. I'm sorry I let you think you were anything less than my favorite person. You were. You are."

Thump. Pump.

Something still feels off. It's not that I don't mean the things I'm saying—I do! Every word. But those are the presentable feelings, the stuff I'd feel comfortable sharing with a room full of people. In here, it's just me and Ally. If I can't be honest with her now, then when? Will I even have another chance?

I stare at the popcorn ceiling, the can lights. *Think, Cam. What is it you really want to say to her?*

"You have to come back, Al."

Softly, at first.

"I need you to come back."

Louder yet, punctuated by sobs.

"Come back, Al. If it ends in disaster, fine. But come back and let's finish what we started. Let's break up. One more fight. Then you never have to talk to me again if you don't want to. Just don't let it end like this. Please, Al, I'm begging you—"

The tears are too much for me to overcome. I can't make a sound. Instead, I lay my head on Ally's chest and listen to her heartbeat. For as long as I can.

39

"Cameron?"

Maizy's driving me crazy.

"Caaaam-roooon."

She's been doing this all morning.

"CameronCameronCameron!"

Peppering me with questions, each one more annoying than the last.

Cameron, are you bringing your stuffed animals with you to college?

Cameron, can I have your room?

Cameron, when are you coming home?

God, I'm gonna miss her.

"One second!" Currently I'm playing a futile game of Tetris, attempting to stack the last of my belongings in the Geo's trunk. With one final push, I throw my shoulder against my duffel, then hurry the hatch closed before anything can come toppling out.

I drag the hem of my shirt across my brow. There's a sticker clinging to it; I must've missed it earlier when I cut the tags. Goodbye, gray STHS basketball T-shirts. Hello, gray UC Maroons basketball T-shirts.

I tear off the sticker, crumple it in my pocket. "Alright, Maiz, what is it this time?" I turn around just in time to snag the soccer ball screaming toward me.

Looking sheepish, Maizy offers a halfhearted "Sorry" as she wanders over. "Who's going to practice with me while you're gone?" Ten years old and already perfected the art of the guilt trip.

"Mom can be your goalie," I suggest.

Maizy makes a face. "Mom doesn't like sports."

"Sure she does."

"Nuh-uh."

"Yeah-huh."

"Nuh-uh!"

I look up at the house. "Where is Mom? We gotta go soon." She was all over my ass this morning about leaving on time so she and Maizy could beat the traffic heading north.

"She's up in her room," Maizy says, snatching her ball out of my hands. "I tried talking to her, but she closed the door. I think she's on the phone."

Just then, I hear ringing. Faint. Muzzled. *Is that my phone?* I pat myself down. Nothing in my pockets. I glance over at the Geo, busting at the seams. *Shit.* A sinking sensation washes over me. *I packed it, didn't I?*

The ringing stops abruptly, only to pick right back up. Whoever's calling won't be ignored. Begrudgingly, I unlock the trunk. Unleash the avalanche.

Maizy is delighted. "Cameron, your stuff fell out." She starts juggling the ball on her knees with a rhythmic *thump-thump*. Almost like a heartbeat.

"Thanks, Maiz."

The ringing stops just as I start riffling through my things. Really regretting stuffing things blindly into trash bags right about now. Duffel's clean. So's my gym bag. *Where the hell did I put it?*

"Hey, Cameron?"

"Yeah, Maiz?"

"What happened to Ally?" *Thump-thump.*

I'm half listening. "Nothing yet. Remember? Mom explained how she's still in the hospital."

"I know that." *Thump-thump.* "But are you gonna talk to her while you're away?"

"What do you mean?" It's ringing again—coming from one of the trash bags. *Gotcha!* It's mostly socks and underwear, but at the bottom, my fingers brush closed around my phone. I'm too late; it's gone to voicemail. Three missed calls from an unknown number with a Shermer area code. Probably spam; they can do that, you know. Make their numbers appear local so you're more likely to pick up. Goddamn snakes.

"Sorry, Maiz, say that again?"

Maizy glares at me without dropping the ball. "I *said*, you used to talk to Ally all the time. I heard you. Then you just stopped."

It takes me a moment to process what she's saying. "Wait, what—"

My phone lights up. Same unknown number. I answer it immediately.

"Hello?"

Breathing . . . just breathing . . . directly into the receiver. And then a voice. From the other side.

"Cam?"

Acknowledgments

This thing took five years to write (and rewrite). So settle in. I'm gonna need a minute.

First and foremost, thank you to my mother. You are the most remarkable person I know and my best friend. This book wouldn't exist without your constant support over the last five years. (And the twenty-three before that.)

To my grandmother, Amo Bishop, my first and favorite English teacher. I know you would be so friggin' proud of me for publishing a book . . . and so horrified by the Band-Aid scene.

To Ari, hands down the best editor working in the game today, who can spot a frivolous scene with her eyes closed. Time after time, I considered giving up on this project, and yet you never wavered. I only hope the finished product lived up to the hype.

To Elise, my confidant, for quite literally saving my life. You're the one who rescued me from plotting hell and provided *A Heavy Dose of Allison Tandy* the shape it needed to get back on track. I can't wait to see where you end up next.

To my agent, Christopher, the kindest man I know. It still

baffles me that a guy with your abilities and credentials took a gamble on a fledgling college student with a TBI. That you have excellent taste in music is an added bonus. Here's to the projects to come; may they take less than an election cycle to complete.

To my Pitch Wars mentor, Alicia, without whom none of this would've been possible. Thank God you decided to go against your better instincts and pick someone who listed you as their number one choice. (If only I'd turned out to be a Nebraska mom catfishing you.)

To Alex, the only person I trust to read my first drafts. Pinky promise we never let the 125K word version of this book see the light of day.

To Jen and Matt, for getting us across the finish line. To everyone at Penguin Teen, especially Theresa, Eileen, Kaitlin, Felicity, and Shannon.

To Diana and Anya, for reading the very first iteration of this book all those years ago and kindly reminding me that there's a difference between writing fiction and journaling. To Hannah, for always keeping me honest.

To Elizabeth, for hiring someone she met on the internet and helping me adjust to life as a (semi) functioning adult. Come back to LA, please. (Reed too.) To Munda, my first real author pal, for coming to my Christmas party and teaching me how to shotgun. To Shannon, my original publishing nemesis, for her design eye and general wisdom. To Prerna, the kindest person in YA. She would *never* walk right past someone without acknowledging them. To Dante, for making dead dad jokes with me at every

opportunity. To Suzanne, for referring to me as *"actually* funny."
To all the ridiculously impressive authors who agreed to read and
blurb my silly little breakup book: Chloe, Kathleen, Jenni & Ted,
Mikki, Gabby, Phil, Cameron, Margot, Lillie, Ryan, and Aiden.
To the Chicago writing crew: Rena, Mia, Layne, and Reese.

To everyone who read early versions of what would eventu-
ally become *A Heavy Dose of Allison Tandy*, especially Tyler, Emily,
Sarah, Vic, Rachel, Mike, and Caitie. To my friends: Julia, Juliana,
George & Tots, Molly, the La Croix boys—Theo, Eric, Silbs, and
Andrew—Jandy and the rest of the ETHS fantasy league, Emma,
Liteau, Mato, and Kiki.

To Ms. Hartley, for encouraging me to write the way I talk.
To Mrs. Mull, for encouraging me to write, *full stop*. To the rest
of the phenomenal teachers who have encouraged me over the
years, especially Ms. Purnell, Mrs. Beckstedt, Mrs. Oberman,
and Prof Baron. To Brad and Carol, for your friendship and for
Project Runway night. To Coach Connelly and Coach Wilson, for
giving a washed-up former benchwarmer nursing a brain injury
something to do besides staring at the wall all day. To Charlie, for
his spiritual guidance on September 1, 2014, and every instance
since. To Terry, for twenty-eight years of unbridled support. To
Dale, for handling the stuff I don't like thinking about.

To the seventy-plus doctors, counselors, and specialists who
worked with me in the weeks, months, and years following
the accident. Special thanks to Dr. Hanus, Dr. Calisoff, Dr.
Fantus, Dr. Raiss, and Dr. Mundjzi. To Camila, for keeping me
off the ledge.

To Alice Dolan, my champion, and Kathleen Loos. A guy couldn't ask for a better legal team.

To the engineers behind the 2010 Honda Accord for saving my life.

To Harry and Emily, as a treat.

To my father, Dr. Finley Bishop. Even though you were a man of science, I hope you would still be proud of your son, *The Creative*. To my stepdad, Steve, for his misty-eyed belief in me and for his corny jokes. Since you are the big softy in our family, I will temporarily lift the moratorium on teary-eyed speeches, so long as the subject matter is me and how amazing I am.

To the ever-expanding Brady Bunch: Tyler, Jessica & Vlad, Emma & Danniel, Jake & Alexa. Special shout-out to Samantha for coining *Delatrix*. To the rest of my family: Aunt Mary, Aunt Ann & Uncle Chuck, Grandma Jessie, and Grandma Lila & Grandpa Sam.

To John Hughes, for filming *Sixteen Candles* two doors down from the house I grew up in.

And finally, to Moira, who has put up with me much longer than she signed up for. Thanks for killing me, Dr. Smalls.